THE EDITOR

STEVEN W. PALMER

WARNING

This book contains themes and scenes of a sexual nature. If you are under 18, or overly sensitive to profanity or anything sexual, then this probably isn't a book you'll like.

The Editor – Steven W. Palmer

saraswati.publishing.cambodia@gmail.com

Cover Art by Sage Greco

https://sagegreco.com/

SARASWATI WRITING AND EDITING SERVICES

CHONBURI, THAILAND

The Editor – Steven W. Palmer

Author's Foreword

First and foremost, this is not a work of erotica. However, it does feature BDSM as a central theme and also has some scenes of a sexual nature.

I wanted to include the BDSM theme for two reasons. Firstly, was the awful and inaccurate portrayal of the lifestyle in a certain book (you know which one). The other reason is I feel that the scene is a perfect example of the duality of human nature; the presentation of a public face that can differ greatly from the reality behind locked doors and closed curtains.

The darker side of human nature, how many perceive it, and how that side is often about control, both external and within, is something that has always fascinated me. That dark side is something that is central to the character of Tom in the book.

To be honest, I'm uncomfortable writing sex scenes and have tried to keep them to a minimum. I'm far more at home with murder, which perhaps says something about me.

One final thing I will ask before you go. Being an independent author can be difficult at times. We don't have big publishing houses behind us nor do we have huge marketing budgets. Reviews are thus very important to us. Ratings are good, and gratefully received, but a few words of review can help other readers to choose a book. So, please take a few minutes to leave reviews on Amazon, Goodreads, or any other platform you use. And if you really enjoyed it, post a review on your social media. A recommendation to family and friends does far more than any advert will ever do. A massive thank you in advance and also thank you for buying the book.

Steven W. Palmer

Chonburi, Thailand. January, 2024

For Kitsune

2015 – 2024

And, as always,

For Cerys

2023

Tom McKay smiled as the business class stewardess took his empty glass and advised him to fasten his seatbelt. He looked out the window at the nearing neon conflagration that was a city of some 11 million souls, though he knew that the unofficial population of Bangkok was likely around 5 million more.

It had been 27 years since he left Thailand and he had mixed emotions about returning after so long. The country had given him so much but had taken in equal measures. He appreciated the irony that what it had given him was why he was returning now, in business class no less, but he wondered if any echoes of the costs still remained.

Tom had first arrived in Thailand in 1994 at the age of 20, a young and naïve backpacker looking to enjoy three months of hedonistic adventures before starting university and then a career. Those three months had ended up stretching to more than two years, a time where adventures had mixed with discovery but which had almost led to his death.

Like most backpackers, his Thai experience had started on Khao San Road, alcohol and drugs freely available and women eager to share the company of this handsome young Englishman who seemed to have a witty observation for every occasion. Unlike many of his peers, the world of transactional sex had not appealed to him though it beckoned often enough. Why pay when liaisons were freely available with girls from almost any nation.

While he didn't think of himself as particularly good looking, it seemed others did so Tom wasn't going to complain. He was six feet tall and slim, dirty blonde hair, intense green eyes with a sensual mouth and an almost patrician nose. He'd inherited his mother's good looks and his father's intelligence, a lethal combination that endeared him to almost any company he was in.

He'd spent a month in the capital before heading north and trekking in the Thai highlands. He had smoked opium with hill tribes, sat and listened to the wisdom of monks, and crossed the borders into Burma and Laos. Every day was a new opportunity to learn, to grow, to experience. It was during his time in the north that he realised that three months would never be enough.

There was little reason to return to England. A university course awaited but it was something he had little enthusiasm for. After all, he'd just spent 12 years sitting on uncomfortable chairs listening to uncomfortable people talking about uncomfortable facts. Three or four more years of the same didn't really appeal to him.

Money wasn't an issue either, though the reasons for that did not fill Tom with much joy. His dad had died 18 months previously and left him enough money and property that Tom didn't have to work unless he wanted to. Not that he wanted to be one of the idle rich forever, one thing his dad had instilled in him was a strong work ethic. But he felt he wanted to learn more about the world beyond the small Oxfordshire village he'd grown up in or the private school that he'd felt had stifled any independence he may have had inside him.

He didn't have much of a relationship with his mum, at least not since she had taken up with a younger guy not long after his dad's death. He'd known they didn't have a perfect marriage and he knew they'd both had affairs, several of them. But he'd thought she could have waited a little longer than four months before moving a new man into the family home. He'd had a massive argument with her, one that had ended with him packing his things and leaving. He hadn't spoken to her since.

So, here he was, young and good looking, though he didn't think he was arrogant with it, and a bank balance that meant he could do as he please for the next few years at least.

Tom was snapped out of his thoughts by the plane hitting turbulence as it descended through the cloud cover towards Suvarnabhumi. Would the city of angels be a city of ghosts or would it let him lay bad memories to rest?

Tom lay back on the King-sized bed in his suite in the Banyan Tree, all paid for by the company of course. It was a far cry from some of the places he'd stayed 27 years previously. He could have afforded to stay in the best hotels back then but had felt he would have been cocooned from the reality of the country so had chosen standard backpacker guesthouses.

He'd had to share most of those accommodations with a bunch of scuttling friends and he still shivered whenever he saw a cockroach. He could cope with snakes and spiders but those little fuckers gave him the creeps ever since a night of opium dreams had been interrupted by the biggest cockroach he had ever seen settling on his chest. There was little chance of that happening here, the suite at the Banyan Tree was as pristine as any accommodation he had stayed in.

As jetlag threatened to pull him into its embrace, he wondered if he'd made the right decision in accepting this post. Then he remembered that there had been little choice in the matter. One of the junior editors at the publishing company where he was the managing editor had accused him of behaving inappropriately at a conference. He had no idea if he had or not, heroic quantities of cocaine and alcohol meant he had little recollection of the evening in question. But his boss, Kevin, had left little room for choice.

"Look, Tom, you're one of the best editors Green-Hayes has, if not the best. And you have an eye for a book that will sell. But in this day and age, that sort of behaviour is just not on. A couple of board members wanted you sacked but I made a case for keeping you and pointed out that the last three books you signed have all been major bestsellers.

I offered a compromise. You know there's a massive demand for Asian literature just now and we just acquired a small publishing house in Bangkok. As it's a city you know well, I suggested we second you there for a year or two, enough time for this nonsense to blow over and for that girl to move on somewhere. Go over, check the new company out, and see if there are any potential sellers on the books. Just keep your nose clean, and I mean that both ways, do your time, then come back as if nothing had happened. Who knows, maybe you'll discover the next Haruki Murakami."

So there really had been little choice. He could have resigned but the publishing industry could be so incestuous that someone would have talked, whispered behind his back, and he knew job offers would have been few and far between. And after 27 years, surely he could put the past behind him?

He wasn't due in the office till Monday, so had three days to recover from jetlag and to explore the city and see what had changed. The view from the window showed a lot of that change; there had been plenty of skyscrapers in Bangkok back in the 90s, but now it seemed they were everywhere, office buildings, condos, malls, and luxury hotels. He knew the real Bangkok probably still existed at street level, but this was now a skyline that could compete with any western metropolis.

Tom knew that one thing that would have definitely changed was his old contacts. Trusted people who could get him anything he wanted likely had families now and had retired from their old ways. Well, that or they were in prison or dead. Operating on the wrong side of the law was always a risky career choice and especially so in a country with severe laws. Though the recent move to some form of cannabis legalisation had caught him unawares. He would never have guessed that Thailand would have relaxed their draconian laws on weed though he knew that like many other things in this land of often fake smiles, the decision had been one driven by the love of money.

He was also conscious that this posting was a form of probation. Tom knew that someone would have been asked to keep an eye on him and that he would have to keep his dark desires and habits hidden from office life. That said, he was here as head honcho to ensure the Bangkok company was integrated into the global family smoothly. That meant there might be some toes that could be trod on. As part of the deal, the former owner of the Thai publishing house was remaining as managing director and may not take kindly to London sending over a hotshot to oversee things for a year or two. So, one of his first tasks was to reassure Aekarach Tortermvasana that Tom wasn't a threat and to make him his new best friend. Tom resolved to invite the Thai to dinner on his first day at work in the first part of a charm war.

Tortermvasana had been successful as a writer before launching the publishing house and, from the reports he'd read over in London, was a better writer than a businessman. Tom had read the translation of Tortermvasana's first book and had been impressed by the powerful writing and the insights into how Thai society worked. He also had something in common with Tom; a good eye for a story that would sell and he had signed a few regional bestsellers as well as one book that had done well in English language markets, and it was that which had caught the eye of Tom's boss. The Thai hadn't written anything in five years, however, and Tom was hoping that the reduction in responsibility and pressure would lead to more books in the future.

Looking at his watch, Tom saw that it was already 3pm. Today was lost as far as exploring was concerned and he decided to grab a few hours' sleep then eat at the hotel restaurant.

It was dark when he awoke, and the jetlag had mostly gone only to be replaced with hunger pangs. He decided he couldn't be bothered showering and heading downstairs so it would be room service then a long, hot bath. Seeing it was past nine, he ordered from the hotel's room service night menu; tiger prawn spring rolls, phad kaprao, and a glass of Chalawan pale ale. He didn't want to drink more than one beer as he wanted to spend the next day seeing the city that had played such a big part in his life.

The food arrived within 45 minutes and was as excellent as he had expected from such a prestigious hotel. With his appetite sated, he lounged on the bed for a couple of hours, bouncing between channels on the large TV but never settling on anything. Bored but tired, he decided to run that bath before retiring for the night. Tomorrow could be interesting.

1994

After two months in Thailand, Tom realised he didn't want to return to the UK anytime soon. Though he had plenty money in the bank to extend his trip as long as he wanted, Tom wanted to explore work options. He briefly – very briefly – toyed with the idea of buying a bar on one of the islands but quickly came to his senses. It would trap him in one place and a sedentary lifestyle was definitely not what he was looking for. He also wanted to avoid the cliché of teaching. But he loved writing, English had been his favourite subject at school. How could he monetise writing while enjoying what he did? He'd had no formal journalism training and he was unsure that *'my English teacher thought I was very talented'* would impress many people. Maybe if he sent examples of his writing to some newspapers and magazines, someone would like what he did. He could also send stuff to Lonely Planet as he knew there were always looking for updates. Hell, even last year's version – which was by his bedside – already had a few outdated entries thanks to restaurants and guesthouses closing or opening.

Of course, all his submissions could be sent back, but he knew he had a good chance with Lonely Planet and he also knew that people back in a usually cold and miserable UK loved glimpses into something better. It also helped that he was a fairly good photographer, maybe not professional level, but skilled enough that he could supply each piece with plenty of photos that would add colour and depth. He'd started on his dad's camera and when his dad had seen the promise in those early shots, he's bought Tom a Nikon F90, one of the best cameras on the market.

His geek mate back home had also been going on about this new thing called internet that had launched a year or two before. He was convinced that this would be the new big thing and would be like an encyclopedia anyone could access and find out about... well anything really.

To be honest, Tom had only half paid attention to what Ben was saying but now he thought about it, the more he realised this could be a real outlet for frustrated writers if it took off. So, he did have ideas and options, though only time would tell if they had been good ideas or realistic options.

He decided to keep a comprehensive travelogue – great idea, Burton Holmes – of everything he did and saw; the guesthouses and hotels, the tourist and non-tourist sites, the food, the transport, everything, as well as photos to accompany each entry. He could then edit that information into different-sized pieces and, once he felt he had enough, he would start sending them to different publications. He wondered if this internet thing would allow for electronic communications and noted to ask Ben when he phoned him next. For now, he would have to rely on good old airmail. He'd give things two months from posting and if he'd had no interest, he could move on to his next idea.

Tom was currently in Chiang Rai, attracted as much by the stunning scenery as by the easily accessible opium. Looking at his map of Thailand, he realised it could be a fortuitous place to start. Tales of the Golden Triangle could be a great hook for an editor looking for something different, something interesting. He could then travel west to Chiang Mai before heading south to the Thai heartland of Sukothai and Phitsanulok. From there, east, and a brief sojourn over the border to Vientiane before forging south through Isaan, the country's rice bowl, and ending up on Bangkok which in itself could produce several pieces.

He wouldn't even have touched the south or the islands and would have enough material for a dozen or more articles as well as plenty of updates for Lonely Planet. If his idea worked and he got signed up to write regular pieces, then he could plan different trips and use Bangkok as a base.

Several weeks later, he was back in a mid-range hotel in Bangkok. The trip had been a success, at least in terms of the amount of material he'd collected. He spent the next few days confined to his hotel room editing text and developing some images, only emerging at night to drink and seek out more opium. He'd sorted all the information into three types of finished material; short listings for Lonely Planet, and both short and long-form pieces to send to magazines and newspapers.

He'd had a long phone call with Ben, who promised to look into sorting some form of email account for him, though he warned Tom that not every publication may have that option yet. He also asked Ben to collate a list of addresses of newspapers and magazines that might be interested in travel pieces. Two days later and Ben called back, providing a long list of physical addresses and fax numbers which Ben jotted down as well as details of an email account Ben had set up for him.

There were a few things in Tom's favour; he had an eye for detail so he often included things in his pieces that other writers may have missed. That eye for detail also extended to his photographs, he always seemed to capture candid moments that made his snaps stand out. Lastly, his witty observations seemed to make his writing stand out, or at least so he had been told. He had a knack of seeing the humour in what others might have seen as bland moments.

Yet despite all those positives, he knew it was going to be a waiting game and his confidence would remain shaky until someone accepted one of his submissions. He didn't want to do any more pieces until he knew whether it was going to be something that brought in money, even a little, and was worth putting effort into.

He'd decided to make Bangkok his base. It was a good jumping-off point for anywhere in the country, or the region for when he wanted to explore further. There were cheap flights from Don Muang if he was heading further afield and plenty of trains and buses for exploring Thailand's countryside and islands.

Tom didn't want to live in an expat cocoon with a comfy condo and all the trappings of privilege. He wanted to immerse himself in everything Thai, from the food to the language to how ordinary people lived. After more than a week of searching, he settled on a first-floor apartment in Suan Luang above a noodle shop on Phatthanakan Road. It was close enough to the transport hubs he'd be using but far enough from the tourist zones that he – mainly – wanted to avoid. Of course, he'd have to dip his toe into those places if he was writing for a living; most visitors to Thailand wanted to tick places like the Grand Palace off their carefully compiled lists. But he really hoped that an editor might want a wider flavour than those oft-trodden places.

One thing he wanted to avoid, or at least only write about if asked to do so, was the sex scene. He'd visited Nana Plaza when he first arrived, more out of curiousity than lust, and had his feelings that it wasn't for him confirmed. Not that he had any prejudice or dislike for those working in the sex industry, it just wasn't to his specific tastes.

Despite his lack of Thai and his new landlady's lack of English, he had somehow managed to negotiate good terms on a one-year contract. He then furnished the apartment simply but comfortably; a good bed was his biggest expense and he also upgraded his aging word processor to a newer model. While his initial submissions had been in easily legible longhand, he knew that any regular work would have to be typewritten. If Ben was right, he'd maybe invest in a computer at some point but he'd wait to see how much it would be useful and needed.

With a base established, the next stage of his plan involved learning the language, or at least enough of it to get by when in the more rural areas. He was under no illusion that fluency would be achieved quickly, enough people had told him how difficult it was to learn, but as long as he knew the basics, he'd be happy. He had found a language school on Phetchaburi Road, only two kilometres from his apartment. Tom had explained to the admin staff that he'd be out of town on a regular basis and couldn't commit to a rigid lesson plan. The secretary had advised him that being part of a class would be no use as his classmates would quickly be ahead of him. She suggested that a one-to-one course would be his best bet though he would have to pay a set fee for a 12-month course.

1992

Tom's public face hid many secrets. To the people he met, whether on his travels or when out socialising, he was an amenable and witty Englishman. His predilection for recreational drugs was a lighter shade of dark, a mere shadow compared to what lurked below, though his recently acquired taste for opium was something that worried even him. But hiding in the darkness was a love for pain, or a love for inflicting pain to be more precise.

While the practice of fagging had disappeared – officially at least – from the English public and boarding school system by the early 1980s, the reality was that it was very much still happening. The victims were too scared to talk about it, and the perpetrators had a strict code of silence that meant nobody outside the school knew it was happening. If you challenged the established order, then you faced being ostracised or beaten.

Tom had been ambivalent about it all, at least until his own fag had crossed a line and stolen from him. Up till then, he had been fairly laidback about the system and saw himself more as a mentor than a master. The boy, Paul Grayson, was a diminutive little thing who would jump at his own shadow. Tom had been heading to a study session and had ordered the boy to clean Tom's room. But when he was halfway to the study group, he realised he had forgotten an important book. When he walked into his room, he found Grayson rifling through Tom's weed stash.

Enraged, he had slapped the boy in the face and then had ordered him to bend over a chest of drawers. Removing his belt, he began to flagellate Grayson, a red mist banishing any and all reason. He knew other seniors administered punishment but this was his first time. As the mist dissipated, he realised to his horror that he was sexually aroused. Disgusted with himself, he told the boy to leave and lay on his bed, his mind a maelstrom of tortured thoughts.

He analysed his actions, and his reactions, and realised it was not the boy that had turned him on, he knew he wasn't gay, it was the power, the control, the inflicting of pain on someone who was totally helpless. It didn't stop a wave of nausea rising in the pit of his stomach though. Although the boy was 16, and despite many of his peers regularly giving out beatings, he knew that if disclosed, his position at the school would be in jeopardy, never mind what his parents would say.

For more than a year, he suppressed these new desires, at least in real life. Once he had left school, he made a trip into London and visited a sex shop and bought some magazines and videos that catered to this niche that had embraced him. His purchases only served to confirm his tastes yet he now faced a dilemma; how did he turn those tastes into more than a masturbatory fantasy?

It was the same sex shop he had visited before that finally supplied an answer to his dilemma. Four months after finishing school, he plucked the courage up to return and questioned the owner – a stereotypically sleazy-looking man of around 40 called Dave – as to whether there were any clubs that catered to his sadistic bent.

"Course there is, mate," said the man in a Cockney accent that was even more stereotypical than his sex shop owner looks.

He'd gone on to explain that there were just as many people who got their kicks from having pain inflicted on them as there were people like Tom who wanted to inflict the pain. Intrigued, Tom had listened as the man told him about a weekly private club, away from the judging eyes of the public – and the police – where people like Tom could be the people they really were beneath the façade. He'd gladly handed over the £100 the man asked for as a 'membership fee'.

So, the following Friday, Tom met the man at the shop as instructed. He'd been unsure if there was any dress code, though he guessed there would be a lot of fetish clothing, so had worn a simple black t-shirt and jeans. Dave had greeted him warmly and, once the shop had been locked up securely, they caught a taxi to Vauxhall, paid for by Tom of course.

Although the area as a whole was undergoing a lot of gentrification, some parts were still laden with shadows, grimy buildings hiding from the light and any progress. Dave led Tom down a side street lined with railway arches on one side and derelict flats on the other. There was graffiti everywhere, ranging from fantastic street art to the assertion that 'Maureen is a slag'. The man stopped outside a non-descript arch, bordered on one side by a car repair shop and on the other by a clothing wholesaler. Dave knocked on the heavy metal door and it was answered by the scariest-looking man Tom had ever seen.

He was around 6'5 in height and was easily around 22 stone. It wasn't his size and weight that scared Tom, however, it was the shaved head, the numerous tattoos, and the fact that he was dressed all in leather complete with a spiked dog collar. Despite his ominous appearance, he greeted Dave and his guest warmly and Tom had to stifle a laugh that such a scary-looking man had such a soft, effeminate voice.

Tom noticed that Dave handed the man two crisp £20 notes, so much for the £100 membership fee. Once through the metal door, they entered a reception area. The old railway arch had been divided up using MDF panels and this front area gave no clue as to what lay beyond. However, Tom could hear the hypnotic sound of techno with a heavy bass and wondered what to expect. The woman behind the desk, similarly attired to the doorman but far less scary, took their names and waved them in.

The main room that lay beyond reception was also the largest. The walls had been dressed in various black drapes and what Tom thought might be parachutes. They made the space feel smaller, almost claustrophobic, and the effect was amplified by the large strobe hanging from the ceiling. Tom estimated that there were around 30 people on the dancefloor, all in various outfits that, till now, he'd only experienced in magazines and videos. There was leather, lots of leather, as well as chains, collars, whips, and various other accessories. Despite feeling a little underdressed for the venue, Tom felt very much at home.

A few of the dancers greeted Dave and looked at Tom curiously. Fresh meat for sure though his outfit didn't give any clues as to his tastes. Dave then led him to an empty table and they both sat down. A gorgeous hostess approached them, her curvaceous figure ensconced in a tight basque with sheer stockings and knee-high boots that made Tom smile. What he wouldn't give for an hour or two alone with this beauty.

She returned a few minutes later with two pints of lager and a seductive smile for Tom.

"Don't even think about it, mate. Well, you can think about it, but don't do anything. That's Mandy, she's the manageress but she's also Bill's wife. Bill was that behemoth on the front door. They only ever play as a couple and Bill's a dom top."

Tom shivered. While the woman was utterly stunning, the idea of being buggered by Bill did not appeal to him in any way. Though he may just be starting on his journey of sexual discovery, he already knew that his tastes were strictly heterosexual. He'd probably join a threesome as long as nothing was expected from him.

Dave had removed a baggie from one of his pockets and was racking up two large lines on the table. Seeing Tom's worried face, he laughed.

"Don't worry, it's a cool venue and anything, and I mean anything, goes. Hell, I even know a couple of cops who are regulars and they're always dusting their noses."

Task completed, he rolled up a note and passed it over. Tom hesitated, not through any reluctance to indulge, but more because he wondered what quality Dave could obtain. The man interpreted his look perfectly.

"Listen, son, I may look like a sleazy bastard, mainly because I am, but I only score quality gear. This is Peruvian flake, very high purity, and probably better than the shit your public schoolboy mates can get."

Tom didn't want to contradict him and tell him that Peruvian flake was what he usually got, so he looked suitably impressed and snorted the line in one go.

"Damn, that's really nice," he offered as he rubbed the detritus from his line onto his gums.

"Told ya," replied Dave as he made short work of his own line. "Right, let's give you the tour."

There were doorways, or at least curtains, to both the left and the right at the back of the room. As Dave led Tom through to the rear, the techno soundtrack began to be underpinned by cries and screams. Tom swallowed. It was all becoming very real, maybe too real. What had appeared both arousing and exciting on a screen was now mere feet away from him and he wasn't sure he was ready.

They had taken the left entrance and the space at the back of the arch had been subdivided into smaller spaces of varying size. As Tom peered nervously in the first one, he gasped as he saw a naked man suspended from a wooden frame while two women were inserting needles all over his body. His initial shock soon disappeared as he realised he was aroused and hard. He watched for a few minutes before Dave tapped him on the shoulder and beckoned him to follow.

The next space had a woman shackled to a strangely-shaped sofa while three men in masks used her.

“Do you want to join in?” asked Dave.

“No. Not tonight. Tonight, I think I’ll just watch. Maybe next time.”

Dave laughed and led him further into the Inferno.

The next space had a leather-clad dominatrix humiliating a couple and the last on this side was just an orgy. ‘Just’ thought Tom in amusement. It said a lot that an orgy could have the tag ‘just’ attached.

As Dave led him back to the entrance, he smiled at Tom.

“So, what do you think so far? Is it everything you hoped it would be?”

‘It’s that and more. I never dreamed a place like this could exist. At least not in London.”

Dave laughed again.

“Where did you think it would exist? These dark tastes you have discovered exist in every town and city. Hell, probably even in every village, perverted desires satiated behind a wall of floral curtains. I know of four other clubs like this in South London alone, not to mention the countless private parties held in unassuming houses.”

Tom was speechless as Dave led him round to the other corridor to see what delights awaited him.

This side was laid out identically to the other, each space containing depravity Tom had only seen in two dimensions but that was now laid bare in all its glory. He was still hard and had to resist the urge to go further, to either participate or to pleasure himself. No, tonight was only about finding his feet in this new world, and he also wanted to be dressed more appropriately in the future as he was the only person other than Dave who was in 'civilian' clothing.

"Seen enough?" asked Dave?

Tom nodded and the older man led them back to the table and ordered fresh drinks.

"I'm guessing your curiousity has been satisfied. Now the question is; was it just curiousity or have you found your path?"

"I think I knew it was more than curiousity, Dave, but I did wonder if it was something that I'd only want to do in private or could I like clubs like this. The answer is both. I'm sorry you've had to babysit me though, feel free to go and join in wherever you want."

Dave laughed. "I'll let you into a secret, well two actually. I'm more of a voyeur than a participant. But when I do join in, I prefer boys. Don't worry by the way, you're too pretty and refined for my tastes. I like boys with tattoos and who are a little rougher round the edges."

It was Tom's turn to laugh. "I wasn't worried in any way, well, only as far as worrying about spoiling your night."

"Not at all. In fact, there's been an almost voyeuristic buzz from showing you round the club. Some of the looks on your face have been most entertaining."

Tom had decided he liked Dave, despite the negative first impressions he'd had. Those impressions had not been that surprising though, given Dave's 'profession' and his obvious lack of care when it came to personal appearance. They spent the rest of the evening drinking together, with the odd line in between, and Dave regaled Tom with stories from the scene.

Glancing at his watch, Tom realised he only had 40 minutes before the last bus to Wallingford.

"Dave, thanks for a brilliant night. I'm going to have to dash for the last bus home. It's been really eye opening and I'll come and see you in the shop so I'm more suitably dressed for my next visit."

"Do you have to go? You're welcome to crash at mine and you'll be perfectly safe."

Tom smiled. "I trust you completely, Dave. But I did say I'd be home on the last bus and don't want to change arrangements at the last minute. I'll be back though, both to the club and to the shop. I was unsure if this was the right path for me but tonight's been a real eye-opener."

"Ok, good, I look forward to seeing you again. Just to let you know, I'm getting new stock in on Thursday if you're looking for some fetish gear. If you can't make it up before the weekend, then I'll put some choice items aside for you."

They shook hands and Tom left the club, his footsteps quickening on the pavement as Bill said goodbye with a very suggestive wink.

1994

As Tom thought back to that first visit to the club in Vauxhall, he reminisced about the many adventures he had been on since that night. Dave had introduced him to a whole new world, one he truly felt a part of. With him still living at home in Wallingford, he had been forced to keep his ever-increasing collection of clothing and equipment, not to mention porn, locked away in case his parents discovered it.

Then his dad had died suddenly, a massive heart attack taking him at only 48, despite his regular squash and golf games. He was just beginning to cope with the loss when his mum moved her lover into the family home. He'd always known that both parents played away from home and had accepted that but to move someone into the family home so quickly had hurt him a lot. Words were exchanged, words they'd probably both regret for years to come, but the damage was done. The next day, Tom moved out to a small flat in Wallingford town centre.

Over the months after his initiation, he had explored different aspects of the BDSM scene with some being to his taste and some not so much. He'd discovered he preferred one-on-one scenarios with completely submissive women. They also had to love pain as that was his favourite kink. He'd been taught about needle insertion as well as the standard practices such as flagellation and hot wax. He'd even formed a couple of relationships, although not in the traditional sense, with women who loved the helplessness and humiliation that came with their couplings. Actual penetrative sex was not always on the menu; for Tom, it was about the power and control.

One woman was much older than him, a barrister who was formidable and dominant in court but who craved the exact opposite when it came to her sex life. The other was a student the same age as him who, like Tom, had recently embarked on a journey of discovery. Both women were single and had their own flats or houses, so Tom was able to store an increasing amount of his fetish gear at their places rather than take it with him every time he visited London though some he still kept at his flat rather than buying duplicates.

But now Thailand beckoned. He had long been thinking about a trip abroad before starting university and originally had planned for India. Then a friend had returned from six months in Thailand and had been exuberant about his experience. He'd regaled Tom with tales of elephants, temples, beaches, and brown-skinned beauties. Tom had been captivated and had visited a bookshop in town to buy some books on the country he knew little about. A few nights of absorbing the books, coupled with the enthusiasm of his friend, and his decision was made.

He knew he would have to – temporarily at least – leave his sexual adventures behind him but traveling was part of his plan when it came to discovering exactly who he was. While the BDSM scene was giving him one aspect of that adventure, he also wanted to experience other cultures, meet new people, try new foods, whatever awaited him.

Once his dad's will was sorted, he'd been shocked to find that he had been left almost everything, the family home and a small allowance for his mum the only exceptions. A lot of his inheritance was property; his dad had built a solid portfolio over the years and Tom had no intention of letting any of it go. It would provide him with a passive income and would only grow in value over the years. The cash part of the inheritance amounted to just over £500,000, an amount that made Tom dizzy.

He knew he could do Thailand in style, but he felt that he wouldn't connect with the real Thailand he wanted to experience. While the money was always there for emergencies, and the odd treat, he'd rather restrict himself to a set budget that would force him to seek out things within that budget. When he booked a flight, he even opted for economy over business or first class as he had this idea that a crappy flight experience would only add to his adventure. Tom also believed that Thai people would treat him as they found him. If he was overly ostentatious in his spending, then he'd more likely attract people who only saw his money.

Less than a month later, he was getting off a plane at Don Mueang Airport in Bangkok, the tropical heat hitting him like a well-crafted right hook. He'd experienced high temperatures on family holidays before but this was something different and he didn't have – or want – the option of air-conditioned refuge.

He took a minivan to Khao San Road, his destination a backpackers' hostel that had received a good report in last year's Lonely Planet guide. Checking in, he found his room basic but comfortable, a ceiling fan offering at least some respite from the heat outside. After a shower to wash away the grime of travelling and the sweat from the journey from the airport, he collapsed on the bed and let jetlag drag him into sleep.

2023

Tom had spent the weekend exploring a city that felt so familiar yet had changed so much. At street level, there were still so many of the reasons he had fallen in love with the place; stalls selling every type of street food and hawkers offering everything from sex toys to tourist tat. There did seem to be less of them, however, and far more western franchises everywhere. It was little surprise that the average Thai he passed seemed to be a little... well, bigger. McDonalds and KFC seemed to be everywhere, two businesses that never got his custom back home and certainly would not be getting it here.

There were definitely more buildings, architectural behemoths soaring to the sky and creating canyons that were untouched by the sun in places. He'd taken the BTS up to On Nut and had been shocked at the transformation. While there were still many old apartments in the area, the night market, a favourite former haunt of his, was gone, and it was another area that had seen condo towers sprout from nothing.

He'd walked the five kilometres or so from On Nut to where he had lived on Phatthanakan Road, quickly realising that one thing that had not changed was the tuk tuk and motosai drivers constantly slowing and asking if he needed a lift. He supposed that even in 2023, a farang walking any distance was still an unusual sight.

When he reached Suan Luang, he was dismayed to see that his former home had fallen to the development that had transformed much of the city. The odd shophouse survived, clinging like drowning men scrabbling for life to the concrete rivers that had forged their way through the district. Roads, intersections, flyovers, condos, it seemed like the very soul had been sucked out of the place he'd grown to love. How often had he walked these streets in an opium stupor, his glazed smile betraying nothing yet betraying everything to his neighbours.

He walked through the district looking for something to eat or even for memories that still existed today. The further he went, the less development he saw and he was happy to recognise buildings and apartments that had survived. There was a noodle shop by the road and, although it was not one from his time living there, he sat and ordered a bowl of Pad See Ew.

Sitting at a flimsy table on a seat not designed for farangs brought back many happy memories. One of his favourite things to do when living in Thailand had been people watching. Whether watching curious tourists navigate the inferno of Nana Plaza or the everyday life of ordinary Thais in his neighbourhood, there had been a voyeuristic delight that had made him think of Dave back in London.

He watched an ancient woman, the lines on her face telling a thousand stories, navigate the broken pavement with that day's shopping. For a moment, he wondered if he had seen this woman before, or at least a younger version of her. He may have watched this same woman more than two decades earlier but now, nearing the end of her life, she would have even more tales to tell.

Tom sighed. So much had changed yet so much remained the same. Bangkok may have become a multi-billion-dollar city but people still struggled, still fought their battles, brought up their families, laughed and joked, everything that may have been forgotten by those in their luxurious bubbles. The disparity he had seen so often still remained and, if anything, it had actually grown worse.

A young university student hurried past him, maybe late for her class at a nearby university or just rushing home for a lunch cooked by a loving mother. For a minute, and just for a minute, he imagined her clad in leather and restrained, powerless to deny his lust. Tom quickly banished those thoughts. He hoped that his lust would be more than satisfied that evening.

To his surprise, and to his delight, an internet search had revealed that the BDSM scene in Bangkok was thriving. Not only were there clubs catering to his deviant tastes, there also seemed to be a number of shops that sold clothing and accessories that he intended visiting. He'd only brought a small number of items with him as he had been a little nervous as to how he would explain a suitcase full of gags, dildos, and other accoutrements to an inquisitive and shocked customs officer.

He'd decided to check out one of the clubs that night. Demonia, located on Sukhumvit's Soi 33, looked good from its online pictures. If he liked it, he'd consider a year's membership. They certainly seemed to have all the right equipment and the girls also looked like they would suit his particular tastes in women. These clubs seemed to also offer the discretion that was a prerequisite, partly because of his new job but also because of the events that had led to him barely escaping Thailand with his life.

With his food finished, he decided to get a taxi back to the hotel. For a minute, he debated waiting for one to pass and flagging it down. Then he remembered the various bad experiences from his past; drivers who wouldn't cross into other districts, drivers who didn't want to follow the meter, drivers who didn't want a drunk farang in their car. Thankfully, this was the age of technology and he had already downloaded several useful apps to his phone. Checking Bolt, he saw there were a few drivers close by so confirmed a booking and was happy when a driver quickly accepted. The app told him it was five minutes till the driver arrived so he lit a cigarette while he waited.

On the drive back to his hotel, he added hellish traffic to the list of things that had definitely worsened. It had always been bad, well at least as far back as he remembered, but it seemed there were now double the number of cars traversing the city. Yet there also seemed to be a thousand new roads and flyovers and expressways, so quite why the chaos was so much worse eluded Tom.

The app had advised him that the 20km journey to the Banyan Tree should take 35 minutes. In reality, it was just over an hour when his driver dropped him off, Tom thanking him in his rusty Thai and adding a 100-baht tip to the fare. Once in the oasis that was his suite, he stripped off his clothes and stood under the power shower for more than 20 minutes, determined to wash the grime of the city from every pore. Once he finally felt clean, he decided to take a nap so he would be fully ready for Demonia that evening.

When he awoke, it was already dark. He didn't plan on heading to the club until 9pm or so though he had been a little disappointed to see it closed at midnight. Still, three hours should suffice for a first visit and would give him the opportunity to see if there would be a second one. He ordered from room service, an Australian Striploin with Basque Cheesecake to follow. While he waited for his food, he booted up his laptop and checked his emails and social media.

There were the usual unsolicited submissions from aspiring writers. Some of these he deleted, a few that piqued his interest were forwarded on to the editor who was filling his role while Tom was in Thailand, and two he kept aside to look at later. He'd developed an almost uncanny sense many years before of when a submission was worth investigating further. As well as being able to follow the basic submission rules on the company's website, Tom found that there was something about a person's tone in the accompanying cover letter – well, email –

that made him think their manuscript would be worth reading. It worked for him anyway, as two of his last three bestsellers had all started life as an unsolicited contact.

A knock on the door announced his food arriving, the waiter entering and setting up his dinner on the table in the lounge area. Tom thanked him with a smile and a 50 baht note then settled down to enjoy his dinner.

With dinner done, he settled on the sofa and stuck on some mindless programme on the ludicrously sized television. It was at least twice the size of the one in the bedroom though he had to admit it provided an almost cinematic experience. He forced himself to watch an entire banal episode of the series before heading for another shower. As he let the hot water cascade over him, he reflected on how much more he preferred books. While he – grudgingly – conceded that there were some good films and programmes, there was something more... well, just more, about a book. He loved the way that strong prose could conjure up mental images of the setting and the characters and when he did watch the adaption of a book he had read; he had often found himself disagreeing with the screen interpretations of both.

After a shave and shower, he faced the dilemma of what to wear to Demonia. He guessed that the clientele would be a mix of regulars, both expats and locals, as well as the inevitable curious tourists eager to dip their toes – and other appendages – into what they perceived as a cesspool of sleaze. Looking through his wardrobe, he decided on a pair of black Oxford trousers paired with a white and grey tribal shirt, both from Ozwald Boateng, an ensemble that had cost him more than £1200.

There were three things in life that Tom valued and spent a significant amount of his generous salary on. Quality clothes was one, high-end hi-fi was the second, and the very best drugs was the last and also the most enduring in his life. Thoughts of the latter were very much on his mind just now and he hoped that someone tonight would be able to source high-purity cocaine. He knew all his former networks would now be defunct and he wasn't so desperate that he was going to chance Soi Four and get some low-quality gear that had spent multiple hours up a Nigerian's arse. No, he'd rather do without than abuse his nose with shit gear; it had to be a minimum of 60% purity or he had no interest.

He dressed efficiently, again marveling at the sensual feel of the expensive silk against his skin. He finished off his outfit with a pair of Amberjack Chelsea boots and a few dabs of Moncler Pour Homme EDP, its sandalwood and sage tones the perfect sensual accessory to his clothes. Tom thought back to his first year in Thailand when his entire wardrobe was probably cheaper than what he was wearing tonight. He laughed. His change in sartorial styles had not come from money. After all, he had been a fairly wealthy backpacker. No, the change had come as he'd worked his way up in the publishing world and had realised that dressing better got him noticed more when it came to networking events and rubbing shoulders with the established literati world. People seemed to listen more to someone who paid attention to the little details like pairing the perfect pocket square with a bespoke suit.

It was really no different to the world of shadows that he inhabited in his other life. People wore masks whether fucking a stranger or looking to close a deal. Both worlds were marked out by lies and games. One thing he hated about his job was the ease with which existing celebrities got a book deal. They may be a great comedian or actor or singer, but could they actually write? In most cases, a ghostwriter, all of the talent and none of the recognition, was the one who filled in the gaps left after the vacuous recollections were complete. That said, they had several celebrities, and the accompanying ghostwriters, on the books at Green-Hayes and the revenue stream contributed plenty to Tom's not insignificant salary. Acknowledging that fact didn't mean he had to like it. It didn't mean he had to like the celebrities either. Masks and lies and games.

Satisfied he was ready, he ordered another taxi from Bolt. He had considered ordering a hotel limo but who knew if the company had anyone on the payroll here, ready to report the slightest indiscretion on Tom's part. He'd learned long ago to have a clear and unbroken demarcation between his two lives though the incident had led to him being here had almost seen those worlds collide.

With a final satisfied glance in the mirror, Tom left his suite and headed down to the lobby, to his awaiting taxi, and to what would hopefully would be a night of sated desires.

1995

Tom had now been in Thailand for nine months. His Thai learning was progressing slowly but steadily. More importantly, his writing had hit the right note back home, several of them in fact. He was now writing regularly for a newspaper and magazine in the UK as well as supplying pieces to Lonely Planet. He was never going to get rich on what he was being paid but that wasn't why he was doing it. As long as the payments allowed him to sustain his lifestyle in Thailand without eroding his inheritance, he'd be more than happy. No, when it came to his writing, Tom craved recognition, maybe even fame. He hoped that one day those travel and food articles he was writing so well would lead to him writing a book, though whether any book would be fiction or what he now knew so well, he had no idea.

His life in Thailand was fairly complete. He had a few friends, both Thai and expat, he travelled several times a month, he knew the best street food spots for miles around, and even his neighbours had come to accept – and like – the only farang living in the building. The only thing missing from his life, or at least the only thing that mattered to him, was any sort of sexual adventures that came close to his tastes.

He'd had several dates complete with ensuing sex in most cases. But they'd all been fairly vanilla and he'd always been left wanting more. As a result, he'd broken his own unwritten rule and ventured into the world of transactional sex. But while the women he'd hired had been complacent enough, the whole experience had felt like theatre. Although the scene was marked by lies and masks, when it came to actual play, things became real, more honest. Tom wanted his partners to show genuine fear but to be aroused at the same time. Boundaries existed for a reason, but how much you could push those boundaries was part of the thrill.

He thought back to Dave's words that first night in the club.

"Where did you think it would exist? These dark tastes you have discovered exist in every town and city."

Bangkok had to have a BDSM scene, even it was well-hidden. After all, it seemed to cater to every other perversion and dark taste known to man so there had to be people here too. A couple of months earlier, he had been introduced to a Russian drug dealer called Yevgeny and Tom was now a regular customer, elated to find that the quality of the cocaine and ecstasy was easily on a par with what he was used to back home. He decided to arrange a meeting with Yevgeny to pick his brains, and he may as well collect an ounce of Charlie to cover the next few weeks.

They met in Saxophone Pub, a smoky jazz and blues bar that attracted the highs and lows of the local population. Tom liked the place; the beer was always cold and the music was always superb. It was the ideal place to meet a friend... or your drug dealer.

The Russian arrived late as usual. He was wearing his usual outfit of a slightly scruffy black suit, an open necked white shirt sans tie, and a midnight-blue Homburg that Tom was sure had escaped from a 1950s jazz club. The man himself was diminutive but had the most piercing green eyes Tom had ever seen. A waitress quickly came over and Yevgeny ordered his usual cognac and another whisky for Tom. Once the waitress had left to fill their order Yevgeny passed a book over to Tom.

"I think you'll enjoy this one, a real tale of human tragedy."

Yevgeny was consistent, not only in the quality of what he sold, but also in the way he delivered his wares; safely hidden inside a hollowed-out book away from the prying eyes of the local police. Tom placed it in his small rucksack and thanked the Russian. He'd pass him the money much later.

"Yevgeny, I want to ask you about something and I know I can rely on your discretion. After all, what use is a drug dealer who can't keep secrets."

Yevgeny smiled. "Maybe one day I will write a book with all those secrets in it. Though of course I would change the names. You'd be surprised how many powerful Thais and expats rely on my services. Maybe you can help me, da? Now, what can I do for you, my young English friend? It can't be drugs as I already know what you like. It's nothing to do with visas as I know you are fully compliant with the laws here. So, what does that leave? I think it must be something to do with sex, da, am I right?"

Tom was a little shocked at the Russian's guess but soldiered on.

"Yes, it's to do with sex. You see, back home I was very into the BDSM scene. I'm a dom and a sadist but for obvious reasons, I keep my tastes hidden. I've been here nearly a year and every sexual encounter I've had so far has been vanilla. An old friend back home once told me that every city has a BDSM scene, even if it happens behind closed doors and drawn curtains. I'm hoping you know of such a scene or at least people who know about it."

"Well my friend, it's not something that really interests me. As you know, outside of recreational substances, I'm a respected expat with an import and export business, a legal one. I'm also happily married and have never been unfaithful to my wonderful Kattiyanee in 12 years of marriage. However, my business interests, not the legal ones, do bring me into contact with other people who thrive in this city's underbelly. Now, I'm not saying the person I'm thinking of can help you but if he can't, no-one can."

"Sounds interesting. Tell me more."

"I'll warn you now, this guy is the biggest bottom feeder I've met in 15 years here. Every time I meet him, which thankfully isn't often, I feel I need to have a shower afterwards. Sleazy doesn't even begin to describe this prick but he says he can get anything you want, no matter how illegal or distasteful. I've heard rumours that he can even supply underage kids but that's never been confirmed. If it ever was, I'd put a fucking bullet in him myself. I have two daughters and anyone that harms a kid is the lowest of the low in my book."

"Sounds like a nasty piece of work."

"He is, even without those rumours. He's also a sniveling streak of piss, a liar, and a coward, so if I arrange a meet, just be careful what you tell him. Give him a fake name, lie about where you live, say you're here temporarily, whatever. I wouldn't trust this guy as far as I can throw him but he knows that if he crossed me, then his death would be a long and very painful one. You understand, da?"

Tom nodded.

"He's a farang, English like you, and he goes by the name of Ronnie Baht. I'd suggest that you meet him somewhere you don't usually go. I'd also suggest that you pay him well. That way, he'll think of you as a cash cow and not someone he might give to the police as a sacrificial cow instead. A good figure would be 5,000 baht when he gives you any info and then a 5,000-baht bonus if the information leads to exactly what you're looking for. "

"Ok, thanks, that's some good advice. Ronnie Baht? I'm presuming that's not his real name?"

"Haha, no, his reasoning for his nickname is that he can get anything for the right amount of baht. I try to avoid doing any business with him unless there's a substantial profit in it for me."

"He sounds like a right charmer but needs must. I guess if he's the only idea you have, then we better arrange a meet."

"I'll phone him on the way home. You should have a layer of protection with me arranging things. The wanker really is shit scared of me which is a good thing. Give me a call at home tomorrow morning and will give you a time to meet. I'm thinking Lucky Luke's in Nana as a meeting place. I know you don't like the place or go there so it offers you a degree of anonymity."

"Thanks," said Tom, 'do I owe you anything for setting this up?"

"No, my friend, I'm happy to help. You're one of my best customers and I actually like you, something I can't say about most of the people I do business with. Just promise me you'll be careful and will follow all my instructions."

The next evening, Tom headed to Nana Plaza just after 7pm. Yevgeny had been right; it was not a place he liked though he did occasionally visit the bars by the entrance to indulge in some people watching. It was still early and girls were still arriving for work, looking nothing like the creatures of the night they would transform into once makeup had been applied and skimpy costumes squeezed into. He had a degree of pity for many of these girls, forced to flee a life of poverty in the rural areas of Northeast Thailand and to support their families by becoming vessels for empty dreams.

Of course, he knew there were some girls who had flourished, multiple sponsors funding them from around the world, supplementing their weekly incomes and extras. But there were others who fell into a downward spiral of drug abuse, seeking some form of anaesthetic to deal with the endless procession of not so hansum men, especially in high season.

Lucky Luke's was empty when he arrived, the cashier looking bored behind the bar and the two hostesses on early shift giving him a surprisingly cursory glance before returning to their food. Tom order a draught beer and waited for Baht to appear.

He was lost in his thoughts when a figure slid onto the stool next to him.

"You must be Paul," the new arrival said.

Tom tried to keep the surprise from his face. If ever someone had fitted a mental image based on a description of his personality, it was this guy. He just screamed sleaze from every pore of his being. The man was overweight, very overweight, and had such sallow skin that Tom wondered if he had hepatitis. He was also short, barely 5' 5 by Tom's estimation and not only was he unshaven, but by the odour that surrounded him, he could be allergic to showers. His skin was pockmarked with acne and his greasy hair clung to his head like a reluctant lover. All those things Tom could have overlooked but the way he looked at the two girls sitting at a table marked him out as the most dangerous type of predator. Every time he glanced at the girls, he licked his lips like some salacious lizard. Tom was unsure whether this was an involuntary response or if the man really was a complete sleazebag. He suspected the latter.

Tom forced a smile of greeting.

"You must be Ronnie." He didn't offer his hand.

"That I am, son, that I am. Any friend, or customer, of our Russian is a friend of mine. Now, why don't you order me a beer then we can grab a table and you can tell me what you're looking for."

Tom ordered the man a beer and another for himself then they moved to a table away from the girls. Ronnie took a long drink from the bottle then licked his lips again.

"Those two lasses are a right little pair. I may barfine them once our business is done but only if they do lezzy stuff. The tall one has a cracking pair of tits too."

Tom shuddered inwardly. This was one of the reasons he avoided the girly bar scene. It attracted lots of Ronnies from almost every country on the planet. Men who saw women as mere commodities to be bought, used, and then discarded. Yes, Tom's tastes might be seen as deviant by many but the scene operated on the basis of trust and consent. People like Ronnie relied on currency to fulfil their sexual desires.

"So, son, what is it I can do for you?"

Tom explained that he was looking for a BDSM scene in Bangkok and an introduction to it.

"Kinky? I like it. Course, most of these girls will do anything for a few thousand baht but I'm guessing you've tried that and it wasn't quite what you were looking for?"

"No, it needs to be mutual and consensual. It's not just about what I like; part of the satisfaction comes from fulfilling their fantasies too."

"Ok. And boys? Girls? Both?"

"Girls."

“What about age? Young? And if so, how young? Or do you prefer something more mature. Not to my tastes, like, I prefer a young lass with a firm body. Can’t be arsed with flabby tits and belly and all those wrinkles.”

Tom was amazed that the man didn’t realise the irony of what he was saying and remembered to increase how much he pitied the girls who had to service walking corpses like Ronnie.

“To be honest, age is immaterial, though they have to be legal of course.”

The little man shot him a hostile glance, making Tom wonder whether the rumours were true or whether Ronnie had simply heard the accusation too often.

“Ok, I might know someone, even a couple of potential contacts who could help. I will say, I thought I had heard every request no matter how depraved, but this is a new one. It may take a few days to touch base with people so let’s meet here again in a week, same time while it is still quiet.”

“Great, thanks.” Business concluded, at least for now, Tom drained his beer and made to leave. The less time he spent with this guy, the better.

“I’ll see you next week then,” Tom said as he started to leave, again not offering his hand.

Ronnie waved a hand absently, his attention already back on the two hostesses.

2023

On Monday morning, Tom was up bright and early to have a shower and breakfast before his first visit to the office.

Demonia had been disappointing, very disappointing, though something good had come out of it. His initial impression had been a positive one; everything seemed on point, from the décor and wide range of equipment to the various girls in roles of either dom or sub. There had been everything from leather-clad dominatrices to coquettish schoolgirls willing to be dominated. He had noticed that most of the customers for the dominatrices appeared to be middle-aged Thai businessmen, wealthy ones too going by the expensive suits they were wearing and the almost equally expensive bottle service to their tables.

This didn't surprise him. Remembering the years he had spent in the country, he had quickly realised that the most important thing to most Thais was face, or how others perceived them. In the Thai business world, showing weakness was a sign of failure. Being able to visit a place like this meant they could be who they really were without their weaknesses being judged. Roles and masks again, everything in life was theatre to some extent.

He had been glad he'd chosen the outfit he had as the venue had an all-black dress code. Tom had been content to sit in the bar area and watch the various interactions, or at least the start of them, that were happening around him. He'd been approached by the mama-san as well as the various girls working in different roles but had politely declined all offers. He appreciated that the club was catering for a wide range of tastes within the scene and was unsurprised to see an affluent-looking farang walk past him clad in a ballet tutu and high heels He was even less surprised to see that he was on a leash and being led by a striking Thai woman in a leather basque and thigh-length boots.

Yet, for him at least, something was missing. Yes, there was all the equipment he knew and loved. And yes, the women were beautiful and fitted in every fantasy scenario. But they were paid, extremely well paid, to fill those roles and he knew he could never be sure where those roles ended and reality began. He was sure that some of those girls reveled in the roles they played and genuinely loved either dominating or being submissive and controlled.

Tom had noticed one girl watching him from the other side of the room, he thought she was perhaps a guest rather than someone working there. She looked to be of Chinese ethnicity, was petite, and was wearing a figure-hugging black catsuit that left little to the imagination. Perfect cheekbones framed emerald-green eyes and deliciously red lips. Though she was small, she had curves that suited her figure. More importantly from Tom's perspective, she exuded a sensuality that ticked all his boxes and he could easily picture her bound and gagged and at his mercy.

He caught her eye and beckoned for her to join him. She hesitated for a moment then crossed the room and sat beside him.

"You're new, in town for business?" Her voice was more of a purr than anything else.

"Yes, definitely new to the club but not to the scene. I've just moved to Bangkok or should I say moved back."

A waitress approached them and, after asking what the girl wanted, Tom ordered a dirty martini for her and a double Balvenie for himself.

"I'm Kanya." That purr again, like spoken velvet massaging his ears.

Tom offered his hand. "Very nice to meet you, Kanya, I'm Tom."

"So, what do you like, Tom?"

Tom knew this wasn't a setting where shyness or a reluctance to talk was an option.

"Very dominant, and I mean very. The usual things, control and humiliation and inflicting pain when it's consensual."

Kanay looked disappointed. "Ah, that's a shame. I had been hoping you were a submissive needing a good pegging."

Tom laughed. "And I'd hoped you were a sub who loved being restrained and pleasing her master."

"Then I guess we're both disappointed then. It really is a shame, though. You're a very attractive man and those are few and far between."

"So, are you a guest or do you work for the club?"

"I'm just a guest. While I have every respect for the women who work here, I'm a little choosy about who I fuck. The idea of some fat and sweaty captain of industry or commerce being naked in my company is quite frankly revolting. But you don't seem very interested in partaking of the various pleasures on offer. Are you in a more voyeuristic mood this evening?"

Tom thought about how honest he should be.

"Not really. It's my first night and this visit was more about seeing what the club was like. Sadly, it feels like just another hostess bar, albeit one with better décor, some interesting rooms, and the occasional very attractive patron."

Kanya blushed, not what Tom had been expecting from the woman.

"There are some girls who genuinely love the scene but they are few and far between. I more come in the hope that some good-looking man is turned on by the idea of being prostrate under me while I fuck him with a strap-on."

Tom gulped, not something that happened very often. Kanya continued.

"May I ask? Do you ever partner up on sessions? As in two doms with one or more subs? I know it sounds strange when we've just met but I feel I'd like to know you more. But if it doesn't involve anything sexual, I'd weirdly be happy with that too."

"Yes, I've partnered up on a few occasions. Let's take it one step at a time though; I'd like to get to know you better too, even if it was just as a friend who I could talk to about the things we both like."

Kanya giggled, an almost childlike sound that belied who she truly was, then offered her hand again.

"Friends it is then, at least for now. Who knows what delights the future has in store for both of us."

Tom took the proffered hand with a warm smile.

"Very nice to make your acquaintance, new friend."

"So, can I suggest we play a game to cement this new friendship? It involves sitting where we are and chatting, getting gloriously drunk, and guessing what some of the guests do in real life."

"That sounds like a very good plan to me, Kanya."

They spent the next two hours drinking and laughing. Most of the latter came from the ludicrous guesses they both offered regarding guest's real occupations. A Thai man dressed as a human baby was an army general with mummy issues. A woman in a furry cat costume was a fervent Buddhist by day and a mother of three. And another man, this one clad from head to toe in leather and chains, became a mild-mannered schoolteacher in their minds.

Tom couldn't remember when he had laughed so much. Nor could he remember the last time he had met someone he felt such an affinity with. That affinity was only confirmed when she returned from the ladies and slipped him a small baggie of cocaine. Once he too had indulged, the ensuing conversation made him realise he now had a source for his favourite substance and, going by the almost immediate effects, the quality and purity were on a par with what he was used to.

It was nearing closing time when Kanya turned to him with a sad smile.

"I'm sorry, it's almost midnight and I need to do a Cinderella on you and flee the ball, not because my carriage is going to turn into a pumpkin though. I'm booked on the 6.10am flight to Chiang Mai. Fuck knows why I booked such an early flight, especially on a Sunday."

"Holiday?"

"Yes and no. I'm going to see my parents and my sister, but it's nice to get a break from Bangkok too. Plus, it gives me the chance to gorge on Khao Soi. There are a few places that do it here but they're never as good as the ones back home."

"Sounds nice. Khao Soi is one of my favourite Thai dishes. Now I'll have to find some."

“I’ll make it for you when I’m back if you want. I’m pretty good in the kitchen but I’m far better in the bedroom.”

That seductive purr again.

“How long are you away for?”

“Just six days. Will you miss me?” Kanya winked and Tom laughed.

“I don’t think I’ll have time to miss you. I’d imagine it’s going to be a pretty hectic week in this new job. Getting to know everyone and ensuring I don’t ruffle too many feathers. I need to wine and dine the former owner as well as a couple of our main authors. I need to reassure everyone that there will be no drastic changes. In fact, this takeover means more exposure for them all.”

Kanya laughed. “I hope your boss has given you a nice expense account.”

“Yes, but I can’t go too mad. They’ll notice if I start ordering vintage champagne all the time and I’d probably get a right bollocking. I plan on making sure I’m free on Saturday to view some condos. Do you want to come along and be my translator? I’ll treat you to a nice lunch, or at least my expense account will.”

“Sounds like a nice plan. In fact, I could cook you that Khao Soi when we finish. And I promise to keep all my strapons locked away.”

Tom, who was in the middle of drinking, spluttered the liquid.

“I really hope the hotel knows how to clean silk or I’ll be sending you the bill,” he joked.

Laughing, Kanya glanced at her phone.

"Ok, my Bolt is here. Are you sure you'll be safe on your own?"

"I think I'm big enough to look after myself. I'm just going to finish this drink and order a taxi too."

Kanya rose and Tom rose with her. They kissed each other on the cheek, a chaste farewell that said much about the uncertainty of where this was going.

Tom watched her head for the cloakroom and sighed. If only Kanya was submissive, then he might have found the perfect partner. He sighed again. Ah well, he'd found a good friend at least, not to mention a reliable source for coke.

Sunday was Tom day. He had no plans to leave the hotel all day, especially given the slightly fuzzy head he was experiencing. He ordered a light lunch to his room then lazed on the sofa with a good book. He booked the 150-minute Royal Banyan spa treatment for 2pm, had a shower, then decided to have some Cantonese food for lunch at the hotel's Bai Yun restaurant.

The spa treatment was fabulous, just what he needed before the week ahead. After a refreshing longan juice by the pool, he went back to his room for a nap before dinner. He awoke just after seven and ordered BBQ pork spare ribs and a portion of gnocchi from the room service menu. Tom day was all about indulgence, although with no alcohol, and pampering. Mission accomplished.

Tom felt ready for anything the week would throw at him. The company's offices took up two floors of the prestigious M Thai Tower on Wireless Road. It was less than three kilometres from the hotel but Tom ordered the hotel car service to take him there. It looked better arriving in a sleek Mercedes rather than a bog-standard Bolt, even if none of the staff actually saw him.

Dressed in his best Hugo Boss suit, the driver dropped him off in front of the building. Looking around All Seasons Place, he felt hemmed in on almost every side by concrete, glass, and steel, mighty edifices dedicated to commerce seeming to be the fashion in this area. He entered the atrium, glancing at the listings board to see the company was located on the 18th and 19th floors, something he'd been told but had somehow forgotten.

Kram-roo (ความรู้) Publishing, Bangkok, Ltd. Tom wondered if the name would be retained. He knew no decision had been taken yet, but he assumed it would stay in some form. Maybe they'd just add something to it, 'A Green-Hayes Company' maybe. After all, the name was known in the region and it would make no sense to get rid of it, even if Green-Hayes itself was a global name. As he approached the barrier before the lifts, he realised he didn't have a pass, and the burly – for a Thai – security guard didn't look the type to accept his word.

Retracing his steps to the main reception desk, he gave his name and that of the company to the girl smiling at him. He was sure that there was some school somewhere churning out clones for reception and front desk work. They all seemed to have those porcelain features with the same gleaming smile. The girl called up to her counterpart at the publishing company then gave Tom another smile.

"Please go up, sir. The reception staff there will issue you with a permanent pass, ka. Welcome to M Thai Tower, ka."

She gestured to the security guard and spoke in rapid Thai. The man smiled, something that made him seem even more intimidating, and opened the gate to the side of the barrier.

When he reached the 15th floor, Tom exited the lift and found himself in a wide-open airy space. As he approached the reception desk, two stunning clones rose in unison and gave him a respectful wai. He was pleased to see that both girls bowed their heads and that their fingertips were at eyebrow-level, a sign that they knew and respected his position. He returned the wai, though without bowing and with his fingertips lower to show them he knew Thai etiquette. The taller of the two girls came from behind the desk.

"Sawasdee ka, sir. Welcome to Kwam-roo publishing. Mr. Tortermvasana is on his way down to meet you. Please take a seat."

Tom had barely sat on the comfortable seating when Tortermvasana appeared. Tom was immediately struck by how... well... bookish the man looked. There was nothing about him that said 'businessman' at all and Tom thought he would more fit into an academic environment rather than what was meant to be one of the best publishers in Thailand.

Tortermvasana was a little over five feet tall, his hair wild and grey, and a patrician's nose, something unusual for a Thai. Tom always looked at a person's eyes when meeting them for the first time and he immediately saw that this man had an intelligence that shone out from them. He could imagine Tortermvasana always questioning things and never accepting facts at face value. His smile was warm and genuine, and Tom hoped that indicated his presence was welcome.

"Khun Tom, welcome to Thailand. I hope you've had a pleasant few days before coming to work. Please, come to my office and we will have a long talk before I introduce you to your team. Would you like a coffee or something else?"

Tom shook his hand, his grip firm but not threatening.

"Coffee would be lovely, thank you, Khun Aekarach."

Tortermvasana spoke to the girls and then led Tom through the office and up some stairs before entering a corner office with stunning views over the city. The office had hundreds of books on shelves and though there seemed to be no order to their chaos, Tom guessed the Thai knew exactly where every tome was. One side of the office was dominated by a large – and very messy – desk, while the other side was more casual with two sofas and a low coffee table almost as messy as the desk. It was here that Tortermvasana led him to and gestured that he should sit on one of the sofas.

"First of all, Khun Tom, let me say that you are very welcome here. I know books, I know good writing, and I can recognise talent when I see or read it. However, business I don't know so well. Balance sheets, overheads, all these things just confuse me. So, I don't want you to think that you are an intruder in any way. And I'm very glad London has sent someone so talented and who knows this country and some of our ways."

"You're too kind, Khun Aekarach. Can I just say that I read *Summer in Isaan* a few years ago, long before Green-Hayes was even thinking about buying your company. It's a wonderful book and gave real insights into the people and the place."

"Ha! Now it is you that is too kind but thank you. I hope that with you taking the business side of things over, I can once again focus on my writing. It's been too long since I had the time to be inspired. That said, I am at your service to help you adjust. My door is always open to you and I hope we can become good friends. I do, however, have one favour to ask. This is the biggest office but I have very much made it my own. It should pass to you but I'd be very grateful if I could keep it."

"Khun Aekarach, I am here to help not hinder. I may be here one year or two years; I don't know yet. But I want to cause as little disruption as possible so of course you can keep this office.

I want us to work closely together to take the company to new heights. I am considering appointing a CFO to handle the business side of things so we can focus on the literature side. I hope we can present great Thai writing and writers to the world as I know there is a lot of talent that has not seen the light of day."

"Thank you. That is very reassuring to hear. You read so many stories about companies taking over other companies and making so many changes, ripping the very soul out of them and getting rid of staff."

Tom smiled.

"The main aim of Green-Hayes is to find good stories, not become the subject of one. While I cannot promise that we will have the same number of staff in a year's time as we have now, I can promise you that the mission and values will not change. The sad fact is that Kwam-roo is losing money and we need to identify what is causing that and get the company back in the black."

"Yes, I understand that and hope we can work together to achieve it."

When the two men finished their coffee, the Thai took Tom on a tour of the office, introducing him to the various departments, from sales and marketing to editorial. Tom would have struggled to remember English names, let alone the tongue-twisting Thai names most of the staff had. He was amused to see that many of the women working in the firm had followed the tradition, if it could be called that, of adopting almost western nicknames. It was going to be easier to learn and remember nicknames such as Mouse and Deer than their real Thai names such as Duangkamon and Laksanara.

He then showed him to the office had had hoped Tom would accept. It wasn't much smaller than Aekarach's own, with floor-to-ceiling windows commanding majestic views of the cityscape. While it was empty and devoid of any personality, Tom knew he could stamp his own tastes on the blank canvas. Aekarach smiled when Tom said he loved the office and that he was more than happy with it.

He then led Tom along the corridor, knocked on a door, and then entered a much smaller office but with the same magnificent views. Tom was surprised to see a farang, his desk piled high with papers, who looked up and smiled as the two men entered.

"Tom, this is John Kopp who was our token farang until you arrived. John's American but don't hold that against him as he works in UK English as well as their own quaint version. John edits all our translated work to make sure that every nuance and idiom has carried over well. He's been here ten years so is pretty fluent in Thai."

Tom shook hands with the man, glad that he wouldn't be quite so isolated in the office.

John smiled again. "I'm sure your first day is busy as hell but let's do drinks later in the week and I can give you all the inside gossip." He winked at Aekarach as he said this and Tom realised he was joking. Or was he?

Once the tour was complete, Tortermvasana showed Tom to his office which was at the far end of the corridor from the Thai's own. Although smaller, it was similar in design to Tortermvasana's though without the piles of paperwork and accumulated books, at least yet.

The morning passed quickly, mainly taken up by administrative tasks including issuing Tom with a permanent pass to the building and assigning him login and email details. It had just gone 12 when Tortermvasana popped his head into the office and invited him to lunch. They walked the short distance to the Conrad Bangkok and had a light lunch at the hotel's City Terrace while formulating plans and ideas as to how to take the company forward.

After returning to the office, Tom spent the afternoon looking over current rosters, sales figures, and plans for the next few months. By the time 5pm came, both his head and his eyes were exhausted and he was even more sure that the company needed a CFO who might know little about books but who would know everything about business.

He called London, aware that it was mid-morning there so was a good time for a chat. He gave Kevin an update of his first day and got authorisation to head-hunt a suitable CFO as soon as possible. Once the call was concluded, Tom decided to call it a day and, saying goodbye to Tortermvasana and the other staff he saw, he headed back to his hotel.

1995.

It had been a week since their meeting and, though he wasn't looking forward to seeing the man, he was hopeful that Ronnie would have some contacts for him.

Lucky Luke's was again empty, and Tom realised it was more a place for late-night revelries than a bar you would usually meet friends in. Ronnie was already here, flanked by the same two girls who had been working the previous week. Their enthusiasm did not come close to matching Ronnie's own, and Tom suspected they were more chasing some lady drinks while hoping to avoid being barfined by the loathsome little man.

When Ronnie say Tom approaching, he rose from his bar stool and greeted Tom warmly.

"Hey, buddy, great to see you again!"

Tom knew two things for sure; he didn't want to be this guy's buddy and it certainly wasn't great to see him again.

"These sweet gals are Porn and Pook. Don't you just love those cute Thai nicknames? Porn's the one with great tits by the way, which makes her nickname even funnier. I took these two honeys to a short time hotel last week. Boy, did they deliver. Though they seemed to spend more time pleasuring each other but it was good to watch. I may take them out for round two tonight."

Tom was unsurprised that the two would rather have girl-on-girl action than girl-on-Ronnie action and he could see from their faces that a second encounter wasn't high on their bucket list.

Ronnie patted the girls on their asses and Tom resisted an involuntary gag reflex.

"Run along for now, girls. Uncle Ronnie needs to talk some business with his friend here.

No, thought Tom, *even if you introduce me to my ideal mate, there is no way in hell you will ever be my friend.*

He ordered a beer for Tom and another for himself.

"So, I have good news for you. It appears there is an underground scene catering to your tastes. For obvious reasons, they don't advertise beyond word of mouth. I actually have two contacts for you, both of whom organise house parties."

He handed Tom a folded piece of paper.

"Now, I've vouched for you since Yevgeny recommended you to me. So, these are their home numbers. When you call, simply say 'Ronnie said you could get me some nice wine.' Nice touch, no? I thought adding a layer of subterfuge suited the shadows that seem to surround this scene."

Tom sighed inwardly. While he knew the scene required, no demanded, a certain level of discretion, he suspected Ronnie had been reading too many spy novels. He slid an envelope across the bar to the man.

"There's 5000 baht in there. If either of the contacts proves useful, there will be another 5,000 for you."

Ronnie doffed an imaginary cap.

"Why thank you, sir. If you ever need my services again, my number is also on that piece of paper. Saves you having to go through Yevgeny."

Tom drained his beer quickly, determined not to spend longer than necessary in this man's company.

"I'll leave you to your pleasures. Thanks for the help."

He walked out the bar, sad at the idea of the two girls having to share uncomfortable embraces with Baht for baht.

He called the first of the numbers the next day and asked for Lamonphet. A deep and obviously well-educated male voice came on the phone asking who was calling and Tom gave the coded message he'd been given by Ronnie. There was a pause then a laugh.

"Ah yes, that stupid code from the stupid man. I think he believes he is in a James Bond film."

Tom immediately felt some affinity with the man.

"I did think it was a bit ridiculous myself but that's what he told me to say."

"I'm guessing this is Paul then? He did say there was a young Englishman looking for some adventures and I only gave him my number yesterday. Please, call me Lam, I know how farangs can struggle with Thai names."

"Yes, it's Paul here, but my real name is Tom. I don't really know this Ronnie Baht guy but a mutual friend, or at least acquaintance, had suggested he might be able to introduce me to people with similar tastes. He also suggested I give him a false name."

He heard a deep throaty laugh.

"Very good advice. So, tell me, Khun Tom, what are your particular tastes and I'll see if I can help you."

Tom hated talking about the things he liked, especially over the phone with someone he didn't know.

"Well, to start with, I'm a dom. I like control, humiliation, master-slave play, bondage, and..." Tom hesitated, "my real kink is I love to inflict pain. But it has to be on a consensual basis."

"Then I think we can accommodate you. We hold regular parties that cater to all of your list and more. There are three or four subs who attend these parties who love pain, within limits of course. In fact, we're hosting a party this coming Saturday. Would you like to come? No initial commitment from you other than a financial one; we charge 5,000 baht for each guest. The charges are purely to cover the costs of the food and drink available. There's a full bar you can help yourself to and a range of sandwiches and cold cuts in the kitchen. None of the people attending are sex workers, purely people with slightly different tastes from what others see as normal."

"Sounds like a plan. Is there a dress code?"

"Very much your choice. If you have fetish wear, then you can of course wear it, though I'd suggest you change into it after you arrive. You may get some strange looks walking through Bangkok otherwise. If you don't have any, that's fine too but I can put you in touch with a very good leather worker who makes custom clothes as well as some equipment such as cuffs and restraints. There is one thing, though. I know that if you have experience on the scene, you'll know how important discretion is. But some of our guests, both Thais and farang, are in the public eye a lot when it comes to their vanilla personae. We therefore respectfully request that you don't discuss what happens at our parties nor disclose anyone's identity."

"That goes without saying. So, Lam, what are the arrangements for attending?"

"As it's your first time, I will have my driver pick you up. Do you know On Nut?"

"Yes, though it's a fair distance from me. I live on Phatthanakan Road."

"Ok, be on the corner of Sukhumvit Road and Sukhumvit 77 at 7pm. I'm sure there won't be many farangs standing about but just in case, my driver will be in a black Mercedes. The fun usually starts around nine but we like to have some drinks and conversation first. It will give you a chance to meet some of our regulars too."

Saturday arrived, and Tom found he was as apprehensive and excited as he had been when visiting the club in Vauxhall for the first time. He wondered if the guests would be much the same as that club; people from all walks of life brought together by a common interest. He was aware that Lam had mentioned that some of the guests would be in the public eye so could understand the need for discretion.

The scene was so misunderstood by people. Everything was based on trust, consent, and a respect for boundaries. It was the very reason safe words existed. People also mistakenly thought that all the power lay with doms and masters, when the reality was that the real power lay with the subs and slaves. It was they who usually had the final decision when it came to boundaries and anything forbidden, and it was they who could instantly stop any play with a word or phrase.

There had been times when Tom had been in that situation, left frustrated because he had been too firm with a partner and had tried to take the pain to the next level. While it had frustrated him, he knew you had to obey the rules. Even in a big city like London, there were lots of interconnections and people knew each other or knew people who attended certain clubs. If someone broke the rules, if they went too far, then they would suddenly find themselves unwelcome at any party or event.

Despite those rules, those boundaries, and despite the fact he had to follow and respect them, Tom yearned for complete control. He wanted domination to be just that, for his sub to obey him completely and to have no safe words or boundary. And yes, he wanted to inflict pain, though not to a level that required hospitalisation, and he wanted the recipient to enjoy it too.

So far, his dream remained elusive, and rules, boundaries, and safe words have been a per of every liaison to date. Maybe tonight would be different.

Tom had dressed simply but smartly, expensive – his most expensive, in fact – black dress trousers paired with a black t-shirt that accentuated his muscles, something that he found women loved. He'd also had two very generous lines of Yevgeny's latest product and he could already feel the confidence and arrogance grow.

He took a motosai to On Nut; he was around 20 minutes early so made his way to the corner and lit a cigarette. There was an urge for another line but there was nowhere he could see to take it. Ah well, it could wait till he was at the party though a small bump in the car might be doable.

A black Mercedes pulled up beside him at one minute to seven, the driver dressed in suit trousers, a crisp white shirt, and black tie. *Whoa*, thought Tom, *this Lam must have a serious amount of money*.

The driver got out the car and, once sure he had the right person, opened the rear door for Tom. The interior still had that new car smell and Tom was now definitely sure that Lam had more than a few baht in the bank. The car headed towards the city centre, Tom managing to sneak a bump of coke while the driver concentrated on the traffic. After about 15 minutes, the car turned off Sukhumvit and into Ek, weaving its way through narrow lanes before turning down one that ended in a cul-de-sac and that appeared to only have around four houses in it, each separated from the other and looking like the higher levels of luxury. The driver stopped in front of a set of large wooden gates and pressed a button on a remote control, causing the gates to swing open automatically.

As the car swept into the grounds, Tom whistled inwardly. This was serious money for sure. As the driver swiftly moved to open the door for him, he saw a figure emerge from the front door. This must be Lam.

The Thai was in his mid-30s, though he could have probably passed for 10 years younger. He retained that thick, black hair that was so envied by the west and had bone structure that could have enabled a modelling career in another life. Those prominent cheekbones framed a sensual mouth and mischievous eyes, giving an overall impression of a bachelor uncle who took you to a brothel when you turned 16, not that Tom had had one, but it's what he imagined one would look like. He was dressed in what looked like a black silk Tang suit paired with matching black silk trousers. He walked up to Tom, a genuinely warm smile ready for him.

"Khun Tom, welcome to my home. It's very nice to meet you, especially given your growing reputation as a travel writer living here."

Tom was dumbfounded.

"Thank you, Khun Lam. But how did you know I was a travel writer?"

"As I said to you, the need for discretion is tantamount. Do you really think I would welcome you into my home without looking into your background? I will confess, I was a little worried when the first information I received said you were a journalist; I had visions of you wanting to expose our scene. But then a good English friend told me you were a travel writer rather than an investigative journalist and I was quite relieved. He also sang your praises rather loudly and said you were destined for greater things than filing copy from Thailand."

Tom didn't know whether to be embarrassed or honoured.

"I'm a little shocked anyone knows me. I don't really drink in expat or tourist bars and none of the publications I write for are available here."

"Tom, you need to understand, people know people here, and those people know other people. The result? It's difficult to keep much secret here unless you make the effort to do so. But come, enough chat, let me show you round the house and introduce you to the early arrivals."

The Thai led Tom into a spacious atrium and Tom was pleasantly surprised by the light. He had expected a marriage of traditional and modern with plenty of dark woods. Instead, this house was very much a marriage of modern and modern, white walls with colourful modern art, chic contemporary furnishings, and flashes of chrome that seemed to have been added as an indulgent afterthought.

He followed Lam through the house and out onto a pool and patio area at the rear of the house. There were already half a dozen people gathered though Tom was a little surprised that nobody seemed to be dressed for the evening ahead. As if sensing his thoughts, Lam laughed.

"The fun doesn't usually start till about nine. People will get changed later if they want to. This early part of the evening is more about socialising. and sometimes business too."

Tom noticed that he was the only farang in attendance, at least so far. The other guests were all Thai and ranged in age from about early 20s to about 60. Four were male and two female and Tom hoped there would be more balance once the rest of the guests arrived.

Lam took him over and introduced him to the group. Tom knew he'd never remember the names, not at first anyway. He was glad that everyone spoke good English as he'd still describe his Thai as very basic. One of the two women was particularly striking, wearing a dress that clung to her in all the right places. She had the petite frame so typical of Thai women but with added curves. What he particularly noticed though was her eyes, a deep-green that made him think of emeralds. His first thought was that she was beyond beautiful. His second thought was wondering what her preferred role was. He had no idea about the etiquette for the night ahead but he hoped that at some point, he would end up with this woman.

Over the next hour or so, another nine guests arrived. Of that number, there were two other farangs, a couple, or so it seemed, aged about 40 who both smiled politely at Tom. Even within secret clubs there were inner circles. Lam had told him that he always kept the guest list to even numbers, though of course there were no restrictions on the permutations of that number that might happen. The only general rule was that everything that took place had to do so under the auspices of consent. While each person might have their own boundaries and rules, it was up to them to tell those to any playmate.

As the evening wore on, people disappeared to change into their outfits. Chic cocktail dresses and smart suit trousers were gradually replaced with leather, rubber, harnesses, and all manner of fetish paraphernalia. Someone, Tom presumed it was either Lam or a very trusted servant, dimmed the lights in the main lounge and adjoining rooms. Soft lounge music began to play, though Tom couldn't see where the speakers were situated.

By now, he was feeling very self-conscious as he was now the only one not wearing some form of fetish clothing. He sipped his wine awkwardly and tried not to stare as the initial couplings commenced, nothing extreme as yet but still arousing from a voyeuristic perspective.

Then he became aware of someone standing behind him and turned. It was the woman with the emerald eyes. Gone was the Audrey Hepburn dress he'd so admired earlier, but it had been replaced by an almost sheer bodysuit, black stockings, and high heels, an outfit that he admired even more. Of particular interest to Tom were the various accessories she had chosen to wear. She wore a black leather collar with a ring for a leash as well as matching wrist and ankle restraint cuffs.

She smiled and then spoke in a voice that reminded Tom of velvet and dark rum.

"So, Khun Tom, or should I just call you sir? You appear a little overdressed but we can rectify that. May I ask, sir, would you like to own me for the evening?"

Tom struggled to speak, not a scenario he was used to.

"I'm...eh, I mean, it's my first time."

The woman laughed. "You don't strike me as a virgin."

Tom could feel his face reddening.

"No, I don't mean that. It's my first time at a party in Thailand. And I left all my outfits and equipment back in London as was a little paranoid what customs might say if they opened my cases."

She laughed again, a sound that was both rich and enticing at the same time.

"Now that would have been funny. I can just imagine one of our conservative female customs officers finding a suitcase full of fetish gear."

"Sorry, may I ask your name again. I know we were introduced earlier but I was too busy staring at your eyes to remember it."

"Alas, sir, my eye colour is false, cosmetic contact lenses that I absolutely love. My name is Ireshi, sir, I hope it pleases you."

"What does it mean? I'm afraid I've only recently begun learning Thai and have been focusing more on the words for noodles and chicken than on the meanings of names."

"No need to aplogise, sir. There are many farangs who live here for years without learning more than the most basic phrases. My name means 'queen', though I promise to always be deferential to my king. But you have not answered my question, sir. Would you like to own me for the evening? If my dress does not please you, I can go and change. But if it is I myself that does not please you, then you have my sincere apologies."

Tom felt his confidence returning.

"No, you please me very much, and you can please me all night, if you wish."

"It is not about what I wish, sir. If you truly want me, then I am yours to do with as you please. I wanted you as soon as I saw you but I also know my place."

Tom fetched them two glasses of wine from a nearby table.

"So, Ireshi, let's get the awkward parts out of the way to start with. Tell me your boundaries and choose a safe word for the evening."

"Hmm, let's keep the safe word simple since you are new to Thailand. If sir really goes too far, then I will cry out 'mai chai' which is one of our ways of saying 'no'. As to boundaries, I have very few. If sir wishes to hurt me, I ask that no marks are left where they might be visible, so please do not mark my face, arms, or legs. And although I do like pain, I am not a fan of burning, so no cigarette play though you can use candle wax. My only other boundary is one of practicality rather than taste. If sir wishes to indulge in anal, I ask him to remember that my asshole is small and tight while sir is obviously well-endowed by the looks of how those trousers are struggling to contain your excitement."

Tom gulped. Not only did this woman appear perfectly suited to his tastes but he hadn't even noticed he was fully aroused.

"I will certainly remember and follow your rules, Ireshi. But tell me, do you indulge in any...em...recreational substances?"

"I only use cocaine when playing, sir, but will also smoke marijuana when home alone relaxing, or home relaxing with a lover."

"I think we should retire to one of Lam's bedrooms, Ireshi. I feel too self-conscious dressed like this but I also want the pleasure of drinking in every inch of you."

***

Tom woke with a shaft of bright sunlight shining directly on his eyes. He groaned and stood up from the bed and padded naked over to the window, closing the thick curtains and returning the room to a more shadowy atmosphere that suited his aching head. He looked back at the bed. Ireshi lay still sleeping, naked except for the wrist cuffs that still connected her to the ornate headboard. What a night. She had been the perfect compliant sub, acceding to his every desire and he was pretty sure they'd managed to work through most of the Kama Sutra. Ireshi had produced a bag containing an assortment of sex toys and he was also pretty sure they'd used all of them at one stage or another over the evening.

His cocaine supply was as exhausted as he felt and Ireshi looked, the quarter ounce he had obtained from Yevgeny only a few days before nothing more than isolated crystals on an empty wrap. He couldn't recall the last time he'd indulged so much, both in sex and coke. He also couldn't recall such an amazing evening. Though it was a scene that hardly encouraged monogamy, it was one where strong relationships were often forged, initial lust being strengthened by a bond of trust as you got to know each other's tastes and boundaries.

There was a gentle knock on the door and Lam entered, wearing a luxurious silk bathrobe.

"Good morning, Tom. I had a feeling when you disappeared with Ireshi that we'd not see you for the rest of the night. She really is a perfect match for you not to mention being incredibly beautiful. One small word of caution, however. Her father is a senior police general and Ireshi can be incredibly jealous below that veneer of obedience. If you see each other regularly, or even just again, be careful not to upset her. And if you decide not to see her again, which I doubt, be sure to let her down gently if she feels the opposite. Even the most compliant sub can have a dark side, or darker than her sexual tastes anyway."

"Thank you, Lam, and thank you for inviting me into your home. Yes, Ireshi is something special for sure. We'll see how things develop."

"You're welcome, Tom. I hope we can have dinner and drinks one evening so we can get to know each other better. I'll let you get back to...well...whatever. If you're hungry, the staff will make you something or you can ring down to the kitchen for coffee and food. Just dial three on the phone by the bed."

With a knowing smile, Lam left the room. Tom looked back at the bed and the still sleeping Ireshi. He could feel himself becoming aroused again and moved onto the bed to wake his new lover.

2023

Three weeks in and Tom felt at home in the office. He'd quickly discovered that the business had a great team. The problem was Tortermvasana. Although a nice guy and a very talented writer, his man management skills left a lot to be desired, not to mention his complete lack of understanding when it came to costs and profit margins. He'd started the business with good enough intentions, wanting to give a platform to emerging Thai writers. But he'd made some poor decisions, thinking that just because he liked a manuscript, then it would be a commercial hit. Poor sales combined with overly-exorbitant advances and stupidly large print runs had quickly pushed the company into the red. While the few successes stood out, they were drowned by the failures.

Tom had explained to Tortermvasana that he wanted him to focus on writing and that any decision regarding signing a writer would lie solely with Tom. While he valued the older man's experience and would happily accept recommendations from him, Tom wanted the business back in the black within two years or less. He'd also realised that some of the younger editors were not only talented, they really had their finger on the pulse of what their peers were reading and what might be a commercial success.

He'd reorganised the submissions system and had one-to-one chats with each of the editorial team to identify their preferred genres. He'd also reduced the submission guidelines to the first three chapters rather than entire manuscripts. His reasoning was that if a book hadn't drawn a reader fully in within those three chapters, then the rest probably weren't worth bothering about.

So, with some changes to the website, including having an English version, submissions now went to one of the editorial team first. If they thought it was good, then they'd pass it up the line to Tom. He'd read the submission then have a meeting with the editor in question who would then explain to Tom why they thought that particular book would sell. He also wanted to see if his own sixth sense would match the expectations of the editors.

He was keeping John concentrating on editing English translations of their Thai language books but any new submissions in English would come directly to Tom. Everything they had published so far had been by Thai authors and he wanted to tap into the rich vein of talent he knew existed in the expat community. But 'talent' meant avoiding the thousands of clichés you could find online. Tom wasn't interested in yet another tale of a bar girl relationship going bad or sick buffalos and brothers helping to drain a farang's bank account. He'd already sent some speculative emails to western writers who seemed more in tune with the Thai psyche than with a bloated divorcee from Barnsley using his redundancy money for one last hurrah.

His two main targets were an enigmatic Englishman who went by the name J.D. Strange and another Englishman, Phil Hall, whose 'From Bangkok to Ben Nevis Backwards' Tom had devoured on the plane. Another thing he was planning to change was the entire publishing model. Till now, Kwam-roo had only released hard copies and Tom felt they were missing out on major revenue streams not releasing eBooks and audiobooks.

He'd already okayed his planned changes with head office who were totally on board with his ideas to increase revenue. After all, though they had a strong belief in the power of the written word, they were in business to make money.

Within a week of instating the changes, Tom had already received 12 submissions. Ten of them had been quickly deleted when Tom has skimmed the submitted chapters and realised they were full of the dreaded clichés. One of the remaining two was a murder-mystery set in Phuket and the first three chapters had hooked Tom enough that he'd requested the full manuscript from the writer, a retired policeman living in Mai Khao in the north of Phuket.

It was the other submission that had really caught his attention though, not just for the content but for the fact that it had been written by a Thai in English. If it hadn't been for the cover letter, then he would have assumed it had been written by a native speaker.

Dear Sir,

My name is Chompoo. I'm a recent graduate of Chulalongkorn University and am now working for a magazine here in Bangkok.

I have had a love of creative writing for many years but I write short stories rather than novels and am unsure whether this is something you would be interested in. Another potential issue is that my stories are quite dark, so much so that one of my teachers suggested I see a psychologist.

However, I find the darker side of human nature fascinating and feel that there is something primeval in some of our thoughts and actions. I wanted to reflect this in my stories.

I have enclosed two stories in this email and hope that you can consider them both. If you were interested, I write about one a week and putting together an anthology of these stories would be fairly straightforward.

I will understand if this length and type of story do not fit with your business model but hope that you at least fully read them.

Yours sincerely,

Chompoo.

Tom knew Chompoo was not the girl's real name. Thais loved nicknames and this one meant 'rose apple'. And given the content in her stories, he was not surprised that she preferred a degree of anonymity. Saying her stories were 'quite dark' might qualify for understatement of the year. They were extremely graphic, both in terms of the sexual aspects and the violence. While they appealed to Tom on a personal level, he could also be detached enough from his own feelings to recognise that this girl was a very talented writer. Any salaciousness was balanced out by a command of English and nuances that many western writers would struggle to emulate.

The first story was about misplaced jealousy and misunderstandings that led to multiple murders, all described in graphic and gory detail. But it was the second that had really piqued Tom's interest. It was the tale of an outwardly conservative Thai woman who led a double life as a dominatrix. The actual writing was again superb, but it was her knowledge of the BDSM scene that struck Tom. It had to be intimate knowledge as it showed an understanding of the scene beyond anything an internet search would provide. It was easy enough to describe the actions, but those alone would have come over as cold and sterile. No, this girl wrote about the feelings, the thoughts, the desires, even the doubts, and she captured them perfectly.

His initial worry was that such stories would never sell. But then he remembered the strange fascination that many Thais had for the macabre, especially on social media. It seemed to be quite acceptable to post photos of the aftermath of the many dreadful accidents that happened every day on Thailand's roads. Horror films and ghost stories were also hugely popular, from modern day horror flicks to traditional tales of bloodthirsty ghosts. Maybe this could work though given the details in the first two, they may need to tone some of the stories down. He'd see how the stories developed over the coming weeks and months.

He created a new folder on his laptop, labelled it 'Chompoo', and downloaded both stories into it as Word documents. There was maybe even a chance of pitching the stories to Netflix or similar. Thai films and series had been proving popular in recent times. He composed a reply to the email.

Hi Chompoo,

Thank you for the submission. I must say, I was very impressed by your standard of English. It was as good as anything a native speaker would manage. I was even more impressed with your two short stories. Yes, they're dark but they are very well-written and definitely draw a reader in.

Of course, we will have to see if that standard is maintained in other stories but if so, then I could see potential in releasing an anthology of your short stories.

If you can send me another three or four, and if they are of the same quality, then I'd like to arrange a meeting to discuss terms and to offer you a contract.

I look forward to hearing from you.

Best,

Tom.

1996

Life was good. In fact, it was almost perfect. His writing was selling on a regular basis and he now had a contract with one UK broadsheet to produce monthly travel articles about Thailand. When you added in the frequent freelance pieces he was writing and the regular contributions to Lonely Planet, then not only did he have a decent revenue stream, but his name was getting well known too.

Ben had set him up a website though he was still technically naïve. After a couple of months of Ben taking sole responsibility for the site, he'd finally grown frustrated and sent what he called 'a dummy's guide to websites' video. Now, Tom had no problem in uploading the hundreds of photographs he was taking; he'd bought a scanner and had spent a week or so learning how to use it. At Ben's suggestion, he'd also started keeping a blog and had found it a good place to post rejected articles or just his own thoughts and observations. He hadn't been sure if the site would be a success but much to his surprise, Ben told him that the site was getting 5,000 hits a week. He'd also said that on a monthly basis, he was growing by about 200 visitors every month.

His blog had the ability for readers to leave comments though there had been a couple of negative ones with the usual sex tourist or colonial attitude remarks. He found both those negatives hilarious. He didn't have any interest in transactional sex though he'd interviewed a few sex workers for a magazine piece. And he felt his attitude was anything but colonial. He'd mostly immersed himself in Thai culture and in the people; it was one of the reasons his articles were doing well as people wanted to read something different from the usual travel articles that talked about the quality of the hotels and beaches or what the best tourist spots were.

His language skills had progressed a lot too. While he wouldn't quite describe himself as fluent, he could conduct a pretty good conversation, though he still found the speed most Thais spoke at quite daunting and usually had to ask them to slow down so he could follow what they were saying. He also struggled when visiting some of the provinces, the dialects meaning he could only have the most basic of conversations.

Then there was the sex, the tremendous, amazing sex. Ireshi was now living with him, was owned by him. She wasn't allowed to fuck anyone else unless he gave permission or was present. Ireshi was only part of that fantastic sex, though she was the major part of it. As he'd hoped, Ireshi had been more than interested in sharing the occasional three-way-relationship and they found a gorgeous dominant Singaporean they had played with a couple of times, a civilised dinner out somewhere followed by intense debauchery that had left Tom feeling drained for days.

He'd converted the spare room into a playroom cum dungeon. As well as the leather worker, who also worked with rubber, that Lam had introduced him to, he'd also introduced him to a sympathetic but bemused carpenter. Lam had given the man a new revenue stream making equipment that the man did not quite understand but didn't care as he was now making twice what he had before each month. The rest of the apartment was completely vanilla, the walls decorated with Tom's own pictures and the shelves full of mementos he had collected on his travels.

The secret room was where he could be himself, and where Ireshi could be herself too. Outside of that room, they were to all intents and purposes a 'normal' couple. When her job allowed it, Ireshi would often accompany him on trips though their sex remained relatively vanilla when away from home. He'd even met her father, the Police General. The General had been disapproving at first, the very idea of his only daughter being in a relationship with a farang something he could never accept, would never accept. But his attitude had softened over the year the couple had been together. Although he may not entirely approve yet, he saw that Tom was not your average farang. His attempts at the language, though amusing to the General at first, came to be appreciated as he recognised that the young man was making a real effort.

Ireshi's mother had been far easier to win over. Though a deferential woman in the shadow of her husband, she was still beautiful and Tom could see where Ireshi had got her looks from. Ireshi had confided in him that her father had a mia noi, a minor wife, a fancy name for what would be called a mistress in the west. Her mother knew all about his mistress but had imposed certain rules on her husband, including never spending an entire night with the other woman. Tom found this sad but also amusing. Their relationship was nothing more than another type of sub-dom relationship. The father may be the domineering one on the surface but his wife, who was the one who had brought money to the marriage, held a lot of power and her husband acceded to the rules she set.

The only shadow in Tom's life was cocaine. Although he mostly kept its use for any play sessions, the amount used each playtime seemed to grow each time. Ireshi almost matched him in her taste for the drug but there had been a number of occasions where it had gone too far, where Tom had blacked out for a few minutes and had come back to reality with Ireshi screaming their safe word. That had scared him and thrilled him at the same time. His dominant side might be about total control but there was something exciting about the idea of going beyond that and losing control completely. Yet it had scared him immensely too, especially the last time. When he'd come to, he had a silken rope around Ireshi's neck and she was close to suffocation or worse. If he'd remained in his blackout a few minutes more, then he shuddered to think what might have happened.

He had made attempts to reduce how much they used but it seemed an almost impossible task. Yevgeny certainly wasn't complaining as Tom was now his best customer by far.

The one thing Tom disliked, hated even, about the relationship with Ireshi was that he had to use condoms. Ireshi had a rare condition, inherited from her mother, that meant if she used contraceptive pills, she was at risk of blood clots that could lead to venous thromboembolism that could possibly be fatal. Neither of them wanted a baby, at least not yet, though it was something they had discussed as a possibility for the future. So for now, he had to use the dreaded condoms every time they had sex.

They still attended Lam's parties, though less regularly than they had. Tom had been surprised to find that he was jealous if he saw Ireshi fucking another man. Though that male selfishness meant he had no problem watching her with another woman or sharing her with one. Lam did socialise with them outside of the parties though, often going out to dinner with the couple with his latest, and usually short-lived, girlfriend accompanying him.

So, yes, life was good and Tom had no plan for that changing or leaving Thailand. He'd grown to love the country and the people though he was yet to say to Ireshi that he loved her? Did he? Maybe. It was certainly the closest he'd come to love in his life so far, and their relationship had developed into something far more than just a dominant and his submissive. It had quickly become apparent that fucking was kept for the playroom or for parties. It was almost as if their secret side was something that only came out in their secret room, an outfit to put on just like the many outfits in the playroom drawers. Outside of those four walls, they made love, usually gently and tenderly but still intensely. He was beginning to believe that he wanted to be with Ireshi forever but was also feeling pressure coming from her parents to formalise the relationship into something, in their eyes anyway, that was more respectable and would be more accepted by her parents and their social circles... even if he was just a farang.

He had a trip to prepare for, one that Ireshi would not be coming on due to work demands and other reasons. This trip was to the southern provinces of Songkla and Pattani, an area he hadn't visited before and possibly the most dangerous area of Thailand due to the Muslim insurgents who wanted to be part of Malaysia. While part of the trip was to be for the usual type of travel article he wrote, the main focus was to be the insurgency. A friend of a friend had introduced him to a man who knew... the usual story. But it meant that he was due to meet one of the insurgents in Hat Yai and then be taken on to one of the bases where the insurgents operated from.

This was to be a serious piece for a major British magazine that would look at the background to the insurgency and what their demands were. He hadn't told Ireshi the real reason for the visit and the magazine had agreed to allow him to use a pseudonym for the byline. Tom knew that if the Thai authorities knew his mission, then he would face some harsh questioning by the police or army and that his very life in Thailand could be threatened.

Tom wasn't sure if 'serious' journalism would be a regular thing. While he did have a feeling that many people thought travel writing was frivolous to an extent, he was damned good at it. If he went down the serious route, then even though he might be the right guy in the right place at the right time, there was the chance that he could cross the wrong people. His piece on sex workers had been serious, but he'd more focused on the people rather than the laws or the mafia and police who exploited those workers. It had been well received. Even feminists back in the UK conceded that, for a man, the piece had shown a great deal of empathy for the women – and ladyboys – who worked in the industry. His growing language skills had helped as the people he interviewed felt they could open up more than to someone who was just in the country for a fleeting visit.

But this was a step up from that. Although the levels of violence weren't particularly high, it was an issue that had been dragging on for decades and one that the government in Bangkok was determined to crush. Tom knew that if his journey and interviews were discovered, Thailand's National Intelligence Agency (NIA) would take more than a passing interest. They might even decide to brand him as an undesirable and deport him. This is why he was using his travel articles as cover. He hoped that the veil of secrecy being cast over his meeting with the insurgents would be enough protection. The magazine had even agreed to delay any publication by six months so nobody would think of Tom once the story was out.

Packing everything he would need, including spare rolls of film and batteries for his tape recorder, he prepared for what might be the most challenging story he had yet written.

2023

Things continued to go well at work. Tom had decided that Chompoo would be his own personal project as he was now convinced that an anthology of her stories could be the first big hit under the new ownership. He'd received another three stories from her and he continued to be impressed with the quality of her writing. She described scenes so well, and not just from a visual perspective but also the sounds and smells so that the reader felt fully immersed in the story and could feel that they were there watching events unfold.

He was worried about the violent aspects of the stories though. How could someone so young have such a vividly dark imagination? He knew that, if the book went to the publication stage, then some elements would have to be toned down. Chompoo was still keeping her true identity secret and had refused all Tom's offers of an in-person meeting. He suspected that she was from a hi-so family as that would explain her reluctance to reveal her identity. Thais had a real belief in the concept of 'saving face' and, if one or both of her parents were in the public eye, then they would be horrified if their daughter was exposed as the author of such graphically violent fiction.

It didn't overly bother him much. After all, thousands of books were published every year under pen names. But he did hope she wouldn't cling to blanket anonymity as he wanted to meet the person behind the words, even if it had to be discretely.

As if she knew he was thinking about her, his laptop pinged to signal that an email had arrived and, when he looked, it was from Chompoo. Another story, great, it had only been three days since the last one. He refilled his mug from his De'Longhi coffee machine – a necessary business expense – and settled back to read her latest offering.

Fifteen minutes later and he sat back in his chair, his coffee cold and untouched, and an unusually disturbed look on his face. Chompoo had been dark before, but this went to places that had never seen light. She'd reached new levels of sexual violence in this story. Tom was no stranger to sexual shadows, there were times he sought them out and embraced them. But this? This was another level from anything he'd previously read or anything he'd witnessed at any of the clubs he'd attended. There had been deaths in some of her previous work and there was only one death in this story, but it went way beyond all the violence of her previous tales combined.

He also wondered if she was mocking him. The protagonist, the killer, in this latest tale was an English expat managing an accountancy firm in Bangkok for the parent company back in England. Yes, he was an editor rather than an accountant but the similarity was undeniable. In the story, the man, tormented by his denial of his own sexuality, abducts a ladyboy sex worker, tortures her for two days, then brutally murders her. There was no denying the prose was powerful but, for Tom at least, any beauty was diluted by the underlying inhumanity contained in almost every sentence.

The solitary bulb cast flickering shadows onto the bare concrete walls, swinging slightly in a breeze from one of the broken windows in this building that had not seen life in more than a decade but that was now witnessing death instead. The shadows themselves seemed to have some form of life, creeping upwards on the walls in synchronicity with the swinging bulb.

The room looked as if it had been drained of colour except when the bulb illuminated the spatter of blood up one wall. A soft but desperate moan escaped from the crushed figure shackled to a chair. That noise would have surprised any other observer but him, for the shattered body had looked as if it had abandoned life though it had only sought temporary refuge in unconsciousness. He smiled but it was a cruel smile as he realised the game was not over yet. Looking carefully at the selection of objects on the nearby table, he chose a corkscrew, already tainted with blood, and approached the figure in the chair. The screams began again but the wind rushing through the smashed panes of glass carried the cries off to where no one could hear them.

What could have happened in this young girl's life to make her write about such horrors? Of course, there was a chance that Chompoo was not who she said she was. He only had her word for that and it could easily be an older woman – or man – masquerading as a new graduate. But what would such deceit achieve? Pretending to be a young girl in her late teens or early twenties would surely be a self-defeating exercise. He knew he had been shocked and surprised at the skill and content from someone so young. It was one thing to write under a pseudonym, quite another to take on a false persona.

Tom couldn't recall any situation in his editing career where he was so unsure about what to do next. He knew that, with some editing, a book of Chompoo's short stories could potentially be a hit. And given that she was writing in English, and writing so well too, the book could appeal to global audiences. Yet there was a small voice in the back of his mind telling him to walk away, to delete everything she'd sent so far, to tell her to look elsewhere for a publisher.

But that small voice was drowned out by ego and pride. He wanted his stint in Bangkok to be more than successful and for his return to the Green-Hayes head office to be in a blaze of glory. It was about more than taking Kwam-roo back into the black, it was about more than having a bestselling book, whether national or even international. This was about Tom, just as it had always been. He wanted the company to see him as indispensable, no matter what indiscretions arose. He wanted the company to welcome him back with open arms, to offer a promotion, maybe even a seat on the board. As ever, it was about control and Tom craved that control in both his public and private life.

Tom may have had to flee Thailand in fear of his life. The shadows of that time still haunted him and had remained a black cloud on the horizon from the moment his boss had told him he was being sent to Bangkok. It would be ironic that something so dark could be the thing that finally signalled an end to the shadows of the past, that something so disturbing could be the thing that brought light into his life. He decided to reply to Chompoo.

Hi Chompoo,

Thank you for another amazing story. The quality so far has been fantastic and I don't think any of your submissions to date would be out of place in an anthology of short stories.

However, I do have some concerns regarding the content. Although your skill as a writer is undeniable, and although there is definitely a market for dark fiction, I worry that perhaps some of your stories go a little too far.

Please do not take offence at this. I am speaking as an experienced editor rather than as a keen reader. And in no way am I suggesting that you completely change course. All I'm saying is that maybe you could consider toning down some of the more graphic aspects of your writing.

I worry that the levels of violence, much of it sexual violence, would reflect badly on Kwam-roo as the publisher but also on you as a writer and a person.

On that note, I would be really grateful if you would agree to a meeting in the near future. I appreciate that you are, for the moment at least, wanting to preserve some distance between you and your stories and I would be happy to meet at a place of your choice, away from the prying eyes that are the mark of any type of office.

I hope you will take my advice and suggestions in the spirit they were intended.

Best,

Tom.

After pressing 'send', Tom wondered if he would hear from the girl again. Would she take offence that he wanted to dilute her thoughts, to sanitise them for public consumption? From a personal perspective, he wouldn't change a thing, though he would tone down that last one a little. The stories seemed to feed the shadows inside him and brought back memories both good and bad. But when he was sitting behind this desk, he had to be professional. Releasing these stories could spark a scandal. And while some said that any form of publicity brought positive benefits, he was unsure whether the powers that be back in London would agree.

No, he had to stand firm on this. He had to be Tom the managing director rather than Tom the person, the dom, the pervert, the man with a dark history. He sat contemplating his thoughts for several minutes until his reverie was interrupted by his laptop announcing a new message. To his surprise, it was a reply from Chompoo.

Tom,

Thank you for your honest message. I'm sorry, but I don't feel ready to meet quite yet but perhaps soon we can. I know you probably suspect that I am not who I say I am, that the darkness in my stories is indicative of someone much older or perhaps even a different gender. All I can do for now is assure you that I have been completely honest in everything except my name. For now at least, I prefer the anonymity of a fake name and the use of emails to communicate.

As to the content, I cannot dilute what my eyes and mind see. If you genuinely feel that there is no way forward, I will cease sending you stories and seek an alternative outlet. But surely, as an editor, it's your role to make changes where needed and I'd be more than happy to listen to your suggestions for edits.

Maybe I see things differently to most people. Bangkok may be the most visited city in the world and those millions of tourists see only the beauty of the city. And yes, there is a lot of beauty for sure, from the majesty of the Grand Palace to the peaceful environs of Wat Arun. Hell, for some strange reason, many tourists even find the chaos of Khao San Road alluring though I've never seen the attraction myself.

But this is my city. I have grown up here, though I will confess that much of my life has been spent in a cocoon of privilege. Yet as I grew older, I felt the urge to escape that cocoon, to scratch the polished veneer that most people see and peer into the dark underbelly of this city of so-called angels. I have flirted with the shadows, walked the dark alleyways of poverty, and seen the side of the city that will never make any tourist brochure.

Bangkok may be a beautiful city but it's also an ugly one. There is violence in the night with only an echo of bloodstains left by morning. There is the desperation of single mothers who sell their child's virginity to predators. There is the hollow despair of the addicts, their only purpose each day to find another brief escape from reality.

For every ray of sunlight, there is an opposite shadow. Bangkok is Yin and Yang and it's perhaps ironic that the Chinese saw fit to make the dark and negative Yin also feminine. Maybe I am the personification of Yin because now I see only the darkness that exists here. That does not mean I do not acknowledge the existence of Yang but rather that I feel the darkness needs documented, that I need to tell stories no-one else will tell.

Few people will walk the twilight alleys of Khlong Toei, yet that so-called slum contains a thousand untold stories. I feel that I must tell some of those stories, that I am the voice of the dispossessed, the people in constant despair, the dead, and the dying. And yes, my stories are violent but that's because for many of these people, life itself is violent. I believe there is some darkness in everyone. Can you truly tell me that you can look in a mirror and see only good?

I hope that we can find a way to continue. If not, I understand.

Best,

Chompoo.

Tom reread the message. He wondered for a minute how she had known about his suspicions over her identity. But if she truly was the age she said she was, then she had a maturity far beyond her years. This was especially true given that she'd confessed to living in a 'cocoon of privilege' for much of her life. He would have understood her insights if she had lived a life in poverty, or at least close to it, but then her standard of English and skill in expressing her thoughts might not have existed.

She had also acknowledged that she was willing to listen to suggested edits, something that had completely escaped him as a possible solution. Yes, he could tone down aspects of her stories without ever losing her message or voice. After all, that was often an editor's role; finding things that didn't work or were too extreme, and working on them with the author to make the finished work more palatable. It would be relatively easy to dilute some of the more violent scenes without losing sight of the end effects.

Once again, he felt nothing but wonder at just how mature this young woman appeared to be. Brave too. To walk the alleys of this sprawling city alone – or at least, he assumed she'd been alone – took a lot of guts. If you looked beyond the main pages of the local newspapers or online sites, you would find daily tales of murder, rape, and suicide. Were her stories really so different from the real-life ones found in the news? She'd given him a lot to think about.

1996

The trip to the south had gone well and he had plenty of copy as well as some great photographs. Of course, the men in the photographs had worn masks in every photo, knowing that anonymity protected them from capture and death. He'd even been forced to wear a hood when travelling to one of their bases, the man who accompanied him determined that their HQ would retain the same veil of secrecy as the identity of the insurgents Tom had met.

He'd been surprised to find them likable. He'd had an image in his mind of hardened terrorists ready to do anything to achieve their aims. But the men he'd met had been farmers, shopkeepers, husbands, fathers, ordinary in every way except what they did in secret. Tom had laughed when he thought of that. It was yet another parallel with his own life; clear demarcation between public and private lives. He'd also expected them to be religious to the point of fundamentalism, but while there were some in the groups he had met who could be described – kindly – as extreme, most were fighting because they genuinely believed their province had more in common with Malaysia than with the Bangkok elites. Most of the insurgent groups were even prepared to accept some form of compromise if Bangkok granted the area more autonomy. But Bangkok was standing firm, determined to hold onto an area they had only ruled for some 200 years.

Though the trip had been both enjoyable and productive, he was glad to be home in Bangkok. More importantly, he was glad to be able to enjoy a cold beer after abstaining for several days to respect his hosts. He was also looking forward to seeing – and enjoying – Ireshi when she returned home from work. His appetite had not been sated since he'd left Bangkok and he was hungry for flesh. There was a certain irony that right on the border lay the town of Sungai Golok, seemingly innocuous by day but once the sun went down it transformed into a den of debauchery, its bars and brothels attracting men from across the river in the strict Muslim province of Kelantan.

When Tom had been told about Sungai Golok, his original plan was to have a little R&R in the town but he'd reconsidered his plans when he realised it would offend his hosts, who seemed to observe the tenets of Islam more closely than some of their Malaysian brethren. So it had been a rare few days of abstinence from him and he planned to fully unleash his sexual frustration on Ireshi in a few hours.

He threw his pungent clothes in the washing machine and spent more than 20 minutes under a scalding shower to wash the long and uncomfortable journey from his body. The drive back to Bangkok had taken some 22 hours, though they had split the journey with a night at a basic guesthouse in Surat Thani that seemed to be popular with cockroaches and bedbugs. The guesthouse shower had consisted of a dribble of cold water that wouldn't have soaked a mouse. On his arrival home, he felt as ripe as the papaya the old lady sold on the corner of his street.

Once he felt human again, he dressed in shorts and a plain white t-shirt. Although he hadn't slept that well the night before, the shower had woken him up so he decided he may as well start developing the photographs he had taken. His playroom, scene of so many torrid sessions with Ireshi and others, also doubled as a darkroom. As he'd painted the room black and had covered the windows with blackout curtains, it was the perfect place for sensitive work with film as well as less sensitive sexual adventures.

He checked and cleaned all his equipment including the developing tank, reels, and chemicals, then carefully began the process. Mistakes could be costly, not just in the sense of losing precious photographs but in having less shots to submit to the magazine. If there were too few, they might use stock photographs which meant less money for him. He went through all the development steps like clockwork and, once happy everything had been done right, hung and left the developed pictures for his usual two hours. Looking at his watch, he saw it was just after 6pm, still two hours till Ireshi arrived home from work.

Rather than laze about, he decided to prepare a special dinner, one that would get them both in the mood for some fun and games. He headed to the local market and picked up some fresh tuna for sashimi and pomegranates to make a dessert. He already had dark chocolate and red wine back in the house so would make an aphrodisiac feast. He was also sure there was a carton of UHT cream in a cupboard, not ideal but it would complement the pomegranates and chocolate.

Once dinner was finished, he would allow them both some time to digest their food before commanding Ireshi to put on an outfit – what, he hadn't decided yet – and then they would move to the playroom to let Tom finally sate his lust. He rolled a spliff and poured a glass of wine and sat back to ponder what outfit Ireshi would wear and what adventures he would put her through.

He must have dozed off, twisted daydreams of his fetishes running through his head. Ireshi's key in the door woke him and she smiled warmly when she saw her lover had returned. The fact that pain would likely figure in the evening ahead was something she welcomed, it's why they made such a good couple. They embraced and shared a long, passionate kiss.

"Go and have a shower while I put dinner out. But don't wear anything sexy yet; I've still not decided what you will wear tonight. So, for now at least, just a t-shirt and shorts will suffice."

She nodded in deference to her dom and headed for the bedroom. A few minutes later, she returned, wearing a red t-shirt with some slogan in Thai that he didn't understand, and a pair of white shorts.

They chatted casually over dinner, Tom regaling her with tales of his adventures in the south and Ireshi telling him of things that had happened at work. It almost verged on banality until Tom started saying how he could empathise with the insurgents and their desire for autonomy or to be cut free from Thailand altogether.

Ireshi may have had a very defined proclivity when it came to the darker side of sexual activity, but when it came to anything to do with the country of her birth, she was fiercely orthodox and conservative. Tom had long learned to keep his republican views to himself, both out of the desire to avoid arguments and out of respect for his adopted home. He even stood respectfully whenever the anthem was played. But they did frequently clash on political issues.

"They're nothing more than fucking terrorists," she stated, her voice rising in anger. "They're Thai and they will remain Thai until the day they die."

"But it's only been Thai for 200 years. It was a Malay sultanate before that and they are closer to Malaysia culturally and in other ways too. Even if the government aren't prepared to grant them independence or cede the territory to Malaysia, they could at least grant them some level of autonomy."

'Ancient history,' she retorted. "If Khun Banharn gave them autonomy then what next? Other provinces would be jealous and would start asking for autonomy for their own province too. Remember, 'The unity of a people come together as a party shall be a guarantor of prosperity'."

Tom sighed. He'd always felt that the country's motto was ironic given how the Bangkok elites looked down on other provinces.

Ireshi went on, "I wouldn't expect a farang to understand these things. We have stood alone and strong while other countries fell to the French or the British. We're not going to let a load of fucking ragheads destroy our country."

Now Tom was angry. "Don't ever use that term in front of me again. You talk about unity then use that fucking horrible word to describe fellow Thais? Is it any surprise they want to leave if this is how you fucking Bangkok hi-so's think of them?"

Ireshi realised she'd crossed a line.

"I'm sorry, sir."

"So you fucking should be."

Tom was as disappointed as he was irate. He drained his glass of wine.

"Go to the bedroom and strip while I choose something for you to wear."

Ireshi didn't reply. Her eyes remained downcast and she merely nodded and headed to the bedroom.

Tom knew he had to control his anger but he wanted to punish Ireshi. He walked over to his desk and opened the drawer where he kept his drug supplies. Damn, he'd forgotten to contact Yevgeny before he returned and there was less than half a gram left. He'd have to give the big Russian a call later or in the morning and organise a meeting. He racked up a healthy line, rolled up a 500 baht note, and snorted the powder in one go, wiping the detritus with a finger and rubbing it on his gums.

Now it was time to play and he planned on making Ireshi pay for her disrespect.

Feeling the cocaine beginning to surge through his system, he made his way to the playroom. Against one wall was a wardrobe and a chest of drawers that contained everything from the finest silk lingerie to leather and rubber costumes. He dismissed the lingerie, he was in no mood for softness tonight. He finally settled on a black flared wetlook minidress. He didn't pick out any underwear as the mood he was in, he'd probably just rip it off.

Crossing to the cabinet that held all their accessories, he picked out the usual ankle and wrist restraints and a collar and leash. He then looked at the three pieces of furniture he had commissioned, deciding that the bondage frame would be the best choice for the evening as it would allow him access from any and every angle. Satisfied with his decisions, he picked up the dress, collar, and leash and went to their bedroom.

Ireshi was standing naked in the middle of the room, her eyes still cast downwards while she waited for her master. While he was still angry, staring at her naked beauty reminded him of how much he loved her.

He handed her the dress and the collar.

"Put these on," he commanded.

"Yes, sir."

She slipped into the dress, the wetlook fabric clinging to every inch it covered. Once the dress was on, she fixed the collar round her neck and Tom clipped the leash to it.

"You've made me very angry with your attitude tonight, especially when we should have been celebrating my return. Now you need to be punished."

"Thank you, sir," replied Ireshi meekly.

He led her through to the playroom and heard her gasp as she saw he had moved the frame to the middle of the room. She knew what to expect now.

"You know where to stand."

She nodded and moved underneath the frame, raising her arms in the air so Tom could bind her wrists to the top bar. He then secured each of her ankles to the side bars so that she was in an almost 'X' position. Tom then unclipped the leash and then, as an afterthought, grabbed a blindfold from the cabinet and tied it round her head so she wouldn't know what was coming next.

Now it was time to play.

Tom woke with the dawn, a ray of sunlight piercing its way through a gap in the curtains and managing to find his eyes. The smell of sex and sweat pervaded the air, a reminder of all that had gone before. He glanced to his right to where Ireshi lay sleeping on her belly, the red welts covering her back and buttocks explaining why she had chosen that position. Their games had been extreme, though not as extreme as they had sometimes been. Tom's anger had manifested itself in the intensity of the sex and they had finally collapsed exhausted into bed around midnight, moving from fast-paced fucking to a tender embrace before sleep claimed them both.

He left Ireshi to sleep and switched on the coffee machine in the kitchen before showering the last traces of their fun away. He had a busy day ahead of him. He needed to finish the copy on his insurgent story and then phone it in later when the magazine office opened. He'd then head for the local internet café and send over scans of all the best photos so the editor had a good choice. And he also had to call Yevgeny and arrange to meet him later in the day. But the session had left him ready to face the world and anything it threw at him.

After all, all work and no play made Tom a very dull boy.

2023

Tom had spent the morning going through some of Chompoo's stories and seeing what changes he could make without losing her message or her voice. People thought that editing was just about finding and fixing spelling and grammar mistakes but the reality was that there was far more too it, especially if you were looking at developmental aspects.

His move into editing had been almost accidental. After his forced exit from Thailand, he'd been at a loss as to what to do next. He'd covered some of the lost work with travel pieces from around Europe but there was a glut of similar writers so he'd seen his workload fall by more than half. One magazine in particular had stuck with him though, commissioning several pieces that weren't always travel. It was also nice to meet people that had previously only been voices on the phone and it was one of those voices that had pointed him towards editing.

Vanessa had been his point of contact and editor since his second commission and it was over lunch one day that she suggested editing.

"Tom, you're a great writer and one of the things I love about you is you make my job so damn easy. Have you had training as an editor?"

"No? Why do you ask?"

"Because nearly every piece you've submitted has been almost perfect. Yes, I had to cut down the length now and again to fit the column space available, but in terms of spelling, grammar, or even sentence construction, I've hardly had anything to do. And trust me, that's unusual. Most of the writers I work with think a colon is part of your digestive system."

Tom laughed. He liked Vanessa. She was one of the few media people that he knew who he regarded as completely honest.

"Don't laugh. I'm being serious. Look, I know you've lost a lot of writing work since you left Thailand, though the story behind that is something that you've yet to tell me and I suspect it's one that couldn't appear in print."

For a moment, a dark cloud crossed Tom's face. Vanessa was right; it was a story that could never appear in print and it was a story that he would never tell anyone. He'd explained his sudden departure away as visa issues that 'suddenly' appeared on the back of his sympathetic piece on the southern insurgents. He'd told people he had no idea how they'd discovered it was him behind the fake byline but that he'd been given 48 hours to leave the country. While most believed him, some, like Vanessa, suspected there was more to the story but did not pry too deeply.

"Anyway, Tom, I have an idea. How about I pass you some small pieces to edit, not big stories, just filler. But it will allow me to see whether that eye for detail you have in your own writing can be applied to the work of others. If you're good, I'll speak to the boss about a contract though you'd have to do a course or two to keep the fascists in HR happy."

Tom had never considered editing before. It was true that he was a stickler for accuracy in his own work, but that had been drummed into him at that expensive school his parents had chosen. In fact, despite the high annual fees, Tom felt he had only learned two things at school; his ability to write almost perfect copy and an understanding that his sexual tastes lay in the shadows.

"Ok, I like the idea and I'll give it a go. But I'm not quite ready to give up writing yet so I'd rather it was part-time."

"Would two days a week work for you? The only thing is that you'd have to work from the office, and by office, I mean a small cramped cubicle. But it would be a seven-hour workday and you can choose those hours anytime between 7am and 10pm, perfect if you've been out the night before."

And so that lunchtime conversation was the first step on his journey from being solely a writer to being one of the best editors in the country. Out of the first eight pieces he'd been given to edit, Vanessa had only had to make corrections to one. True to her word, she'd arranged to send him on a couple of editing and proofreading courses, though she still felt he didn't actually need them.

He'd split his week between two days of editing in the office and three days of writing pieces on a diverse range of subjects. He still did some travel writing, but it now tended to be specially-commissioned pieces on unusual or exclusive travel experiences.

For the first six months, he'd worked on smaller articles, sometimes as short as a single column. Vanessa gradually increased the size – and importance – of the pieces he worked on till finally, he was given the responsibility of editing that week's cover story. After 12 months, he truly felt like an editor.

It was Vanessa again who spotted something special and it was again over lunch that she brought it up.

"Tom, your editing is great and it's also made me look good for discovering you, and that's never a bad thing in the cutthroat world of the media. But I'll be honest with you, you're wasted in magazine work."

He looked puzzled, he thought he was doing really well.

"You've forwarded me a few pieces where you felt things were missing or perspectives could be changed, things I hadn't even noticed till you suggested them. And every one of your suggestions has led to an improved article. Now, copy and line editing are skills that can be taught like many others, though you seem to have had those skills already."

"Well, to be fair, I was taught those skills by an incredible but strict English teacher. He did not suffer fools or mistakes gladly and I quickly learnt that perfection, or close to it, was preferable to detention."

"Ah, that explains a lot. As I was saying, copy and line editing can be taught but developmental editing is something that people either have or don't have. Yes, there are courses on it too, but in my opinion, they're worthless. For every ten developmental editors out there, only one of them is truly great. Again, it may only be my opinion but you know I'm rarely wrong. It's a little like sports; you may be able to be taught new techniques and to hone your chosen discipline, but you need that innate talent to go anywhere."

Tom could feel his neck reddening. Though he'd never describe himself as modest, such praise from someone like Vanessa, who'd spent more than 30 years working as an editor, really got to him.

"You have that innate talent I mentioned, and you have it in droves. The problem for you just now is that there isn't really a demand for developmental editing in magazine or newspaper work. Where it's really needed is in the book publishing sector. A good developmental editor can make a real difference to everything from reviews to sales. Look, and I'm going to hate myself for doing this if I lose you, but my friend Farrell works for Macmillan. He's having a dinner party next weekend so why don't you come as my plus one? You've nothing to lose and everything to gain and, knowing Farrell, there will be plenty pretty but vacuous interns for you to charm the knickers off."

Tom thought for a minute. He'd never considered working with books before, though he did plan on writing his own one day. But then he'd never considered working as an editor either.

"Why not, Ness. As you say it's a dinner party so it's not like a formal interview or anything. And those interns sound just perfect too," he said laughing.

The rest, as they say, is history. Though some of the history was stuff Tom would rather forget. He went to the party with Vanessa, got on like a house on fire with Farrell, and was invited to come into the Macmillan offices the following week for an informal interview. As an added bonus, he ended taking home a posh little intern called Gillian who turned out to be more flexible than an Olympic gymnast.

The informal interview led to a formal one, and that in turn led to a job offer. The money on offer far exceeded what he had been previously earning and the only real downside was that it was full-time and full-on, so his writing career was effectively over though he still had that book in his head.

He was a perfect fit, and Vanessa's sense of his skills was bang on too. Within his first year, he had worked as developmental editor on two major bestsellers, something unheard of at Macmillan for someone who was effectively a trainee. His second year proved he'd been no flash in the pan with four bestselling clients. At the start of his third year, he was promoted to senior editor, the youngest to be appointed in 32 years.

He'd probably have been happy to stay at Macmillan forever, but in 2007, two of the senior managers decided it was time to set up their own publishing house. There was an in-joke at the office that David Green and Paul Hayes had been with the company since the days of Charles Dickens but that was now going to be a defunct joke.

It was little surprise that they took quite a few staff with them but Tom was surprised when they approached him. Other than the odd cursory nod in the lift, he'd had no real interaction with either man. But as Paul Hayes explained, they wanted the new company to have the best of the best and that's how Tom was viewed. The financial package offered was almost double what he was already getting, and the two partners threw in some lucrative bonuses including stock options and profit sharing. Of course, those bonuses would be dependent on Tom getting off his backside and finding new clients and, perhaps most importantly, producing bestsellers.

Macmillan countered with an improved financial package but Tom was attracted by the challenge. Working at Macmillan had become just a little too comfortable and authors were assigned to him rather than him choosing. That sense of freedom was what made up his mind for him.

His lucky streak, though it was really not that much to do with luck, continued apace. He received some submissions direct but also nurtured relationships with some of the best agents in town so that he often got first pick when they had a promising new client. The agents knew that if Tom liked a manuscript, then it would likely sell, and the more copies the final book sold, the higher their commission payments.

In 2017, Green and Hayes sold the company for £220 million to an American investment group. Despite the new ownership, both men retained a position on the board and a percentage of the stock. Two months after the sale, Tom was promoted to managing editor, reporting only to the board and to Kevin Jones, his immediate boss.

That was the public face of Tom; the dazzling, talented, and handsome young managing editor who seemed to have the Midas touch when it came to both fiction and non-fiction titles. He'd been profiled in magazines, had appeared on television, and had dated a string of actresses and celebrities.

That public face was partly a lie though. The actresses and celebrities he dated were all vanilla relationships but allowed him to maintain the persona everyone knew, loved, and were often jealous of. His private face and his private life remained hidden in the shadows. He only attended private clubs where discretion was paramount. In those clubs, it was often the case that his status was minor when compared to some of the other members. He'd recognised several of his peers, ranging from politicians to film and TV stars.

And just as there was a string of pretty women in public when the paparazzi were watching, so there was a string of compliant subs ready to explore his own flavour of darkness.

He had found it ironic that at least two of those subs had been well-known in their own right. One was the daughter of a wealthy Tory MP and the other had been a presenter of a daytime chat show on Channel 4. He had managed to keep public and private demarcated for years, until that one incident at the conference.

Tom had been in a celebratory mood. One of his closest clients, already a best-selling author, had just signed a three-film deal for her most recent trilogy. He wasn't just happy for her though, well thought-out clauses in her contract meant that a percentage would go to both Tom and the firm.

The man who loved to be in control lost control that evening and he still wasn't sure what exactly had happened. He remembered the copious amounts of Veuve Clicquot. He remembered the copious amounts of high-quality Peruvian flake his contact had obtained the previous weeks. And he remembered the copious breasts of the young intern who he'd been sure was flirting with him all night. She'd accused him of groping her in his room and trying to force himself on her. For someone who knew and valued the idea of consent, something integral to people who understood the BDSM scene, it was a self-administered red card.

He'd sent a sincere letter of apology and hadn't tried to defend his actions but he had fully expected to be sacked. Kevin had thrown the drowning man a lifeline, convincing the board that Tom was too valuable to lose. The price was to spend some time in purgatory and that purgatory had to be Bangkok, a place Tom really didn't want to return to even after all these years. There was again irony in that, as punishment for forgetting the rule of consent, he was going to be sent to the only other place where he had lost control.

And here he was now, reading and editing perhaps the most talented writer he'd encountered in over a decade. His worries had dissipated over the months he had been there and he was convinced that the shadows of his past had been left in the past. Almost everyone he had known then was dead, in prison, or would have hopefully forgotten him apart from the odd malicious thought. The one ghost from his past was one that he didn't think he had to worry about.

He'd been shocked one evening to see his old friend Lam on TV, and even more shocked to find out that Lam was now a senior member of government. He had considered contacting the man; they had always got on well but Tom decided it was better to let sleeping politicians lie. After all, lying seemed to be a prerequisite for a career in politics no matter where in the world you were.

It had been one of life's weird synchronicities that a couple of weeks after seeing Lam in TV, he met him in person. It had been at the launch of a new online media outlet. Tom hated these sorts of events but, once you were in any sort of senior position, networking became one of your necessary skillsets.

Their eyes had met across the room and Lam just acknowledged him with a slight nod. It wasn't till later, when Tom nipped outside for some fresh air and a cigarette, that Lam followed him. There was none of the former friendliness in his face or voice when he spoke.

"I had heard you were back. I must say I'm surprised that you dared return to Thailand, even after so long. My life is very different now and I'm in a position of power, something you would do well to remember. If I hear even the slightest hint of gossip about my previous predilections, you will pay a heavy price. I already have a safety net in place to deal with you should anything be disclosed."

Without giving Tom a chance to reply, Lam turned and walked back into the building. *'Wow,'* Tom thought*, 'no hello or anything. Surely he knows how much I value discretion and privacy?'* He wondered what Lam had meant by a 'safety net'. He assumed that with Lam's power and connections, he meant that his visa could easily be cancelled and Tom deported.

Strangely enough, Tom had been even more careful now about keeping his dark side hidden. He'd decided against returning to Demonia. The fact that it seemed popular with curious businessmen and others in high positions meant it was inevitable that he'd eventually meet someone who knew who he was.

Thankfully, there was Kanya. After the meeting at Demonia, they had kept in regular contact and she had gone from being his coke dealer to his friend within weeks. She'd finally confessed that she was willing to play sub for Tom as the attraction was too great to resist. Her only condition was that she was to be allowed to 'play away' so that she could still exert her dominant side on others. He'd accepted the condition and the relationship had grown, though it was founded on lust rather than love.

They enjoyed each other's company outside the bedroom anyway, so to anyone that knew or saw them, they were just another normal couple. If only they knew.

The fact that he was enjoying life in Bangkok had surprised him. But the shadows had evaporated, the ghosts had been exorcised, work was good, and he was in a satisfying relationship where Kanya had no expectations.

Now his main focus was on Chompoo, or whatever her real name was. He genuinely wanted her to be a success, though there was again the selfish aspect of how it would make him look good.

By the time lunchtime arrived, he'd edited – and reedited – three of her submissions. He didn't want to do any more than that until she had read them and told him her thoughts. If they could reach full agreement, or at least some form of middle ground, then he would forge onwards and hopefully have a book out by the end of the year.

1996

Tom knew that discretion was key to living in Thailand, at least if you were involved in anything that was either illegal under Thai law or immoral in Thais' eyes. Tom's drug use was, of course, completely illegal. Though the level of punishment, if there was any, was intrinsically linked to how much money you had. Corruption was rife and, if caught with any illegal drugs, a substantial 'donation' to the arresting officer would guarantee your freedom. He preferred to avoid that risk though; his meetings with Yevgeny were the only time he really carried any drugs outside his home.

Those meetings tended to happen in places where police were highly unlikely to be carrying out random checks. Yevgeny liked to meet in the city's better restaurants and bars, so a surprise raid was improbable. When you added in the fact that Yevgeny had several senior police officers in his 'employ', the chances of arrest reduced exponentially. The only real risk was one of the urine tests that police carried out in busy areas of town, usually with the purpose of emptying a tourist's wallet than upholding the law.

Tom had only been stopped at one of these roadside tests once, and when the police realised he was not a tourist and had a good command of Thai, they let him go on his way without having to fill one of the dreaded plastic cups.

The other side of his life was a bit of a grey area when it came to legality. He was living in a country where prostitution was illegal yet sex work brought in a huge amount of currency to the Thai economy. And the sex industry catering to farangs was just the tip of a very sordid iceberg. Almost every town had a brothel, or a brothel masquerading as a KTV or a beer garden, catering to the locals.

So, while Tom knew his own tastes would be viewed with distaste by many, he didn't think there would ever be the risk of prosecution. Besides, he only really indulged in those tastes in the comfort of his own home, though less comfortable for Ireshi. There was still the occasional party at Lam's but even that was becoming rarer. And he and Ireshi now had two choices if they wanted to involve a third in any sessions, both of them women they had met at Lam's house, so both of them people who knew how important discretion was.

Tom and Ireshi both liked to socialise, though like his meetings with Yevgeny, they tended to visit the nicer restaurants, clubs, and bars rather than the places inhabited by freelancers and backpackers who reeked of sweat and patchouli oil. Of course, his work often took him places that were a little less salubrious than his usual haunts, but they were usually all outside Bangkok. It was the double life thing yet again. Just as he had a public and private face in Bangkok, so his travels allowed him to see the other side of Thailand, a side away from five-star hotels yet a side that usually contained a lot more honesty than the deceit of the luxury travel market.

It was rare for him to have any work assignments within the city itself. He'd covered all the tourist attractions in his first year, both the main ones and those off the beaten track. But one of the magazines he freelanced for had asked him to write an article on the methamphetamine problem in Thailand. It was most common to find the drug here in pill form, mixed with caffeine and known as yaba, which was the Thai phrase for 'crazy medicine', very appropriate. It was popular with the lorry and bus drivers who drove the long-distance routes around the country, and it was also popular with the city's sex workers, often seeking a way to anaesthetise themselves from their often-unattractive customers.

These poisonous little pills had led to a plague of addiction across the country. Now they were spreading their way around the world and the magazine had sensed a story in the making, one that could be cautionary yet sensationalist.

While Tom had nurtured many different contracts in many different areas, this was a new world to him. He'd turned to Yevgeny for advice or help over one of their regular lunch meetings, this one at the recently opened Sheraton Grande Sukhumvit hotel.

"Fucking horrible stuff," muttered the Russian. "I've never really liked amphetamines, though ecstasy is the one exception to that. There's a fucking world of difference between using drugs and abusing drugs and people who take or smoke yaba tend to be the lowest of the low."

"Come on, tovarich, I'm not looking to buy or use the shit, but I need to speak to someone in the trade, ideally higher up. It's easy enough to find users and addicts; I just need to wander down Soi 4 after midnight. But I want to know more about where they come from and who's making them, without actual names of course."

"I don't actually know anyone that sells it or makes it. But I do know someone who probably does."

"Of course you do. They may talk about that whole six degrees of separation but with you, that's reduced to two or three."

Yevgeny laughed loudly, attracting disapproving stares from the next table.

"I'd protest but you are totally right, my English friend. Though there are many people in this city I would rather have 10 degrees of separation from. Ok, I will make some phone calls later and see if I can hook you up with mid-level dealer or higher. Now, too much talking and not enough drinking vodka."

Ten days passed before Yevgeny got back in contact by phone.

"So, I have someone who has agreed to meet you. They run the yaba trade in Khlong Toei so they are a fairly serious player. He knows I have vouched for you so you will be completely safe but he demands anonymity; you have to take no photos and not even describe him."

"I'd assumed that would be the case anyway. So where do I meet this guy?"

"On his own turf, of course, deep in the heart of Khlong Toei. One of his men will meet you outside Khlong Toei Market on Rama IV Road at 3pm tomorrow. Wear a red t-shirt so he recognises you. He will take you to the meeting point. Don't be scared if you see others following you. This guy is paranoid and will want to be sure that no-one is following you other than his own men."

"Oh, I love a bit of subterfuge," joked Tom. "Thank you, tovarich, I owe you one."

"You owe me a lot more than one but you know I like you so in reality, you owe me nothing. Just promise me that you won't try this shit. I know you like your drugs but I also know you favour quality. This shit is the equivalent of a warm glass of Chang after a chilled bottle of the finest champagne."

Tom laughed again. "For a Russian, you sure come up with some good analogies."

"For a Russian? You're lucky I do not take that as an insult, Tom!"

Tom was outside Khlong Toei Market at just before 3pm the next day. He was wearing a red t-shirt as instructed and Yevgeny had also told him the name of the seafood stall to stand beside. He saw a man looking at him, hardly someone that would be snapped up as the next big model. The man was emaciated, a sure sign of yaba addiction, his hair was matted and greasy and his eyes were sunken orbs that were almost empty of life. The man walked over to him.

"Khun Tom?"

Tom nodded.

The man beckoned Tom to follow him and he guessed the man spoke little or no English.

They walked through the maze of narrow alleys, the smell of cooking from almost every shack failing to mask the stench of raw sewage from the discoloured waters below. The shacks themselves were ramshackle affairs with no real pattern of construction. The walls were often recycled bits of wood and almost every roof was rusting corrugated iron.

The deeper the man led him into the slum, the worse it seemed to get. Suspicious eyes gazed at him from every other doorway, many of those eyes as empty of life as Tom's guide. The only real vitality Tom saw was from the gossiping women, matriarchs who probably kept their families together even in these harsh conditions. Then there were the children, usually naked, playing in the narrow alleys or splashing in water that likely contained a multitude of parasites and diseases.

But there were still signs of life in those children's eyes, an innocence born of their tender years and a lack of understanding that fate had not been kind to them when it came to their lot in life. Tom knew that the light he saw would fade in time. Many of those children would suffer abuse, both physical and sexual. For some of them, there would be a different type of abuse; solvents, drugs, and alcohol to block out the memories or simply to block out reality. For many, their future lay in sex work, catering to the depraved tastes of both locals and tourists.

These thoughts saddened Tom, especially when he knew the very drug he was researching would be one that might dominate their often short lives. But he was a storyteller and not a crusader. The most he could do was to spread awareness, to inject a degree of discomfort into the cocooned lives of the affluent tourists a mere kilometre or two away.

The man finally stopped outside a shack that looked a little better put together than its neighbours. Tom realised it was a restaurant, though that description might be a little grandiose for this place. An old Thai woman of indeterminate age stood at the doorway. Given the harshness of life in the slum, she could have been anywhere between 40 and 65. Inside the shack, there were four small tables, each with four mismatched cheap plastic chairs around them.

On one of the chairs sat a man who Tom hoped he would never meet on a dark night. Though as skinny as the guide, this man had a sinewy strength about him, with hair cropped almost down to the skin, and a vicious-looking scar that ran from just below his left eye to the underside of his chin, as well as the customary collection of amulets hanging round his neck and arms covered with Sak Yant tattoos. Tom estimated he was about 25 to 30. He looked up, saw Tom, and smiled, revealing teeth that, other than the lack of moss, resembled a row of ancient and neglected gravestones.

He rose and shook Tom's hand.

"My boss tell me you good man. I can talk about yaba but no pics, ok?"

"Sure," said Tom, 'I won't even take any photos around here in case this is where you do business."

The man smiled again.

"Good, good. You want coffee? Beer?"

"Coffee would be great, thanks." He would have liked an iced coffee but didn't trust the ice to be hygienic.

"Okay, okay."

The man shouted at the old, or oldish, woman in rapid Thai that Tom found impossible to follow.

Tom took out a packet of cigarettes and offered one to his host who greedily grabbed one.

"So, what you want know? Cannot say names of people but can tell other things."

"Yeah, I know you can't give too many details. The magazine is in UK but I'm happy to keep things anonymous."

The man looked puzzled.

"Anonymous means I use no names and do not even describe you too much."

The man nodded in understanding.

"Ok, you call me Wachirawit, not real name but mean diamond or lightning. Funny, yes? Yaba make you go fast like lightning."

"Yes, a very good name."

"I already know name you is Tom, I say right?"

"Yes, that's right. So, let's start with you. Tell me about your life."

The man sat and thought for a few minutes.

"I born here, I grow up here, I probably die here. Mother die when I five, father die when I ten. I go live with uncle. Leave school when I 12. But need money. Uncle always drunk and we poor. So I start as person running between person with yaba and person who want yaba."

"Did you start using yaba then too?"

The man shook his head vehemently,

"No, and not use yaba now too. Yaba is very bad but, like other things, people want buy so I sell."

Tom was surprised. He'd expected anyone involved in the yaba trade to be an addict or user. Of course, the higher up you went, that expectation would be null and void. He very much doubted that the drug lords or even chemists were getting high on the poison that made them money.

"So, you started as a runner, a delivery boy. How did you move upwards? How did you get better jobs?"

"Four years I deliver for small dealer. Then he die. Bigger dealer come ask me to take dead man's place. So then I make more money and have young boys deliver for me. Big dealer like me because never use yaba and always have money on time. For two years, I small dealer. Then big dealer get me work with him."

"Another promotion then? I mean, another better job?"

"Yes, now I deliver again. But now deliver to small dealer not customer. Then collect money when pills all sold. Big dealer trust me."

"And how big was he? How much of Khlong Toei did he control?"

"He in charge for whole area. Very important, make much money."

"He trusted you a lot then. What happened next?"

“Yes, he trust me. Become like my brother. He get me better house to live. Then he give me new job. I collect all his yaba from man who work for his boss.”

“Wow, that was a big job for sure. How many pills would you collect?”

“Depend. Sometime I get bag with 5,000 pills, sometime 10,000. And he have me take money when collect pills. Very important job.”

“I bet. So that’s your job now?”

The man swelled with pride, puffing his chest out as he looked Tom in the eye.

“No, now I big boss for all of Khlong Toei. I in charge.”

“How did that happen?”

Wachirawit frowned, his chest deflating again at the question.

“My brother die. Someone try rob him and shoot him dead. Steal money and some yaba. But my brother not stupid. Most yaba and money he hide somewhere only we knew. But I find man who kill him and he die too, very slowly.”

“Was the next boss up line happy with you becoming new boss here?”

“Yes, he knew can trust me as I collect pills and bring right money. But he want meet me first. Say hello but warn me what happen if I try rip him off. I already have good friend work with me so he took my place and collect pills and pay money.”

“Ok, so now you big boss of Khlong Toei. Tell me about how it all works above you.”

“Small district have big boss like me. Then there is bigger boss who run several districts. And another bigger boss above him.

On and on then you have boss of all city but I know only my boss."

"Clever, all compartmentalised"

Wachirawit looked puzzled again.

"It means is safe from police. Different areas, different bosses. And the very big boss probably never sees a yaba pill."

"Yes, I think very rich man. Lot of people work for him because lot of people use yaba."

"Do you know where the yaba comes from?"

"My boss say Burma. Many people make there then send to Thailand. Much come to Bangkok because big city."

Tom was considering his next question when he saw something out of the corner of his eye. It was definitely a farang, and even though he had his back to Tom, there was something familiar about him. What was of more concern to Tom was that he was with a young girl, a very young girl. She couldn't have been more than ten-years-old. As the couple, though even thinking that term made Tom's stomach turn, entered a shack on the other side of the water, the man turned for a moment to see if anyone was watching. As he did, Tom instantly recognised him even though the man could not see him sitting in the interior of the coffee shop.

Ronnie fucking Baht!

He'd heard that Ronnie could procure anything, including underage kids, but he hadn't realised the bastard was a child molester himself. He wouldn't even be surprised if the girl's parents knew about it, the attraction of a sheaf of notes outweighing any disgust they might feel.

As the two disappeared inside, Tom turned to Wachirawit,

"You know that man?"

Wachirawit scowled.

"He bad man. He fuck children. I want kill him but my boss say no. Kill him and many police come here. Dead farang not good for business."

"I know him but he is not a friend. How many times does he come here?"

The Thai spat on the floor, an action that gained him a foul look from the shop owner.

"I not always see him but he come maybe two times a week. That girl or other one. Always same. I speak parents but they have no money so sell daughter. I sell drugs but what that man do is real bad thing."

Tom was lost in thought. One strand was thinking that some form of expose would make a great article. But the other focused on getting this bastard off the streets. He'd speak to Yevgeny. The Russian made a point of knowing where everyone he did any business with lived. He'd also be as disgusted as Tom to know that Baht was molesting vulnerable children.

He turned his attention back to Wachirawit.

"Leave it with me. I'll make sure this man does not come back to Khlong Toei."

The little Thai man smiled. "Thank you, Tom. I hate that bad man but nothing can do."

"Anyway, I think I have all the information I need. Thank you for speaking to me. How do I get back to Rama IV Road?"

"I call my man. He come get you, take you back where he meet you."

Wachirawit pulled a mobile phone from his pocket, one of the better models, he was definitely doing well.

"He come five minutes, ok?"

"Yes, thank you again."

Tom finished his coffee which had been surprisingly good. A few minutes later, his guide appeared and Tom got up to leave. Wachirawit also stood. He took Tom's hand in both of his and looked him in the eyes.

"You good farang. I know I bad man as sell yaba but I not like that bad man. If he stop coming, I make sure family get money so they not need sell girl again."

Tom found himself liking the little man. Sure, he was selling a dangerous drug that could lead to addiction and even death. But you could say he was a victim of circumstances and had done what he had to do to survive. There was also a well-worn cliché in the world of criminals that there was an actual hierarchy of the crimes you had committed. And molesting and raping kids was very firmly at the bottom of that hierarchy.

As his guide led him back through the maze of Khlong Toei, Tom was already scheming Baht's downfall in his head.

2023

Tom had a routine that he followed almost religiously every day. The only exceptions were the mornings after he'd had a session with Kanya, cocaine, or alcohol, or often some combination of the three. Those sessions usually only happened at the weekends so his routine happened five days a week or more. His alarm would wake him at 6.30am, he'd go and spend 30 to 40 minutes in the condo gym, return to his unit, shower, and then have breakfast.

Once dressed, he'd head for his local BTS station at Phrom Pong, collecting a coffee from one of the street vendors outside the station. He'd alight at Phloen Chit and walk to the office, collecting a copy of that day's Bangkok Post and a fresh coffee on the way.

Even though he arrived before business began, the office was usually already quite busy with fresh-faced interns keen to make their mark or staff with deadlines to meet. His secretary, Mai, was always at her desk before he arrived and he often wondered if she slept there because he was yet to arrive before her. Within five minutes of him arriving, Mai would bring him another coffee, his third of the day. Tom felt he wasn't fully functional until he'd had four cups of caffeine to fire up his systems.

He'd spend around 15 minutes reading the Bangkok Post before checking his emails and moving onto the first tasks of the day. He settled in one of the comfier seats by the window to complete his morning ritual. It was a shorter ritual than back in London as there he would have had several newspapers to browse – and the occasional trade magazine – though he tended to skim those while the Post was more cover to cover. The only other daily English language newspaper here was The Nation, but it had been online only since 2019.

The first few pages were the usual stories; political machinations (one of Thailand's favourite pastimes), international headlines, and the occasional story on some multi-billion-baht deal or sporting victory for a Thai team or individual athlete. Then a story on page five caught his attention.

POLICEMAN KILLED IN RITUAL MURDER

He read the story then reread it again slowly.

A policeman in Nong Khaem, one of Bangkok's western districts, had been found brutally murdered the previous day. The officer had been suspended from duty while allegations against him of being involved in several rapes were investigated. A police spokesman said that it had been a particularly vicious killing, and that the officer appeared to have been tortured for hours before being killed and dumped in a quiet alley.

The spokesman went on to say that they suspected the killing was linked to the rape allegations and that the officer's penis had been completely severed. There was some suggestion that black magic was involved, something that many Thais still strongly believed in. Police were still looking for the missing organ. The journalist had even inserted some dark humour to the story, wondering if any ducks in the area were being rounded up as 'feeding the ducks' was a popular Thai idiom referring to severed penises, though the idiom more referred to the actions of angry and jealous wives rather than a vicious killer.

He shook his head. Once could be put down to coincidence, but twice was just, well, fucking weird to say the least. Abandoning his coffee and the newspaper, he crossed to his desk to see just how weird it might be.

Booting up his laptop, he opened his secret folder and opened one of the files. He sat in stunned silence as he read through it.

The figure in the shadows laughed. 'Your uniform can't protect you from the crimes you have committed. Do you feel helpless? Good. Think about how helpless your victims felt while you raped and brutalised them. They trusted you because you wore a uniform but to you, the uniform represented power and you used your power to violate them.' The man, chained to a metal bedframe, moaned in pain. His naked body was covered in dozens of tiny cuts, cuts inflicted to cause pain without any fatal damage. The figure approached. 'Look at that pathetic little worm between your legs. Pathetic yet it has caused so much pain and suffering to others. I think it's time we cut the head off the worm so it is never responsible for suffering again.'

The figure moved to a small table beside the man. It had various knives and scalpels on it as the figure had been very careful to not cause any damage that would lead to the man bleeding out. Yet. They picked up a vicious-looking hunting knife, its blade glinting even in the dim light of the warehouse. The man moaned again, this time in fear as he knew what was coming rather than the pain of previous wounds.

Now the figure moved closer, grasping the man's limp penis in one gloved hand while the other hand brought the knife towards his limp cock. As the blade began to slice into flesh, the moans turned into screams of pain, though they were largely muted by the duct tape covering. Within minutes, the penis had been completely severed and the figure placed the appendage into a bag they had for just that purpose.

Blood was pumping onto the floor, but the figure knew it was unlikely the rapist would bleed to death. They just wanted to watch the pain, to enjoy the man's suffering, for a few minutes more. As the man lapsed into the refuge of unconsciousness, the figure sighed, stepped forward, and plunged the hunting knife deep into the man's heart, ending his suffering, but more importantly, ending the chance of him every inflicting suffering on others again.

Now they had to clean up the scene before dumping the body in an alley somewhere close. They placed the various knives and scalpels into a bag so that they could dump them in different khlongs during the day. The body itself was wrapped in plastic and securely taped. Then they doused the area in bleach before scrubbing it as clean as possible. Tonight, there would be one less rapist walking the streets of Bangkok.

Tom held his head in his hands for several minutes. What the fuck was going on? Two stories from this girl that bore far too close a resemblance to real murders that happened after she'd sent them. Was she the killer? Did she know the killer? Just as he was beginning to feel that the ghosts of his past had been banished, new ghosts seemed to be appearing to haunt his new life. He began to ask the same questions he had before. Was Chompoo really a young girl? The very fact that she had so far refused to meet made him even more suspicious after that newspaper story. He knew he had to confront her, and not by email either. Only by meeting face to face could he look into her eyes and see what truths lay hidden there.

He stood up and walked to the window gazing on the beautiful bustling city that had played such a major part in his life, both good and bad. His office on the 19th floor offered views across the city and, when he glanced down to street level, he could see thousands of dots scurrying around like busy little insects. For a moment, he wondered how many of those dots had secrets they kept hidden. How many were killers or other criminals? How many had mistresses? He knew the answer to that last question was probably a lot of them. Though Thais had sanitised the concept of extra-marital relationships with the idea of mia nois or minor wives in English.

Maybe he was being overly paranoid and it was just coincidence. There had been no mention of links to other crimes in that morning's story. The story about the transgender had only borne a slight resemblance to the actual crime. But this? A policeman accused of rape? Paranoia? Coincidence? Or was there something darker lurking in the shadows of these events? His mind was a maelstrom of confusion and worry. He needed answers and only one person could provide them, though he knew those answers may not be the truth. He sat at his desk and composed an email to Chompoo.

Hi Chompoo,

I've been working on some edits for your stories and had planned to send them over in the next few days for you to look at.

However, something has come up this morning that is causing me a great deal of concern. There was a report in today's Bangkok Post about a policeman being murdered. He was under investigation for rape and was viciously tortured and his penis was severed before he was killed.

Under normal circumstances, I might have allowed myself a small smile at this story. After all, it's been alleged that he was a rapist so, if guilty, he probably deserved what happened to him though of course, there is also a chance he was innocent of these allegations so maybe I'm being unfair to him.

But my concerns come from your story, Karma, where a rapist who is a policeman meets an almost identical grisly end. There are some differences of course. You've made his guilt quite plain for all to read and he finally dies from being garroted rather than stabbed through the heart. But the similarities are there and just too strong. Can you offer any explanation? I also think it's imperative that we meet soon. We have lots to discuss in regards to moving forward with your stories and it would be easier and more effective to talk in person rather than by exchanging emails all the time.

Best,

Tom.

Once he'd pressed send, he knew there was no way he could concentrate on work. He told Mai that he had a bad migraine and headed home, hoping to find a temporary peace until he heard from Chompoo.

1996

His thoughts about Yevgeny had been right. Though the Russian had known that Baht had a reputation for finding young girls for some of his clients, he'd always thought the girls were around 15 or 16 so, while he'd found it distasteful, he'd put it to the back of his mind.

Tom's news that the man was an active molester, and the approximate age of the girls he seemed to prefer, had made the usually stoic Russian become more animated than Tom had ever seen him.

"I mean, I don't know if he's finding girls that young for other people, but that doesn't really matter. He's abusing girls himself, ones from the most vulnerable backgrounds imaginable. The meth guy in Khlong Toei said he'd have killed him long ago if it weren't for the fact that his boss didn't want a sudden increase in the police presence in the district.

"Bastard," swore Yevgeny. "I have never liked him, never trusted him, there was just something about him that made you feel you needed a shower after meeting him. But this is no problem. He will be dead within 48 hours."

"Now just calm down, tovarich. A slow and painful death was my first thought too. But even a slow death is too quick for this scumbag. A far better fate would be a few years in Bang Kwang. Think how the Thai prisoners, and the farangs too for that matter, would treat someone who'd been molesting kids? Fair enough, he might not survive that long, but he'd learn what it feels like to be raped."

The Russian looked thoughtful and then his face broke out in a huge smile.

"You are one devious bastard, Englishman. This is one of the reasons I like you. Yes, I do not think he would live to ever be free again, but any time he would have left would be spent in fear, pain, or ideally, both. So, how do we go about it? Have him arrested when he meets with his victim? Does he take these poor girls to his house?"

"I have no idea, I only saw the one he visits in Khlong Toei, and the guy there said he visits once or twice a week. And I don't really want the police to bust him there. No, the first thing we need to do is get into his house or apartment and see if there's any evidence there. These evil bastards often like to keep some trophies of what they have done. Maybe he has pictures or even video that the police would find and could use as evidence."

"Ok, that is no problem. I know people that can get past any lock, any security system. But what if there is no evidence? Do we have my men plant some?"

"Fuck no. That would make us almost as bad as him. Obtaining kiddy porn photos is abuse by proxy. If your men don't find anything, then we'll need a backup plan."

Five days later, and Tom and Yevgeny met at the Sheraton Grande Sukhumvit. They didn't want to discuss anything over the phone and had agreed that personal meetings were the only way to be guaranteed safety.

The Russian was smiling at first but the smile soon evaporated as he thought about the actual details of what he had to tell Tom.

"So, the good news is there is plenty of evidence. The bad news is it looks like he has been doing this for a while and he has multiple victims. Are you sure we just can't kill him ourselves? I have places where we can keep him alive for weeks and make every waking second a hell of pain."

"It's tempting but we don't even want the smallest risk of it coming back to us. What did they find?"

"It's more a case of what they didn't find. Lots of photographs and videos, many of them with him in it, so a solid case. Clothes too, though we have no idea whether these are trophies or clothes he has bought. Some porn magazines too, pretty hardcore stuff and some with animals in them. This really is one sick bastard, Tom. I want to be in court when they sentence him. How long do you think he will get if...when found guilty?"

"I've looked into and some of it is complicated. I know it sounds mad but, unless they can prove he had distributed or intended to distribute the phots and videos, they can't prosecute him for any of them."

Yevgeny looked stunned. "What the fuck? How can anyone be allowed to possess shit like that?"

"I know, I know. I was shocked myself when I found that out. However, because he appears in some of the pictures and videos, the police do not need to catch him in the act having sex with a minor. And because the girls are obviously so young, maybe nine or ten, the sentencing options increase dramatically. It depends what they charge him with but sex with a minor has a sentence of up to 20 years, as does rape. Depending on how many victims are in the material, he could be facing multiple sentences. My only real worry is the Thai legal system. What if he has money hidden away and buys off the judge? With no juries here, it could be relatively easy to get a mistrial if he bribes the judge."

"No fucking way," exclaimed Yevgeny. "No matter how much money he has salted away, I have more. I'll have someone visit the judge and make sure he knows, what is your English saying again? We'll make sure he knows what side his cake is buttered on."

Tom laughed. "It's bread. I mean, who the fuck would put butter on a cake?"

"Well, who knows with some of the crazy food you English eat, Ok, bread. The point is, no way is this bastard walking away from his crimes."

"Good, now we just need to find a way to let the police know and to make sure they take any tip seriously."

"Again, just leave to Yevgeny. I have a couple of police generals on my payroll and they've never really had to earn the money I send them every month. I shall stress to them both how important it is to me that this man is arrested. And I'll also stress how upset I would be if anything went wrong. I may even suggest to one of them that it would be a great shame if the press were tipped off and there were TV and newspaper journalists there to cover his arrest."

Tom laughed again. "And you had the cheek to call me a devious bastard? I hadn't even considered the press angle. Having his face plastered all over papers and TV screens around the world would be the icing on the cake."

"Icing? So, you put that on instead of butter? No matter, we have a plan and it's a good one. I think we should celebrate with lots of vodka."

"Find out the details of the arrest. I want to be there when he's marched out his property in chains and bundled into a van."

"Da, my friend, we will be there and also there on his final day in court."

It was another eight days before Tom received word from Yevgeny that the operation would be happening the next day. The police had wanted to monitor his movements, keep him under observation, and carry out risk assessments before they raided his house. Baht lived in a small but busy side soi off Sukhumvit Soi 77. His house was a two-storey traditional shophouse with a front entrance on the soi and an exit onto a narrow alley at the rear. The arrest team were waiting on Suk 77 in an unmarked van and already had officers covering the back alley should their target try to escape.

Yevgeny and Tom had settled at one of the outside tables of a coffee shop about 100 metres from Baht's house. Front row seats for what might be the event of the year. Yevgeny looked at his watch as Tom sipped his coffee.

"Two minutes till 11. Two minutes till our friend gets the fright of his life."

Sure enough, as it got closer to 11, the arrest team appeared at the top of the soi. They clung to the shopfronts on the same side of the lane as Baht's house, rendering themselves almost invisible should he chance to look out a window. There were five in the team; one carried a battering ram for the front door, two carried some type of sub-machine gun, and the other two held revolvers.

They split into pairs on either side of the door with the officer holding the ram taking position in front of the open security gates, ready to smash open the internal door as soon as he received the signal. Almost exactly at 11am, one of the officers nodded his head and the man with the ram stepped forward and smashed the inside door open. The other four officers rushed inside and, even from their observation point, Yevgeny and Tom could hear one shout in English:

"ARMED POLICE. COME OUT WITH YOUR HANDS ON HEAD. IF WE SEE A WEAPON, WE WILL SHOOT."

There then followed several minutes of silence, the tension growing in the two watchers as they wondered what would happen next. Then the van that had carried the arrest team reversed at speed down the soi, stopping just outside Baht's house. It just looked like an ordinary black minivan you would see doing runs to the provinces or the borders with neighbouring countries. Another couple of minutes passed then the team appeared from the front door, a shackled figure between them, his head bowed as he realised fate had dealt him a very shitty hand. It took less than two minutes for the police to load Baht into the van then the other two officers who had been covering the rear appeared and jumped in the back too.

As the van sped up the soi, Tom stared at it. As it passed, his eyes locked with Baht's, eyes that one minute were filled with despair and the next lit up with fury as he realised who was responsible – or partly responsible – for his arrest.

The legal process was surprisingly swift. It took prosecutors three weeks to sift through the evidence and they ended up charging Baht, whose real name had now been revealed as Hollings, with four counts of sex with a minor and three counts of rape. He pled guilty in the hope that there would be some leniency shown. No fucking chance. He was sentenced the day after he pled guilty, his lawyer having nothing that could possibly mitigate the offences. Yevgeny, who was fluent in Thai, translated the judge's statement to Tom, who was still a good way short of fluent.

"This is the most disturbing case I have presided over in 15 years of being a judge. Your victims have suffered mental and physical trauma they may never recover from and while they have suffered the most, their families have also suffered and both will continue to suffer, maybe for the rest of their lives. The fact that you recorded your crimes so you could relive them over and over again is utterly sickening. If the death penalty was allowed in this case, I would not hesitate to impose it. As it is, it is in my power to make sure you never harm a child again. Ronald Hollings, on the three counts of rape, I sentence you to ten years in prison for each count. For the four counts of sex with a minor, and considering the ages of your victims, I sentence you to 15 years on each count. These sentences are all to be served consecutively."

There were cheers around the courtroom and Yevgeny high-fived his English friend. A total of 90 years in prison. There was no chance that Baht would ever be released, no chance that he could ever be able to molest or rape another child. As he was led from the court, he looked over at Tom with a gaze of pure, unadulterated hate.

2023

Tom had deliberately avoided logging into his work accounts for the rest of the day. While he really wanted to see Chompoo's response, he felt he needed time to focus on himself, to relax, and to put everything that was bothering him out of his mind. He'd spent some time in the condo gym, then lazed about his apartment watching Netflix, eating comfort food, and generally doing nothing that would overtax his brain.

He arrived back at the office the next morning feeling refreshed and ready to face anything. Of course, the first thing he hoped to face was some sort of explanation from Chompoo that would put his mind at rest. Mai brought him his usual coffee, the booted up his laptop, and logged into his work email account to see if she, or was it a he, had replied. Sure enough. Amongst all the usual work-related and spam emails was her reply. He immediately clicked on it.

Hi Tom,

I can fully understand your concerns. Trust me, I was as shocked as you were when I read the story yesterday while on the plane. And yes, there are a lot of similarities between that awful event and my story. But similarities are all they are and I truly hope you don't think I had anything to do with that horrible crime. Even if the policeman was a rapist, whoever killed him has denied justice being done and possibly prevented real closure for any victims.

I actually wrote 'Karma' more than a year ago. The idea was based on a number of factors, well two main ones to be precise. There had been a story in the news about a policeman who had been convicted of four rapes. He wasn't murdered or even attacked – though I'd like to think that the latter might have happened in prison – and he was sentenced to 25 years.

A few days later, there was a feature on the increasing prevalence of wives cutting off their unfaithful husbands' penises and then disposing of them in different ways; everything from just throwing it out a window to destroying it in a food blender. You know yourself that writers often take several ideas from different sources and combine them with 'what if?" to create a new story. That was very much the case here. I took elements of both stories; the rapist policeman and the angry wives, and wrote something that, though dark, I felt contained poetic justice as well as being an entertaining read (well, I hope it was to some).

However, there is also another possible explanation, one that worries me. I have posted several of my stories, including 'Karma', on my own blog as well as on a couple of sites, though those versions were all in Thai. What if someone read the story and made it real? I've read about criminals copying things they read in books or similar. What do you think I should do?

As to meeting, I can see that you are impatient and will not be dissuaded from this. Unfortunately, I am out of the country for the next three weeks, first in Singapore (where I am now) and then Shanghai. But as soon as I return, let's make arrangements to meet though I would prefer it to be away from your office.

Best wishes,

Chompoo

Tom sat back in his chair. Her explanation made a lot of sense so it could just be coincidence. Bangkok was a violent city at times and she'd said herself that her writing reflected the darker side of the city. But her other suggestion worried him a lot. He hadn't realized that any of her writing had been published online, even if in Thai. What if someone was copying her stories in real life or even just taking inspiration from them?

He wondered for a moment if he should contact the police but quickly dismissed the idea. Other than the loose connection, he had no evidence that the killer had read any of Chompoo's stories. They would either not bother listening to him or they would interrogate him in a tiny room for hours. Neither option particularly appealed to him at this point. Plus, Chompoo's explanation had him leaning more and more towards it all being a coincidence. He read the Post every day, though some stories he just skimmed rather than reading in detail.

Bangkok could be a violent city, but then again, so were many other cities. But the darkness that had inspired Chompoo was perhaps more prevalent here. Tourists - and most expats - only ever saw the bright and shiny, their only real views of poverty being the beggars on some streets or the ramshackle huts that lined some khlongs. There were also the shanty towns that were often juxtaposed beside luxury condo blocks, abject poverty existing side by side with luxurious comfort.

He thought back to Chompoo saying that Bangkok truly was a city of Yin and Yang and realised how right she'd been. But that was not to say that only Thais inhabited those shows. For a start, there were the migrant workers, usually from Laos or Myanmar and very often undocumented. They often lived in conditions that made the shanty towns seem like five-star resorts. And not every expat lived in those comfortable bubbles either. Even without thinking about the overstayers, there were plenty of cheap Charlies who lived on what was a pittance to them but would be riches to many poor Thais.

Their shadows often overlapped with the shadows of the city, drugs, alcoholism, and crime meaning they were often trapped in never-ending cycles of self-abuse. His thoughts led him to picking up that day's Bangkok Post from his desk and he began to flick through it.

Of course, the main stories were national ones, politics or economics or the two intertwined. But once you got past those stories, you found smaller tales of violence or death, of another expat jumping in despair, or another foreigner consigned to the hell of Bang Kwang, which could often be a death sentence in itself. And of course, the many deaths of locals reported too, from drunken – or yaba-induced – road accidents to senseless violence.

The city could be both a kind and cruel mistress; that was something that Tom knew better than anyone. She could lovingly caress and nurture you or she could turn on you, chew your very existence up, and spit you out, discarded in a foreign land like the fast food wrappers that littered the streets of the city that never slept. During his first stint here, he'd hardly seen any destitute farangs at all. Alcoholics on their last legs, yes, but never fully destitute. Yet now they seemed to be everywhere, in the parks, in the side sois, or simply on the main thoroughfares looking for handouts. Even worse, at least in Tom's eyes, were this new breed of begpackers. He'd met plenty travelers in the 90s who were on tight budgets but they were still self-funded. This lot were entitled fuckers though, expecting others to fund whatever travel plan they were on.

He'd seen both sides of the city when he had lived here before, but during this stint, he hadn't really explored the shadows. It seemed that not much had changed when it came to the darker side of the metropolis, even while glittering spires of commerce reached higher into the sky.

Tom sighed. While his own secret life might appear to the uninformed as violent, the reality was that consent took away the true notion of violence. After all, it was hardly likely that someone would walk up to a thug in the street and say, 'please stab me'. His world may have been one of shadows and secrets but it was also one of boundaries and trust.

Kanya trusted him when she was at her most vulnerable; restrained and unable to resist anything he wanted to do. Well, almost anything, she still retained the powers of setting rules for their sessions and being able to stop it with a single word. These victims of violence had no such powers. Kanya begging for mercy was part of their roleplaying, a victim begging for mercy was often a desperate but pointless exercise.

He had to trust Chompoo as Kanya trusted him. Well, not exactly the same, of course. And she had agreed to meet, albeit after she returned from her travels. He would wait for her return. Before returning to his work, he sent her a quick email.

Chompoo,

My apologies. Maybe I overreacted when I realised the similarities. I had not thought to first ask what had inspired your story rather than covertly accusing you of being involved. Hopefully, your other suggestion is just speculation and we don't have someone copying the crimes and acts in your stories.

Enjoy your trip. I look forward to meeting you when you get back to Bangkok.

Best,

Tom

1996

Tom felt good again. With Hollings in prison, he felt he had really achieved something – with Yevgeny's help, of course – and that their actions meant that some children would be safer with the bastard behind bars. He wasn't naïve enough to think they'd made a huge difference; it was only one predator after all. But one less molester on the streets was still a result.

The whole experience had made him determined to write an in-depth article on child abuse. His problem was that the western editors he'd spoken to so far had all wanted sensationalism and a focus on child sex tourism. Although this was undoubtedly a problem across the region, Tom knew it was just a small percentage of the total abuse that took place in Thailand, or any country to be fair. Most abuse took place in familial settings, and most abusers were either family members or close friends of the family.

He'd spoken to a lovely Englishwoman, Maggie, who worked for an NGO that helped street kids across the city. Her knowledge had been both enlightening and frightening. He'd always assumed that 'paedophile' was just another term for 'child molester', but Maggie told him that many child molesters were not actual paedophiles. As with other sexual crimes, it was often about power and control. Tom enjoyed the feelings that power and control gave him but the idea of controlling a child for sexual reasons turned his stomach.

Maggie had also told him that many of the street kids had fled an abusive home life, but the sad irony was that their life on the streets would likely lead to more abuse and some would inevitably find their way into sex work. The NGO she worked for, Karn-Pong-Kan (Protection), tried to offer as much support as possible, and housed more than 80 children in two houses they had rented. They also tried to get the kids back into education so that they would have choices as to their futures.

She'd said that the problems were often worse in isolated rural areas where there were fewer NGOs operating and that the normalising of the abuse often meant the patterns and cycles would be repeated across generations. Tom had been as shocked by Maggie revealing the extent of abuse as he had been when he'd found out that possession of child porn was not illegal in Thailand.

Maggie's talks had made him even more determined to write the article, maybe even a series of articles, and not to give in to editorial demands that he focus on the more sensationalist aspects of westerners travelling to Thailand to sexually abuse children. It was all or nothing as far as he was concerned. He'd even thought about pitching the idea to some TV companies though he knew they would likely want their own 'star' fronting the programme. He didn't really care about that, he just wanted to get the story out there and had already decided that any fees he received would be donated to Karn-Pong-Kan.

For now, he felt as if he needed some time off. The whole episode around ensuring Baht/Hollings had been mentally draining and Tom thought a week at the beach or on an island would be the perfect antidote and would allow him to charge his batteries. Ireshi had loved the idea when he had suggested it the previous evening; her work had been stressful too in the last few months.

It would be time away from their play sessions, at least the more strenuous and intense ones. There would be some light roleplay but nothing more. They didn't want any neighbours complaining about the noise that Tom knew Ireshi would inevitably make. Even though their playroom was soundproofed, he still occasionally worried as she was one noisy woman when she had – or was close to – an orgasm.

Ireshi had suggested Koh Tao and Tom had quickly agreed. It was an island he had not yet visited but the reports he had heard, including Ireshi's own exuberant enthusiasm, had meant he needed no persuading. It was an easy enough route too; he knew there was a train to Chumphon from Bangkok that had sleeper berths. It would get them in just as dawn was breaking so they could either catch the earliest ferry to the island or hang about for some food and catch a later ferry.

They'd sort out accommodation once on the island. Tom knew that the island's pier would be crowded with hawkers extolling the virtues of their particular hotel. But he wanted something a little better, or even a lot better, than your bog-standard guesthouse. He doubted the better hotels would have staff down at the pier but he knew there would be various transportation options available and waving an extra couple of hundred baht would ensure good service and a recommendation of the best hotels on the island.

They planned to leave this coming Thursday evening. Ireshi was going to tell her work today that she'd be away for a week. She had holidays due anyway so there wouldn't be an issue about the short notice. Tom planned on nipping to Hua Lamphong station today to make sure they got decent sleeper berths. He also wanted to go book shopping as, other than making love to Ireshi, turning pages and lifting cocktail glasses was as much activity as he had planned.

Thursday came and they made their way to Hua Lamphong and got settled in their basic but comfortable sleeper compartment. The train arrived in Chumphon just after 6am and they decided to grab some breakfast rather than rush for the first ferry of the day. As Tom had predicted, when the ferry arrived at Koh Tao, the pier was crowded with hawkers offering everything from fresh seafood to the 'best guesthouse on island, honest, sir'. Tom was surprised to see no tuk tuks on the pier. Transportation options seemed to be either motosai taxis or songthaew-style pickups that took multiple passengers.

With their luggage, Tom didn't fancy a precarious balancing act on a motorcycle and the problem with the pickups were that you might be unlucky and be the last people dropped off. He spoke to Ireshi who approached one of the empty pickups and explained their proposal as well as the type of hotel they were looking for. The promise of 200 baht added to a probable commission from the hotel were more than enough to persuade the driver that a couple with money was a better option than a horde of backpackers at 10 baht a pop.

Once they were on board with their luggage, the driver set off, giving his fellow drivers a smug grin as he passed them, knowing a single fare would make him more than they would in two or three trips. He headed east from the pier, passing houses, shops, and guesthouses that gradually faded until the view to their left was nothing but gently-sloping verdant hills. It was a short journey; the island was only about eight miles square. As they neared their destination, the road narrowed to single track before they emerged from the surrounding trees to a beautiful little cove with turquoise waters. *'Perfect'*, thought Tom.

The truck stopped outside a traditional teak house with the original name of 'Sawasdee Ka' painted in gold on a sign hanging above the door. The driver spoke to Ireshi in the usual rapid Thai. She turned to Tom.

"He says this is the best hotel on the island. Beautiful house, beautiful rooms, and beautiful view."

Tom laughed. "Or to translate further, it's a good hotel but it's also the one that pays him the highest commission. But it does look nice and this little bay is utterly gorgeous."

He handed the driver 250 baht which was greeted by a grateful smile coupled with an enthusiastic wai. The driver then carried their luggage into the hotel's reception are before wai'ing again and saying goodbye.

As they walked over to the desk, they received yet another wait, this time from a middle-aged Thai woman with a welcoming warm smile. She spoke in – very good – English.

"Welcome to Sawasdee Ka. Do you have a reservation? I wasn't expecting any guest to arrive today."

"Sorry, no," replied Tom, "the driver recommended you so I hope you have some vacancies."

"Yes, we have a few rooms available. In fact, our best room has been free since yesterday. How long did you want to stay for?"

"Seven days ideally, but if that messes with any bookings, then we'd happily accept less."

"No, no, seven days is fine. Are you on holiday?"

Tom wondered if she thought he was just a holidaymaker that had found a girl in a bar somewhere, not that Ireshi looked anything like a bar girl."

"Well, yes and no. We live and work in Bangkok, or Ireshi does. I'm a travel writer so my work can take me all over Thailand."

"Oh, I better be careful then. I don't want you to write anything bad about my little hotel."

Tom laughed.

"If first impressions are anything to go by, I don't think you have anything to worry about."

"I'm glad to hear that. My name is Lawan, by the way. We have a small restaurant that serves breakfast, lunch, and dinner. There are also a few other restaurants nearby or you can travel to Ban Mae Haad or beyond. With it being such a small island, you can get anywhere in a short time. I also have scooters for rent if you want to explore the island without relying on a taxi."

"That sounds like a great idea but we'll maybe leave it till tomorrow. We took the overnight train from Bangkok so don't really have the energy to go further than the beach today."

"Ok, good. Now let's get you checked in. If you'd just fill in this book. I'll need to see your passport and your girlfriend's ID card."

Tom and Ireshi handed over their identification and Tom filled out the details in the guest book. He then took out his wallet.

"No, you can just pay when you check out. That way you can pay everything at once; room, food, drinks, scooter rental, and anything else you need or have used. There is a small mini-bar in your room and I've tried to keep the prices reasonable and no different from what you'd be charged at our bar."

This surprised Tom. He was used to hotels charging extortionate prices when it came to mini-bars. He completed their registration and the woman came from behind the desk.

"I'll show you up to your room. Sorry, but you arrived on the one day my assistant has off, so you'll have to carry your own luggage. We don't have a big staff; just a cook, waitress, a barman in the evenings, and my assistant who helps me with everything."

Tom smiled. “That’s ok. It’s not that heavy anyway and we’ve had to carry it most of the time ourselves.”

Lawan led the way up the stairway to the first floor. Everything, the stairs, the walls, the floor, was that glorious dark teak found throughout Thailand. The walls were decorated with paintings of pastoral and fishing scenes, simple subjects but executed with a surprisingly skillful hand. She stopped outside a door and unlocked it before leading them inside.

“You have a bathroom to your left; the hot water is usually plentiful so you can have a shower at any time. The television is old, I’m afraid, and only has local channels.”

She walked further into the room. A large double bed dominated the room and on one wall was storage for clothes.

“The fridge is under the television but it’s this that I feel makes this such a special room.”

Lawan opened the balcony doors and let Tom and Ireshi walk out. The view was simply stunning, the balcony looking out on the bay and the beach below the hotel. Tom realised that sunrise here would be spectacular and was glad he’d brought his camera. They could easily check out sunsets on the other side of the island one evening, but they had no plans to move beyond the environs of the hotel today other than a possible trip down to the beach later.

“I’ll leave you to settle in. I’m guessing that you’ll both want a long shower after that journey.”

Tom thanked her and Lawan left the room. Ireshi jumped onto the bed and lay back.

“This is heavenly. What sheer luck to find the perfect hotel in the perfect spot. Just think, if we’d asked another driver, then we might be somewhere else. It might have been good too, but I just feel that this is where we were meant to be."

"Yes, I don't usually like too much wood in a hotel but it works perfectly here. You're right, it's the perfect place to unwind and leave all our problems behind. I'm looking forward to a week of doing absolutely nothing that requires any effort. Now why don't you grab the first shower then we'll head downstairs for something to eat. That breakfast hardly filled me at all."

Ireshi looked at him mischievously.

"Why don't we both grab the first shower?"

The week that followed was the most idyllic Tom had ever experienced. After their first day, they got two scooters from Lawan and spent a little time each day exploring the island, from John-Suwan viewpoint at the southern tip to Mango Bay at the north of the island. As well as eating at the hotel, where the food was magnificent, they ate everything from local street food to extravagant dinners. They even found a little restaurant at Mango Bay where the seafood was mostly caught to order; the cook's husband heading out in a small boat to catch the freshest fish either of them had ever tasted.

Tom's prediction had been correct. The sunrise views from the hotel were spectacular. Lawan had recommended that for the best sunset view, they had to take a boat to the small neighbouring island of Koh Nang Yuan and climb to the viewpoint there. Her recommendation proved as accurate as Tom's sunrise prediction, the sun setting gloriously behind the hills on the mainland.

The did most of their exploring in the mornings while it was a little cooler, preferring to spend the afternoons lazing on the beach with a book and some refreshing drinks. In the evenings, they would often go and eat at restaurants on the western side of the island, sharing a bottle of wine before returning to the hotel and making love gently until they were both exhausted. They found there was no need for any of their usual games and it may have been the longest period in their relationship where their lovemaking was purely vanilla.

All too soon, the week was over and it was time to depart for the realities of life in Bangkok. They bid a fond farewell to Lawan with a promise to return one day. Even the weather seemed to understand their feelings as on the morning they left, storm clouds had begun to gather on the eastern horizon. Thankfully, they were heading west then north to the capital so were unlikely to be affected.

As the train began to trundle north, there was little conversation. A week of perfection that always had to end and would forever be in their memories meant that there was little to say.

2023

Tom hated going to the dentist. In fact, he'd always hated dentists. He knew it all stemmed from the fact that the family dentist when he was a child was nothing short of a butcher, and Tom had often – facetiously – suspected that the dentist had once served in a Nazi concentration camp. Adulthood and the better dentistry services available had done little to reduce the anxiety he felt whenever he had a scheduled visit or when, as in this case, it was a matter of necessity.

He'd been in considerable pain for a couple of weeks now, and his probing tongue had found a sizeable hole at the back of one of his molars. His anxiety wasn't helped by the fact that he had turned up at Edelweiss Dental House more than an hour early. The receptionist had been apologetic and said that his dentist was in the middle of an implant procedure and he would have to wait.

Tom sighed and took a seat in the well-appointed waiting area. He was disappointed to find that most of the reading material was in Thai, and what little there was in English has mostly been claimed by the four farang also waiting to be seen. He found an old – more than two months' old – copy of the Bangkok Post behind a Thai fashion magazine and decided it was better than nothing. It was dated a week before his arrival in August but at least it would while away some of the time. Tom had always seen his phone as purely functional. He had no games or streaming on it, just useful apps for ordering food or navigating his way around a city that had changes so much. Given the industry he was in, it was no surprise that he read a lot and he cursed that he hadn't thought to bring a book with him today.

He tried to be interested in what he was reading but, given that most of it was out of date, it was, quite literally, old news. He saw that all of page four was taken up with the list of pardons granted on the occasion of King Vajiralongkorn's birthday. This was a yearly occurrence and usually pardoned low risk prisoners, minor crimes, those that had been in in prison for many years, and compassionate cases or foreigners when the Thai government wanted to seek favour with the country involved.

To a western mind, the number of pardons granted was truly staggering, and the article opened with a note of the total number, some 205,000. Of course, the article was never going to list every prisoner pardoned but instead focused on the cases where the names were well-known – such as celebrities or politicians – and any farang who would finally see the real light of day again. He browsed the piece with half-interest until one name leapt off the page at him.

Ronald Hollings, aged 67, convicted in 1996 for sex with a minor and rape.

Tom gasped. He had assumed the man would have died in prison, either from natural causes or from prison justice, and the name had hardly entered his mind before or after he'd traveled to Thailand. He would have thought that Hollings would have been immediately deported but there was no mention of that, despite it being mentioned in relation to some of the other pardoned farangs. Was he still in Thailand? More importantly, would he know Tom was back in Thailand? Although he'd hardly thought about him recently, that last look of utter hatred in the courtroom was something Tom would never forget.

He checked the byline on the article and realised it was a journalist he had met, albeit briefly, at an event a few weeks previously. They had exchanged business cards and, although there was little chance that Tom would ever use the majority of the cards he was given, he still kept them all, with meticulous notes on who the person was. You just never knew when that five-minutes of talking at some event could prove useful in the future.

Tom resolved to look the card out when he got back to the office and contact the journalist to see if he had any further information. He could also do a Google search to see if Hollings was mentioned anywhere in the media back home. UK newspapers took great delight in sensationalist headlines when it came to returning offenders, especially when the crimes were as heinous as Hollings' had been.

The one good thing to come out of his shock that time passed quickly and, even once in the dentist's chair, his anxiety was so distracted that the procedure went smoothly. His mouth still numb from Novocaine, he took a taxi back to the office, declining Mai's offer of a coffee as he hurried to his desk. He opened the drawer where he kept his business card binders. He was so meticulous with his storage that everything was in chronological order so it only took him a few minutes to find the card he was looking for.

The card reminded him that the journalist's name was Prasit Jitpleecheep and that he was a senior writer for the Post. He didn't want to call him directly and thought an email was a better option. He thought for a few minutes – how exactly was he going to frame his inquiry?

Hi Prasit,

I hope you remember me. It's Tom McKay from Kram-roo Publishing. We met at the launch party for Subsib Bangkok's website a few weeks ago.

I have quite a strange request. I was at the dentist's this morning and the only thing they had to read was an old copy of the Post. I can only assume that it had missed any regular cleaning up of their newspapers and magazines. Anyway, your piece on it was about the pardons granted on the occasion of His Majesty's last birthday.

One name stood out in the article as the original case happened when I last lived in Thailand. Ronald Hollings. He was convicted for rape and sex with a minor. Your article didn't mention him being deported home though that was mentioned for several other farangs.

Call it sheer curiousity but I'd love to know if he was also deported. It seemed strange that it wasn't mentioned given the seriousness of his crimes. I'd be really grateful if you could let me know what happened to him.

Also, we really should have dinner sometime. I have some really big plans for Kram-roo and would love to give you an exclusive.

Kind regards,

Tom McKay.

He'd used curiousity as an excuse, but the real reason he wanted to know was for his own peace of mind. Tom's appointment had been covered in several newspapers and magazines, but most of the coverage had been in Thai. That said, Tom suspected that in 27 years in prison, Hollings would likely have become more fluent than the pidgin-Thai he had spoken when Tom knew him.

He knew that this was going to be another day where he couldn't fully focus until he had the answers he needed. Nevertheless, he opened the folder on his laptop where he kept submissions that had been forwarded onto him by junior editors who thought he might have interest. Opening one of the files, he tried to distract his mind by starting to read a memoir from a woman whose family had lived on Koh Samui for eight generations.

The reply from Prasit came around 90 minutes later. Tom was relieved as he'd found himself rereading pages several times as he just wasn't taking things in.

Hi Tom,

Of course I remember you. That was quite an event too, even if Subsib Bangkok thrives on gossip and who's doing what to who.

I'm quite shocked that such an old copy of the paper was in their reading section. I mean, I'm guessing you were at one of the better dentists and they're usually quite up to date when it comes to the newspapers and magazines they offer.

Anyway, sorry about the delay. I had to do some digging and also speak to one of my contacts in the Immigration Department. It would appear that this Hollings guy hasn't been deported, nor did my contact know of any plans to deport him. As you said, most strange given the seriousness of the crimes he was convicted for. I can only assume that some money has exchanged hands somewhere. Do you know if this guy was wealthy? I've also checked the archives from when he was arrested and when he appeared in court and there's nothing that tells me that.

I sense a story here but, as you can appreciate, I need to tread carefully when it comes to accusations of corruption, especially if it reaches higher levels than the usual standard of bribery we're used to. Do you have any more information on this guy? Did you ever meet him? If he's stayed in Thailand, would he remain in Bangkok or are there other areas he might have traveled to? While I am thinking about a story, my main concern is whether this bastard would offend again. If he's in a more rural area, then there's a greater chance of him reoffending. I really want to speak to someone in the police about this, but until I have some idea of how he's managed to evade deportation, I'm hesitant to approach even my most trusted contacts.

As for dinner, it sounds like a great idea. I'm a great supporter of Thai literature and while I was hesitant at first about the Green-Hayes takeover, time has let me see that this may be a chance for Thai writers 'to reach a wider audience. So, I'd love to hear more about your vision and ideas. Just drop me a line whenever you want to meet.

Best,

Prasit.

Damn. He'd hoped it was just an omission in the article but it appeared Hollings had bought his way to staying in Thailand. He didn't want to give Prasit any information. There was nothing to link him to Hollings, even if there were still serving police officers from that time. Everything had been done through Yevgeny's contacts and Tom knew his name would not have been mentioned. Yevgeny himself was long dead, killed in a helicopter crash in 2016. That meant that the only person other than Tom that knew he had any hand in Hollings being convicted was Hollings. Whether he knew Tom was in Thailand remained an unknown factor, but Tom had to proceed as if he did. That meant being more aware of his surrounding, especially when traveling to and from the office. Tom composed a quick reply to Prasit.

Hi again Prasit,

Thanks for the information. I'm shocked that someone like that would be allowed to remain, no matter how much he paid.

To answer your question, no, I didn't know the guy and certainly never met him. I just remember it being such a big story at the time given his offences and how determined the government at the time seemed to be to send a message that they were cracking down on child sex tourism. Sorry I couldn't be of more help but hope you find out more.

I'll be in touch soon to arrange that dinner. My shout (well, the company's) so you can choose the venue.

Best,

Tom.

Though he knew there was nothing that linked him to Hollings, Tom did worry that any digging into that time might unearth some of his own secrets. He knew that nothing official had ever happened, he'd kept in contact with people who would have known if that were the case for a couple of years after he left. It was more the unofficial side of life that Tom worried about. The Thais, much like the elephants they loved so much, had very long memories and, from that perspective, 27 years was really nothing.

1996

Reality could be a real bummer. Perhaps no more so than when you have come back from a perfect holiday. Both Tom and Ireshi were in low moods, their depression causing an almost palpable feeling of oppression in their home life. While Ireshi was at work, Tom tried to focus on his plan for an article around child sexual abuse. He'd met up with Maggie a couple of times and her help and input were invaluable. She'd even photocopied a lot of material the NGO held; everything from statistics and academics studies to witness statements and stories from survivors, all anonymised of course.

It was gloomy reading which didn't help the way Tom was feeling generally. He'd only worked his way through a small part of it but he was in no hurry as there was yet to be any real interest shown by editors back home. When Ireshi returned home in the evening, she was usually quiet and withdrawn. They hadn't even had sex since they returned, something that was most unusual. Tom had tried to initiate some play sessions but she had always expressed unwillingness or had some excuse, including the clichéd 'headache'.

Tom hoped it was a temporary malaise and that the week spent on Koh Tao did not somehow represent the peak of their relationship. They had gone out for dinner a number of times but there was definitely a spark missing. Conversation was stilted and awkward and it was almost always Tom who had to ask questions. He even tried to ensure that any question he asked was open-ended so that Ireshi might open up to him, but she just seemed reluctant to engage with him.

He did worry that it marked a decline in their relationship, at least from her perspective. He was feeling down too but nothing had changed as far as his feelings for Ireshi were concerned. There were times when he would just sit in silence instead of working, racking his brain as how to revive the passion.

He'd spoken to Yevgeny – the only male friend he felt he could confide in – over lunch one day. The Russian had been his usual stoic self.

"Bah, women. They never know when they're happy. When my wife is in a funny mood, I just go to the golf course or meet a friend for lunch like now. I try everything, buy her gifts, give her attention, take her out, everything. But when she is in a funny mood, it is best just to leave her alone till she feels better or wants to talk."

"Yeah, I've tried everything but nothing seems to help."

"We men sometimes forget that women are in fact the stronger gender. Not only do they give birth, something that frightens me immensely, but they are often the glue that holds a family together. Maybe we will never truly understand them. Men are simple creatures and are often easily pleased. Women are far more complicated and sometimes it is best that we just shut up. Rather say nothing at all rather than the wrong thing."

"So, you think I should make less effort?"

"No, not necessarily. It's not about effort so much as trying to get inside their heads. Do some of the things you are doing; having dinner ready when she comes home from work, hugging her in bed, whatever your usual couple things are. I more mean don't ask questions, don't try to find out what's troubling her, at least for now. If she wants to talk, she will do in her own time. Ireshi is a good woman, a strong woman, but she is also a Thai woman, a conservatively-raised Thai woman to be precise. Parts of your relationship are...well...unusual to say the least, and this is something that conflicts with how she was brought up. Her father may accept you more now than when you first met, but he will never truly accept you. And that's not just because you're not Thai but because you're not the right type of Thai. If she had brought home a boyfriend who was from a poor family or, Buddha forbid, from Isaan or one of the other northern provinces, he would have been just as horrified, maybe even more so. In your favour, you are making a real effort to learn Thai and you are also writing some very positive things about the country, so those will have contributed to his acceptance of you, or rather, the partial-acceptance he has shown."

"You really know the country and people so well, tovarich, I really should interview you sometime."

"Given some of my business interests, I don't think that would be a good idea. But I have been here nearly 25 years now, I have a Thai wife, I have three luk-kreung, and I also have several legitimate businesses that do well. My rolodex contains the contact numbers of some minor royals, several police and army generals, and countless celebrities. I'd even count some of those people as true friends. But am I completely accepted? No, and I probably never will be. I will always be a farang, an outsider, and though I now have a better understanding of the Thai psyche, I will never fully understand it. There's an irony in the fact that we will never be fully accepted by the Thais but the key to thriving here is to accept that fact."

The waiter arrived with their main courses and proceeded to top up their wine glasses. When he'd gone, they switched their conversation to lighter topics. Once they'd finished eating, they moved out onto the hotel's terrace, ordered a couple of cognacs, and lit up their favourite cigars.

As the rich smoke curled up from Yevgeny's mouth, he continued.

"So, where was I? Yes, do not try and force Ireshi to talk, she will only withdraw further into her shell. What you do need to do is be there when she is ready. Listen to anything she says and only speak when you are unsure of something or when she asks for your thoughts or opinion. Women are complicated, Thai women can be more complicated, and a Thai woman like Ireshi, who may feel pulled in two directions, can be more complicated still. So the two key words to remember if you want a successful relationship are acceptance as I mentioned, but also patience. She will open up to you when she is ready and not a moment sooner. Now, other than your relationship, how are things? How is your idea about an article on child abuse coming along?"

"Bloody slowly. I've had some interest from newspapers and magazines, but they want to only focus on the sensationalist side; the fucking creeps who travel to Asia purely to have sex with minors. That Maggie from Karn-Pong-Kan has been amazing. She's given me lots of information that really disturbed me. I could write a whole series of articles and not even begin to cover how big a problem it is."

"Why not write a book then? If even a series of articles would not cover it, then maybe a book would. You're already friendly with this Maggie woman and I'm sure she could link you up with other professionals and NGOs."

"Yeah, and that's going to sell lots of copies."

"I thought you weren't in it for the money and that any payment for an article would go to Maggie's NGO anyway?"

"I'm not talking about the money. But if you have a piece in a newspaper or magazine, at least you know it will have readers. Outside of the folk who work in that sector, who's going to be interested in buying it? It could be months of work or longer. Then nobody reads it?"

"Why don't I publish it then?"

"What the fuck are you talking about now, you mad Russian?"

'Look, you know that some of my businesses are very much under the table and out of sight. But you also know I have quite a few legitimate businesses too. They're good for my image and also quite handy for the odd spot of money laundering. You never know, maybe this could be one of the successful ones. So, you write the book, in your own time of course, and I'll pay for printing and any marketing. Maybe we could send copies to universities that do anything on child abuse as well as some bookshops. Come on, Tom, what have you got to lose?"

"Other than a year or so of my life? I'll tell you what; give me another month or so. If there's no interest from newspapers or magazines, we can talk again. And I suppose that if we did a book, I could sell those editors the sensationalist shit they want."

"Exactly! You could have the book more focused on the abuse within families and just keep one chapter about those bastards that travel here. I mean, aren't you always saying the tourism angle is just the tip of a very ugly iceberg?"

"Ok, I'm liking the idea more. Give me six weeks for some last throws of the dice. If nothing, then we can sit down and talk more seriously about it."

Yevgeny laughed and raised his glass.

"A toast, tovarich, to me becoming a publisher and you becoming a best-selling author."

The two friends continued drinking into the afternoon, switching from their post-lunch cognacs to beer and then to whisky, managing to demolish most of a bottle of Bunnahabhain between them. Finally, Yevgeny announced it was time to call it a day.

"If I leave now, I can be home before Keow and the kids. That means I can be asleep when they get in and they won't disturb me. And if Keow does not disturb me, then she will not know how drunk I am, even if she suspects it. If I leave in an hour, they will already be home and I will be in a very deep hole of shit."

Tom smiled. "I don't think it matters in my case. Ireshi can't be in any worse a mood than she already is."

There was a heart guffaw from the big Russian and he put his arm around Tom's shoulder.

"My poor little Tom. Damned if you do, damned if you don't. I've already told you; give her time and she will talk when she is ready, just be ready to listen."

"I hope you're right, Yevgeny."

"Oh, I nearly forgot. I have something special arriving next week that you might want to try. It's called ketamine, have you heard of it?"

"Is that not the shit vets use?"

"Partly myth. It's used on humans too. This is coming from India where they use it as a children's sedative and anaesthetic. But that is in its liquid form. If you cook it, it becomes a powder and you can then snort just like your beloved cocaine. Apparently, it acts like a discocia...disstia..dissocati...oh fuck it, it makes you crazy.'

Tom laughed aloud. He wasn't sure if it was the alcohol or the word itself that was causing Yevgeny problems.

"I think you mean dissociative. Yes, sounds fun. Sure, I'll give it a try when it arrives."

"My friend loves it. But he says not to do it on its own if you're out at a club or bar. It's better to do at home or out in the country somewhere. He also says, it's very nice if you mix it 50:50 with coke. The coke takes a little of the edge off the ketamine. Now he is one crazy bastard, crazier even than you. So if he's saying to be careful with it, it's worth taking his advice."

"I can't see there being an issue, though of course I'll start off with small doses. I'm a big fan of psychedelics so this sounds like it might be close to that. And anything that mixes well with Charlie is good in my book."

"Just don't take it too lightly, Tom. He's told me some real horror stories about it. People totally freaking out and thinking they were in a movie or TV programme. It's not for me, that's for sure. I'll stick to whisky and the occasional little line of coke. Even that occasional is rarer these days. If Keow suspected I was on coke, then it would be spicy meatballs on the menu that night, and no pigs or chickens would be harmed, just a poor Russian bastard."

"Ok, ok, I get the message. Order me an eighth then. I'll try a few small doses on its own first then try a few with a wee bump of coke."

"I know common sense is not a phrase you like when associated with drug use, but trust me, from what I've heard, it's needed here. You may have started as nothing more than a customer, but I now consider you a close friend. I don't want to end up trying to have a conversation with a dribbling wreck in Somdet Chao Phraya Hospital."

They walked outside and Yevgeny hailed an approaching taxi. He hugged Tom again.

"Remember, give Ireshi the space she needs. I'll give you a call when the ketamine arrives and, for Buddha's sake, don't do it in the house with Ireshi if you've not sorted things out."

As the taxi sped away from the hotel, Tom waved his friend off. That had been some good advice on dealing with Ireshi, maybe she just needed some space. But never mind that, a new drug? Interesting.

2023

Tom was beginning to feel as if the walls were closing in on him. When he'd returned to Bangkok, he'd hoped that all the ghosts of his past were long gone. But already, two of them had come back to haunt him. First of all, there was Lam and his mysterious 'safety net' comment. Tom could understand that he would want to protect himself now he was in the lofty spires of political power. But if he'd known Tom was back in town, surely he'd know that Tom had a pretty important job too and wouldn't want to jeopardise anything by revealing Lam's past – or even present – indiscretions. Besides, they had been friends, hadn't they? Maybe Lam was just being paranoid. But maybe he'd also gone to extreme lengths to make sure nobody could expose him.

Worry about Lam was secondary to that about Hollings though. Last time he had seen Hollings; it was as the man was being led away to what should have been a life sentence. The look Hollings had given him had left nothing to the imagination as to what Hollings would do to Tom if left alone in a room with him. Now the man was free thanks to the King's generosity. And he now spoke fluent Thai and there was little doubt in Tom's mind that he would have made friends, or at least acquaintances, with some equally evil bastards while in prison.

Hollings could be a very real threat, though of course, Tom had no idea if his presence in Thailand was known to the man. But Tom had found out – purely by accident - about Hollings' release through reading an old Bangkok Post while at the dentists. Hollings could just as easily – or accidentally – learned about Tom's return and appointment a similar way.

He thought for a moment about phoning Kevin back in London and asking if he could come home. But that would entail either telling Kevin the whole story or pretending he couldn't handle the pressure that came with his job. If he went the former route, it would mean his boss, or bosses, would know more about him than he wanted them to. If he chose the latter option, then that proverbial tail between his legs could fuck up any chance of promotion he ever had. Hell, it might even mean the end of his job.

No, he had to handle this himself, if there was even something to handle. He decided there were two courses of action he could take. The first would be for his own protection and a quick search on Google identified a few companies providing security and bodyguard services. One lengthy phone call later and he had an appointment the next day to discuss a review of his apartment's security provisions as well as some personal protection services.

Another Google search and he had a list of private detective services in the city. He didn't want one that was purely farang-owned and run as they belonged in the pages of some noir novel. After browsing several websites, he found one owned by an American and his Thai wife but where most of the staff were Thai. He felt a Thai would be more likely to get answers and to have connections with people who might know where Hollings was. He made a phone call, spoke to one of the owners, and arranged an interview for two hours after his meeting with the security company.

He had no idea what he'd do when – or if – he found Hollings, but he'd cross that bridge when he came to it. He considered sending Lam an email to assure him that there was no danger from Tom, but he decided that it might just serve as a further reminder of the potential danger. Power bred paranoia. He'd leave Lam for now but if he happened to meet him again at an event, he'd try and have a quiet word.

His problems were mounting, a situation that he'd never imagined. And that was without considering Chompoo. The girl – if indeed, she was a girl as he still had doubts despite her protestations – could be the greatest writer he'd ever discovered but she was also his biggest work-related headache. Depending how much latitude she gave him when it came to editing, they could produce the best example of contemporary fiction yet seen in Thailand. But he had to reduce some of the violence, tone it down a little and take a leaf from Hitchcock's playbook and have the violent scenes more implicit. He was aware that he had to do this without diluting her voice or changing her message. That was the sign of a good editor.

Tom hoped she was being sincere about the meeting. While they'd exchanged countless emails by now, a face-to-face discussion would be much more involved and there would be the potential for a level of candour that simply didn't, couldn't, exist with electronic communication.

He also had to remember that he had other duties, other clients. Anything in Thai was mainly handled by Aekarach, though Tom still had to sign off on any contracts or print runs. He trusted the man implicitly and Aekarach would send him a single-sheet summary with his recommendation at the end. So far, Tom had accepted every one of his suggestions, just having to scrawl his signature at the bottom of the sheet before returning it to the man.

They also made a point of having lunch at least once a week and regularly meeting for coffee. This gave them the chance to chat about any projects that showed promise or any issues that had been encountered. And, of course, they had an open-door policy when it came to each other's offices, something that could save waiting for an arranged meeting. Though to be fair, they'd only had to do this once.

Tom had also implemented a weekly team meeting that included both the senior and junior editors. He'd made it clear from the first one that these meetings were not to be structured and that anyone could bring up concerns or ask questions. He knew that it would take time for this to be fully accepted and to work the way he wanted. But many of the staff were younger and less restrained by conservative upbringings or the old-fashioned Thai psyche. He'd already identified a couple of the junior editors who definitely had something special. Tom firmly believed that while there were many elements of editing that could be taught, to be a really great editor, you had to have an almost preternatural talent, especially when it came to developmental editing.

Most of the editing staff were at almost fluent levels when it came to English. The only thing Tom felt was lacking was an understanding of the nuances and idioms that native speakers often employed. However, he was equally aware that those nuances and idioms were factors in Thai too. Not to mention the fact that, being a tonal language, two words that looked the same on paper could mean something very different when spoken.

He'd suggested to Kevin during their last weekly call that, at some point in the future, they could look at having some of the most promising editing staff serve an internship at the London offices. Many of them had studied abroad at some point, but Tim felt that immersion in a related work environment would elevate them to a different level.

Long term, his plan was to have a solid team, led by Aekarach, in place for when his exile ended. Of course, head office would want someone in place to handle the financial and business side. The very fact that Green-Hayes had got the company for such a good price was testament to the fact that those were areas where Aekarach certainly did not excel.

Kevin had confided in him that the board's own long-term view included expansion across the region; Vietnam first and then the burgeouning market in Cambodia where there had been a recent explosion in young Khmer writers who were looking forward rather than back to the horrors of the 1970s and 1980s. The book market – and the number of readers - was continuing to grow across the entire region. The two anomalies, at least as far as the Green-Hayes model was concerned, was the desire for digital formats and the popularity of online serialisation of books.

Kevin had tasked Tom with researching what the demand was in the primary markets they were targeting. They'd already decided that they would never make inroads into China, and Japan seemed to have a preference for anime and graphic novels. E-books had always been secondary to the Green-Hayes plan but they had been releasing e-book versions of every release for a couple of years now and that had added to their overall revenue streams, and profits, those all-important profits.

Asia had a huge percentage of users who were doing almost everything from mobile devices. From shopping to games to books, these devices were now being used by more than 60% of the region's population and Green-Hayes wanted a slice of the lucrative pie. Kevin had asked Tom to set up a working group to look at how they could capitalise on the demand for digital content of all types, including the serialisation idea.

It wasn't something that appealed to Tom; when he read a book, he wanted to read it at his pace, even if that meant finishing it in one sitting. Even the streaming services were releasing most of their series in one fell swoop so people could binge watch if they wanted. But as the saying went, the customer is always right... even when they're wrong. It may not be his thing but he could see people reading that day's chapter on the commute to work.

If the numbers showed demand, as Tom expected they would, then it would be a case of finding the right books to serialise. It may even be the case of commissioning some as Tom couldn't think of many books he'd read which would suit this format. Conscious that his 'to-do' pile was growing bigger by the day, Tom determined to put his problems – and Chompoo – out of his mind for the day and try and make that pile a little smaller.

The next morning, his first meeting was on Sukhumvit 31. He'd expected a sleek office building and was surprised to find that the company operated from a villa, albeit a very fancy one that had been converted to their needs. He passed through the metal detectors and was greeted by a smiling and immaculate receptionist with almost perfect English.

"Mr. McKay? Please take a seat. Mr. Carrell will be with you in a few minutes."

Less than three minutes later, a door opened and a figure approached.

"Tom? Please, call me Matt. Come on through to the office. Do you want anything? Coffee? Tea? Water?"

"A coffee would be nice, thanks. Milk, two sugars if possible."

The man spoke to the receptionist in Thai and she nodded and smiled. Carrell then led Tom into a large and luxurious office, all black leather and chrome, definitely something that suited Tom's aesthetic tastes. He was a little surprised. He'd expected the CEO of a security company to be a walking cliché, all bulges and muscles and obviously ex-forces, probably special.

Instead, Matt was a portly Englishman with a genial smile.

"Please, take a seat," he said, gesturing to a large chair in front of the expansive desk. "I know what you're thinking, every new client thinks the same. This doesn't look like a guy who should be running a security company. Don't let looks deceive you. I did serve, though some 30 years ago now. I always had to be at peak fitness then, and even maintained it for a few years after I went into the private sector. But I have a taste for the finer things in life, good food and better wine. I leave the grunt work to others now and I can assure you, my mind is fitter than any other in the building."

Tom laughed. "Thanks for the comprehensive explanation, and yes, I was wondering. You look nothing like the image I had in my mind."

"Let me guess. A musclebound American with a dangerous glint in his eye?"

"Pretty close, yes."

"It's the job of my staff to have those dangerous glints now. My job is to run and grow a business, and it's something I'm damned good at."

There was a knock on the door and the receptionist/secretary entered with coffees on a tray along with a sugar bowl and milk jug.

"Thanks Som," said Matt as the girl left the room. "Now, Tom, what is it you think we can help you with. You didn't go into much detail on the phone.

Tom decided it was best to start at the beginning.

"I lived in Bangkok for a couple of years back in the 90s. I got to know this guy who was a fixer and who could – allegedly – arrange anything, no matter how illegal. Purely by accident, I discovered the guy was a child molester. So, with the help of a friend, we set him up and made sure the police raided his home and arrested him. With the evidence they found, he was given several long sentences to be served consecutively. In retrospect, it may have been a mistake, but I wanted to be in court when he was sentenced. He saw me sitting there and I think he realised I was responsible for his arrest. I'd assumed he'd be in prison for life, or even that he'd die there with a little prison justice. But I discovered the other day that he'd been released as part of the King's birthday pardon list. I have no idea where he is, or even if he knows I'm back in Bangkok, but as you can understand, I'm a little worried about the whole thing."

Matt shook his head. "These bloody pardon lists. While I can understand releasing some lower level prisoners or people with not long left to serve, when real bastards get released, I get annoyed. One thing you need to understand is that none of the blame can be apportioned to His Majesty. You think he has the time to look through thousands of names? He relies on lists of recommendations being put forward, and sometimes a place on those lists can be bought. I suspect this was the case with your guy. Is he Thai or farang?"

"English, name of Ronnie Hollings."

Matt scribbled the name down.

"Was he a violent man when you knew him?"

"Anything but. He was a scrawny streak of piss who would likely have jumped if he saw his own shadow. But surviving nearly two decades in Bang Kwang, he won't only be fluent in Thai, he'll likely have made a lot of very dangerous friends."

"Yes for sure. Given the fact that he was a farang imprisoned for the most heinous of crimes, surviving for that long meant he had protection, possibly guards as well as other inmates. And it would have to have been another prisoner with power and influence. And you have no idea where he is now?"

"Not a clue. He'd obviously paid even more people off to ensure he wasn't deported. I have two worries, or even both combined in one. He could be reoffending again, though I suspect that if that's the case, then he may be in a more rural area. And, of course, I'm worried about my own safety. I have a meeting with a private investigations company later today."

"Which one?"

Tom said the name.

"Ok, they're good. They have mostly Thai staff which is far more effective than some wannabe gumshoe who used to be a beat copper in Slough and who's read too many detective novels. If anyone can find him, they will."

Matt sat and thought for a few minutes.

"There are several services that might help you but as you can imagine, we're not cheap. Our client list includes Thai celebrities and even some of the royal family. And we have also worked with a lot of visiting dignitaries and celebrities, so be assured, you'll be in good hands. I'm going to suggest two things initially, though we'd start one immediately and do the other in the next day or two. I want to assign a close protection officer who will cover most of the day with you. He'd collect you from your home in the morning, be in or outside your office all day, including taking you to any sort of meeting, formal or otherwise. He'd then drive you home and ensure your apartment is secure before leaving for the night. If you have any social functions in the evening, I'd assign someone else to do the same duties then. Now I don't care who you're dating, where you're going, whatever. My only concern is that you're safe going anywhere at any time. The other thing I want to do, ideally tomorrow, is to check your apartment and the building for security risks. How easy it to gain access to the building, to the upper floors, and how secure your unit is. Depending on what my guys think, I'll make recommendations to you regarding any need to upgrade or install security measures."

"That sounds like exactly what I'm looking for. The million-dollar question, though I hope it's not the answer, is how much is this going to cost me?"

"As I said, we're not cheap, but we're good, better than anyone else in the city in my opinion. This consultation is free. The security audit is 30,000 baht but that doesn't include any equipment we recommend. The close protection cost is 10,000 baht per day, but that covers you from whenever you leave the apartment until you arrive home for the night. No extra charges for any social events you might go to. The car hire is 7,000 baht per day but not only are our cars armoured and bulletproof, but all our protection staff are trained in evasive driving. Take the full package I've suggested and we'll call it a round 60,000 baht per week."

Tom whistled through his teeth.

"Ok. After all, what price can you put on peace of mind?"

Matt leaned forward, both arms on his desk, and lowered his voice.

"So, tell me, Tom, what are your plans if you find this Hollings guy?"

"I honestly haven't thought that far ahead. If he is offending again, then my obvious recourse is the police. If there's no evidence of him offending and he's just living a quiet life upcountry, then I guess I can stop worrying. But if he's in Bangkok and there is a credible threat... well, I don't know what I'd do."

Matt's voice lowered again to an almost conspiratorial whisper.

“If it is that last scenario, there are solutions. But they’d be off the books and there would be absolutely no paperwork.”

“What do you mean,” asked Tom.

“Come on, Tom. You can work it out. All my protection staff are either ex-military or have worked at a high level for one of the world’s intelligence agencies. Without giving too much detail, I have guys from Mossad, MI5, and even the CIA. Some of them have done ‘special’ work in the past and have the experience needed to make a problem disappear… permanently. I had you checked out before you came today just to make sure this wasn’t part of a sting operation. Better careful than careless in this game.”

“So, how much would this cost me and what would it entail.”

“You’d leave all the details to us. The less you know, the better. But we would make sure you were in a public place with multiple alibis just in case. Ideally, we’d make the target disappear forever but best to plan for every eventuality. Thinking like that is why I’m the boss and can go enjoy great meals. As to cost, there’s a flat fee of one million baht. When you think about it, it’s not a high price to pay for permanent peace of mind. You’d never even have to think about this bastard’s name again.”

“Ok, let’s cross that bridge if and when we come to it. What if I transfer 240,000 baht to you now? That would cover the first four weeks and we can reevaluate at the end of that period.”

“Sounds good to me. Here…” Matt slid a laminated card with the company’s bank QR code on it. “I’ll have a team at your apartment at 8am tomorrow morning. One guy to drive you to work and watch you, the other two will take your entry card and give the apartment the onceover. I’ll have a report on your condo's security needs and recommendations by tomorrow evening."

"Wow, that's bloody efficient."

"If a client's in danger, or even potential danger, there's no point in wasting time. And as soon as you transfer that payment, you're a client. I'm guessing you can't invoice Green-Hayes for this?"

"No, I can hardly explain that some murderous child molester might be looking for me."

"Yes, I can understand that. I'll be providing regular reports if any of the team spot anything. Also, please update me if anything comes from the private investigator."

Matt stood up and walked Tom to the door. He shook his hand warmly.

"Hopefully, all this will come to nothing. But at least you'll have a little more peace of mind knowing you have someone watching your back. Very good to meet you and hope to see you soon."

Once Tom was back on the street, he realised he still had 90 minutes until his next meeting and that was only around 10 minutes from here. He'd noticed what looked like a good restaurant, Ministry of Crab, as he'd passed in the taxi. It was only a couple of minutes walked from the villa so he strolled up so he could have some lunch before the next step.

He was at the next appointment 10 minutes early. The building, a slightly older office block, was a good way down Sukhumvit 23, well past the famous – or infamous – Soi Cowboy. While the agency's office wasn't as plush or modern as the security firm's villa, it exuded a sense of something Tom couldn't quite put his finger on, but one that definitely suited the business it was in.

The receptionist was as immaculate and smiling as the last one, though her English was perhaps not quite so perfect. The man who came out to greet him was far from Matt's polished sartorialism, an off-the-peg suit instead of the tailored one Matt had worn, his hair almost gone instead of Matt's well-coiffured lustrous locks. But again, his look fitted his profession perfectly in Tom's opinion. Would you trust a private detective in an Amani suit? What this guy lacked in dress sense was made up for by the warm and trustworthy smile he gave Tom.

The man spoke, and the twang made Tom think he was probably from the American Midwest.

"Mr. McKay? I'm Bill Hall. Come on in and let's have a chat."

The office continued the same theme; slightly worn-looking but perfect for a private detective. There were two desks in the room and a Thai woman of about 40 was sitting behind one, looking a lot more businesslike in a two-piece mauve suit and perfect hair.

"This is my wife and business partner, Nan. Nan, this is Tom McKay. Tom, grab a seat. You want a coffee?"

Tom noticed that there was an ancient-looking vending machine in the corner and decided his taste buds wouldn't be too grateful.

"Thanks, literally just had one with lunch so I'll pass. A bottle of water would be nice."

Bill fetched a small bottle from the mini-fridge beside the coffee machine then sat down.

"What's the problem then. Tom? An ex-girlfriend or wife ripped you off? You suspect your girl of cheating on you? Business deal gone wrong? Don't be shy, we've heard every story.

"Probably not this one though."

Tom went through his story once again, Bill and Nan listening attentively with open mouths. When he finished, there was a couple of minutes of silence. Then Bill spoke.

"Fucking hell, mate. I hate these kiddy-fiddling bastards and it definitely sounds like a big pile of baht has exchanged hands. Now, depending on just how much money has been paid, there's a chance he's gone completely dark and is so far under the fucking radar, it would take coal miners to find him. But I think that's very unlikely. Even if he's paid his way out of prison, and out of a deportation order, he's still got to follow certain rules. He'll definitely have to have a visa of some type and he, or his landlord, will have filled out a TM30 at some point. So, we'll know where he's been even if we don't immediately know where he is. Of course, he may have bought a fake passport but it will still need a visa in it and it won't have a legitimate entry stamp."

"So, do you think you can find him?"

"Fucking right, we can. It's just how long it takes. We have some pretty high-ranking contacts in immigration so if he's using his own passport..."

"But wait," interrupted Tom, "he was in jail for nearly 20 years so his passport would have expired."

"Not a big problem. In fact, it could help us. As I was saying, if he has gone the legitimate route, then we can find out when and where any visa was issued. Same with the TM30. It might tell us exactly where he's living. Now, if he has gone the legitimate route, then he would have had to apply for a new passport and you Brits can only do that with the VFS agency. And again, we have a contact in there too so can find out if he applied and when one was issued."

"And what if he's not gone the legitimate route and is using a fake passport? Your contacts won't be able to help you then."

"Not ones working for any of the authorities, no. But we have a hacker we sometimes use, or an ethical hacker as he prefers to be called. He doesn't do anything for personal gain and his fees are pretty reasonable. Remember that massive child sex scandal in Cambodia a few years back? The one where the bastards were broadcasting abuse around the world?"

"Yeah, some English journalist was killed during the investigation, wasn't he?"

"Him and loads of kids, mate. They were some right evil bastards. Well, Zed played a big part in that. In fact, if it wasn't for him, they might not have blown it as wide open as they did."

"Zed? I'm guessing he's not Thai then?"

"That's just the name he uses. None of us know his real name. None of us know what he looks like or even if he's in Bangkok. We do know he's Thai because he had a long chat with Nan once, though his voice was put through one of those robotic voice changer things."

"How can he help us though? Unless Hollings is accessing stuff online."

"Basic math, Tom. If this guy does have a fake passport, it will still need a visa but the entry stamp will be fake. Zed just needs to do, well whatever it is he does, and see how many visas have been issued and how many entry stamps have been issued and then list the names that don't match. Now, if he does have a fake passport, he probably won't be the only one. But we're talking about reducing the search to maybe a few dozen people rather than hundreds of thousands."

"How much will he cost?"

"I'll be frank with you. He'll probably do it for free because it involves a child molester. Hell, I'm going to discount our services too. I'd do it for free but we need to pay our guys with boots on the ground as well as kickbacks to the contacts we use. But don't worry about that now. Let's just get the search started immediately and work our way down the possible scenarios. I'll call our guy in VFS today and Nan will phone our general in immigration later on when he's home. That gets the ball rolling and we should have answers from both within 48 hours. It's anyone's guess how long it might take to find him. It could be a few days but it could be a few weeks too. It all depends on how much effort he's put into staying hidden. Does he know you'll be looking for him?"

"I doubt it. He may not even know I'm back in Thailand. But there were a few articles in the press when I was appointed to my company, and there has been one profile cum interview in a magazine, so there is a chance he does know. But even if he does, I doubt he'll think I'm looking for him. He's more likely to think I've forgotten all about him. Maybe he really is just leading a quiet life somewhere."

"These bastards don't change their behaviour. Wherever he is, there's a pretty good chance that he's molesting kids again, so the quicker we find him, the better. Which leads me to my next question. What do you want to do when we do find him?"

"If there's any evidence that he is offending again, I think you can send the information to your police contacts. The higher the better, though. If he bought his way onto the pardon list and out of deportation, then it's likely he has some pet coppers in his pocket. If he's not offending, just pass all the details onto me and that's your part over."

"Ok, we'll get things started. As soon as we have any info, I'll give you a call. Give me the best number to contact you on."

Bill slid a pad of paper and a pen across the desk and Tom scribbled down his mobile number.

"Thanks. Hopefully you can find him quickly. I hate the idea of him walking free. But I hate the idea of him ruining more kids' lives even more."

They said their goodbyes and Tom headed back onto the street, hailing the first taxi he saw with its meter on.

1996

Things hadn't improved with Ireshi. In fact, they'd had a massive argument the night before, resulting in her packing a bag and fleeing to her parents' house to 'get some space'. Tom knew he should have listened to Yevgeny but two more rejections had left him in a foul temper by the time she arrived home. So, all that good advice had gone straight out the window and he'd called her a moody and selfish bitch.

Her father would definitely be happy to see her return home, and he'd be hoping it would be permanent rather than just some temporary refuge. His acceptance of Tom had always been a grudging one, despite every best effort from Tom to show he was a good man. Calling Ireshi a moody and selfish bitch was hardly the sign of a good man, though he wasn't sure exactly how much she would tell her parents.

As had always been his response, Tom sought refuge in a bottle of whisky, hardly even noticing the taste and quality as he downed glass after glass. Of course, copious amounts of coke offset the immediate effects of the whisky though he knew he'd pay a heavy price for his indulgence the following morning. Luckily, he only had about a gram left, his meeting with Yevgeny arranged for two days from now to replenish his coke and to collect the ketamine his friend had ordered for him.

He'd resorted to his special collection of porn on VHS tapes, collected from a special vendor in Chatuchak Market. But the whisky and coke meant that he couldn't get hard, yet another frustration to add to the list that was annoying him. He finally gave up on the porn, switching to a pirated copy of Fargo that had come from the same dodgy VHS vendor. Though he was enjoying it, his focus was deteriorating by the minute and he switched it off halfway through, deciding that music was the best option. Putting on Belle and Sebastian's 'If You're Feeling Sinister', he slumped in a semi-comatose state on the sofa, gradually falling into unconsciousness as the whiskey overtook the cocaine.

Tom woke just after dawn, a beam of sunlight somehow precisely targeting his eyes and sending shards of pain throughout his head. He swore aloud and half-walked, half-stumbled through to the bedroom. Setting the air conditioning to eight degrees and making sure the blackout curtains were fully closed. Satisfied that his room would offer refuge from the realities of daylight – and his hangover – he took a bottle of water from the mini-fridge beside the bed, drained it in one, then collapsed fully-dressed onto his bed.

When he next awoke, noon was already past. His head felt like a Norwegian death metal band was playing live in his skull and he groaned and reached for a bottle of water from the fridge. He walked into the living room, pausing to fill and switch on his coffee machine in the kitchen area. The living room looked like a bomb had gone off. A bottle of Lagavulin, with perhaps one measure left in it, lay abandoned on the middle of the rug. CD cases still speckled with white detritus lay in various places. Cigarette papers were scattered around the room like wedding confetti. He'd tidy up, but not until a few cups of caffeine had returned him to some semblance of reality.

Maybe it was the hangover, or maybe it was just a result of genuine reflection on his actions, but he felt overwhelmed by a feeling of contriteness. He resolved that he would phone Ireshi's parent's house later and offer a sincere apology and beg her to come back. They were too perfect a match for him not to make an effort. And he vowed to himself that he would follow Yevgeny's advice and wait for Ireshi to be ready to talk, and to listen to what she said too.

Where else would he find someone who shared his tastes? Most of the women who attended Lam's parties were spoken for, at least outwith what happened at those parties. Sex workers were no use; any submission by them would just be an act to earn the promised baht, and Tom needed full submission and submission that the other person wanted and enjoyed.

No, contriteness was the way forward and he had to show it was genuine and not just a way of winning her back. Besides, their relationship went way beyond sex, even the week on Koh Tao had shown that. He loved just cuddling with her on the sofa while they watched a good movie, he loved going out for dinner, whether with friends or just the two of them. Hell, he even loved traipsing round the shops as she flitted from one to the other, her indecisiveness sometimes lasting hours. Life without her would be empty, it was empty even after only 24 hours.

His second cup of coffee combined with a couple of paracetamol had made him feel at least partly alive again. He needed a plan. First thing to do was tidy up this shithole. The cleaner wasn't due for another two days and, if he did persuade Ireshi to come home, she wouldn't appreciate the mess. Once the place was tidied, he'd go for a shave and a long shower to clear the last vestiges of the previous night's indulgence.

Two hours later and everything was back to being shipshape, both him and the apartment. He poured another coffee, lit a cigarette, and dialed Ireshi's home, well her family home. A female voice answered in Thai. Thank fuck, Tom had dreaded it being her father answering. Instead, it was Taeng-mo, the family's maid and someone that thought Tom was wonderful.

"Sawasdee krub, Taeng-mo, it's Tom here."

"Oh, Khun Tom, so good to hear from you. You want speak Khun Ireshi?"

"Yes please, if she'll speak to me."

"One minute, I go get her."

One minute turned into two, then three, then four, and finally five. Then Tom heard the receiver being picked up again.

"Hello."

Ireshi's voice was neutral, which Tom supposed was better than cold and hostile,"

"Hello darling, how are you?"

"I'm fine." She wasn't making this easy and Tom wondered how much influence her father had exerted on her mood.

"Look, I'm sorry, really sorry. I was totally out of order. I'd had a shit day at work and two more rejections but that's no excuse. I've had bad days before and never reacted like that. But things have been different since we came back from Koh Tao and I just keep wondering what I've done wrong. Yevgeny told me to..."

"What? You talked to Yevgeny about us? How fucking dare you."

"Babe, I didn't go into great details, just said that we weren't talking. He is my only real male friend here, after all. Can you tell me you haven't talked to any of your girlfriends about things?"

There was a long pause.

"Ok, ok, I can see why you spoke to Yevgeny."

"I just wish I'd listened to him. He told me not to harass you, to give you all the time and space you needed and to listen when you were ready to talk. I didn't follow any of that advice. Again, I'm sorry."

"Oh, Tom. It's not you. I've just felt so down after that holiday. It was so perfect and coming back to Bangkok, coming back to work, just felt so horrible after that wonderful time. I wanted to tell you but didn't know what to say or how to say it."

"Ireshi, that was the most perfect seven days of my life. I promise you, we'll go back to the island again, back to the same hotel if you want, and we'll do it as often as your work allows. We can even go for long weekends when there are Holy Days."

"I'd like that."

"So, will you come home? The apartment feels so cold without you."

"I can't come home today. My aunt and uncle and cousins are down in Bangkok from Chiang Rai and are coming to dinner tonight. Why don't you come and join us?"

Tom laughed.

"I'm sure that would make your father very happy. I'm surprised he didn't organise a celebration when you returned to their house.

It was Ireshi's turn to laugh.

"Ok, good point. And yes, there was a big smile on his face when I said I'd left you. So maybe dinner tonight is not such a good idea, even though it would be worth it to see the look on his face when you walked in."

This time, they both laughed, and Tom had a feeling that everything was going to be alright.

Ireshi lowered her voice.

"I'll come back tomorrow, probably before lunchtime. Will you be home?"

"Yeah, still trying to find an editor to take on this story. Yevgeny's suggested I do a book instead and he'll publish it."

"Yevgeny? Since when was he a publisher?"

"Oh come on, baby. This is Yevgeny we're talking about. There's virtually no type of business he doesn't have some sort of stake in, and that's both legal and illegal businesses. He says he'll set up a legitimate publishing company. Worst case scenario, he has yet another way of laundering money from his dodgy businesses."

"I knew there had to be a catch."

"Hey, thanks for the confidence in me. Maybe the book will sell well."

"Tom, your writing is fantastic, but it's a big jump from writing a 2,000-word article to a book of what, 70 to 80,000 words?"

"If I do it, and I haven't yet decided that I will, it will be a long-term project. Maybe a year or more."

"Ok, you know that whatever you decide, I'll support you. Look, I better go. Father's just arrived home and I'm not looking forward to telling him I'm coming back to you; I think things are about to get stormy here. I'll see you tomorrow, ok? Love you."

"Good luck with your dad. And yes, will see you tomorrow and love you too."

The next morning, Tom was up early. He did some work on a couple of articles due for submission by the end of the month then turned his attention to housework. He wanted the place sparkling for Ireshi's return and wanted to be sure there was no evidence left of the madness he'd descended into for a while. With the apartment sparkling, he found he was bored. He couldn't focus on any more work, there was nothing on television, so he settled on the sofa with a copy of Jack Reynolds' 'A Woman of Bangkok', a book he'd bought months previously but had never got round to reading.

Although some of the writing style was archaic by modern standards, he found the glimpses into the Bangkok of the past, albeit only a few decades ago, fascinating. What was it about Thailand that seemed to draw so many westerners to its exotic flame like curious moths? Of course, he knew that for many it was the sex industry, nominally illegal yet openly tolerated. Yet there had to be more than that as not every tourist came here to hire compliant sex workers for the night.

He'd visited Pattaya a few months ago, its reputation as the capital of sleaze still clinging to it from its origins as an R&R destination for American soldiers during the Vietnam War. Yet the city had surprised him. Yes, there were a lot of girly bars but they tended to be focused in small geographical locations. Garish neon signs and scantily-clad Isaan girls promising nights beyond your wildest dreams.

It was always going to be a self-perpetuating cycle. As long as the authorities in Bangkok ignored the needs of Isaan and other poor northern provinces, and as long as bloated tourists with wallets full of cash flew in from the four corners of the globe, there would always be a sex industry. He just wished that the government, rather than just turning a blind eye, actually legalised sex work. At least that way, there would be some measure of legal protection for the girls arriving fresh and untouched off the buses from Khon Kaen and other cities.

He'd heard that the bus stations would be crowded with mamasans and pimps when buses were due to arrive, eager to entice new girls into their clutches. If they were virgins, all the better, as their virginity could be auctioned off to wealthy Thais and Chinese.

While he found that whole scene distasteful, he also found it understandable and could empathise with the girls – and boys – who made the journey south. But he would never understand the child sex part of the scene, a truly murky underbelly to something that already contained a lot of darkness. They often started as street kids, forced by their parents or the local mafia to sell everything from tourist tat to chewing gum until they were old enough to switch to selling their bodies instead.

The wandering of his thoughts – a common occurrence for Tom – finally made his decision for him. He would write the book, not because he wanted to, not because it might make money, but because it was a story that needed to be told. The western media gave some coverage to the issue, but usually in a sensationalist way that focused on the westerners who traveled to the region to fulfill their sick fantasies. Although he wasn't denying that was part of the problem, it was a drop in the ocean compared to the familial abuse that took place in nearly every village, the trafficking of their children by impoverished and desperate parents, and the auctioning off of a child's virginity to the highest bidder.

He grabbed a pen and paper and began sketching out some rough ideas. He wanted to open with a list of statistics – Maggie could help with that – and then move on to the western perverts who brought their unnatural desires east with them. But he wanted the bulk of the book to highlight the more localized issues. He wondered if Maggie could provide him with some case studies, maybe even let him interview some of the kids, all anonymised of course. He knew that many of the kids would still be traumatised, some even for life, but she'd know of ones who'd shown resilience and moved from survival to thriving. He hazarded a guess that if she did allow any interviews, it would likely be with older teenagers or even young adults. The wounds in the younger ones' psyches would likely still be fresh and raw and the last thing he wanted was to cause them any more pain.

He was still scribbling furiously when he heard the key in the lock. Ireshi was home! He leapt off the sofa as the door opened, a tired-looking Ireshi entering with her bag over her shoulder. Tom ran towards her and held her in his arms, so tight that she gasped for breath as she dropped her bag.

"Baby, I'm so, so sorry. Thank you for coming back to me."

He kissed her on the lips, passion taking them back to the magic of the island just for a moment.

"How did things go with your dad?"

"What do you think? We were up till past one this morning arguing. He even threatened to have you deported and banned from the country."

"Jesus. Did you manage to calm him down?"

"I told him that if you were deported, he would never see me again. And that I'd leave Thailand to join you, no matter where you were. While that did not exactly calm him, it did make him realise that I was very serious and that if he did anything, he stood to lose me forever. He may not like you much, but I'm his only daughter and he's rather see me with some farang than not see me at all."

"Wow. Would you really do that for me?"

"It would break my heart to do so, but yes. My mother was amazing too. I don't think I've ever seen her lose her temper or swear, but she called him a stupid and stubborn old man and that if he caused me to leave Thailand, she would leave him too. Father went on about our argument and asked how many times I would come running home. Then mother reminded him that in the early days of their marriage, she returned to her parents several times because he was always out drinking and coming home in the early hours of the morning."

"You can tell where you get your strength from. Your mum's an amazing woman... and so are you. Again, I'm sorry. I should never have lost my temper with you."

"Tom, it was as much my fault as it was yours. I should at least have told you why I was feeling down and asked for some time. Instead, I just ignored you and withdrew into my own little world. Now my stupidity has spoilt the memories of our holiday."

"Don't be silly. It was a perfect holiday and one we'll have again. I felt down too coming back to the chaos of Bangkok after spending time in our own little corner of paradise. All that matters is that you're home now."

He took her by the hand and led her to the bedroom, showering her with kisses as he gently undressed her. No kinks, no fetishes, no equipment, just tender lovemaking. Afterwards, they lay exhausted and naked in each other's arms, drenched in sweat until Tom got up and turned the fan on.

As her fingers traced circles in his chest hair, he whispered to her.

"I've made up my mind, I'm going to write this book. If it does make any money, it will all go to Maggie's NGO. If it doesn't, well, at least Yevgeny has a new laundry and I can ask him to make a donation to the organisation. It may take a year or longer, but this is a story that the world needs to hear. They need to see beyond the lurid headlines of the western tabloids. It's not just about Thailand either. This is a problem in every country in the world and it needs to be more in the open."

"I'm so proud of you, Tom. I'll do anything I can to support you."

With a contented smile on her face, Ireshi fell asleep. Tom watched her for a few minutes, wondering how he'd been so lucky to find this amazing woman. Then he too sank into slumber.

2023

Tom was feeling better than he had done in weeks. The detective agency was already on the case tracking down Hollings and he now had the protection of the security company. Once they'd inspected his condo, they'd advised a complete overhaul of his security system. He now had CCTV covering the corridor outside his apartment as well as cameras covering the balcony and the main living area. They'd upgraded the burglar alarm too, a state-of-the-art system that took Tom days to understand. They'd also given him a small panic button that he wore on a pendant round his neck. If he felt threatened in any way, he just had to press it to alert the company's HQ. If it was during daylight hours, or if he was out socialising, a close protection officer was always two minutes away. If it was during the night, their office was only ten minutes away.

With everything that had been going on, he'd almost forgotten about Chompoo until he received an email from her the day before.

Tom,

Sorry for being out of touch. Singapore was hectic as many of my family live there and it seemed like it was an endless merry-go-round of aunts, uncles, and cousins. I never seemed to have a minute to myself.

I will be honest though, Shanghai was more about indulgence. I was out partying with friends every night and I swear I must have put on at least six kilos. Not to mention that I don't want to see a drop of alcohol for a couple of months at least.

Anyway, enough of my adventures. My friends have flown onto Hong Kong so the rest of my time here in Shanghai is doing some business for my father. I will be returning to Bangkok in around 10 days so give me a day or two to recover, and then we'll arrange to meet for dinner. Somewhere discrete and out the way but with good food. As you've probably guessed, I'm a bit of a foodie 555.

Be in touch soon,

Chompoo.

So, he'd finally get to meet the girl with the dark imagination. One of his suspicions had been confirmed though; she was definitely from a wealthy family. Singapore and Shanghai were hardly budget destinations and doing business for her father suggested something beyond the norm too. Hopefully, the rest of his questions would soon be answered.

Tom showered and dressed for work. He had an important meeting that morning. One of his junior editors, Anong – a girl that he had already marked out for promotion – had come into his office a couple of weeks before raving about a manuscript she had received. It was historical fiction set in the reign of Rama V, Thailand's great reformer. The author was a professor of history at Chulalongkorn University and, amazingly, he had submitted the manuscript in both Thai and English. While the English was not quite perfect, it wasn't far off it, and Tom had been as gripped by the story as his editor had been. The professor was meeting them to discuss a three-book contract as he already had two sequels sketched out. If everything went well, then the junior editor wouldn't be junior for long.

He texted his bodyguard/driver and advised he would be downstairs in five minutes. He knew the car would be there waiting for him as soon as he emerged from the building, the driver waiting for him by the door and then escorting him over to the car. Despite the potentially dangerous reasons for his security arrangements, it also gave him a slight thrill, a feeling of inflated self-importance. Of course, he'd had chauffeurs before, back in London, but that was usually for attending major events and award ceremonies. This was totally different, especially as he knew this driver was carrying a gun.

Once he arrived at the office, he ordered a coffee then phoned Anong to come to his office so they could discuss tactics. While Tom would have the final say on whether they would sign the professor, not to mention any benefits he would receive, he wanted Anong to be involved at every step of the process. After all, she had spotted the potential in the manuscript, something that only happened for one in fifty submissions. Most manuscripts they received were rejected and would receive a polite email of varying detail.

If there was some potential, one of the editors would give feedback and encourage the author to submit again in the future. If the manuscript had absolutely no merit whatsoever, then it would be a rejection template signed off by one of the juniors.

Tom knew that Thais loved their history, and Rama V was one of their most beloved monarchs. He had started the process of modernising the country, a process that had elevated it to one of the leading economies in the region. If they could agree a deal, and if the next two books were of the same quality, then Tom knew it would be a feather in his cap and a feather in Anong's cap, not to mention a promotion and salary increase for the talented and dedicated young editor.

A few minutes later, Anong arrived and took a seat in front of Tom's desk. She was an attractive girl of 25 but chose to wear very conservative clothing at work as she wanted to be judged on her intellect and not her curves. Like many countries, misogyny was still rampant in Thailand's workplaces. Tom knew she had a boyfriend who worked in IT and that they were planning to marry next summer, but outside of those scant details, he knew little about her.

"Good morning, Anong. A big day for you; this could be your first major signing."

"I hope so, boss."

Despite him insisting – multiple times – that she should call him Tom, the young Thai always called him boss.

"You've met Professor Rattanakosin. What do you think he will want in any contract?"

Anong thought for a moment.

"I've met him twice. I'm no psychologist but I got the feeling that he writes out of passion rather than a desire for money or fame. He will be on a good salary at the university as he is head of department, but I don't think we should lowball him. That would be disrespectful and you know how we Thais feel about disrespect and losing face."

"Oh, I definitely have no intention of lowballing him. Not only does he write well, but he submitted his manuscript in both Thai and English which means we don't have to have the work translated. If he signs, and I have no reason to think he won't, I want you to edit the Thai version and I'll edit the English manuscript."

Anong blushed slightly. She knew this was her big break, her opportunity to move from the sometimes-faceless pool of junior editors to a role where her name could become known.

"Now, I've thought about the financial side of things and wanted to run my ideas past you. If he signs a three-book deal, then we'll give him an advance of 250,000 baht and a royalty rate of 15%. Those are fairly generous figures but I have a good feeling about this professor and you did an excellent job in spotting the potential."

There was that blush again but Tom didn't hold it against her. He could still remember his first promotion and the unbridled joy he felt when he heard his then boss's praise.

"I don't think he'll have any problem with those figures as they are indeed generous. I think he'll be more interested in the distribution and marketing side of any contract."

"Well, my initial thought was to produce a print run of 2,000 for the Thai version and 1,000 for the English one. I also think this could act as the flagship launch of our move to eBooks. As well as our website, I'd want them distributed to the major bookstores in every city. But I also want to send some – maybe 200 – to a couple of stores in London. There's a lot of interest in Asian literature just now and it will be a good test as to whether to expand distribution in the West. If received well by the media, it may also be worth considering translating into other languages. As to marketing, I have a really good feeling about this first book, so let's do print media adverts, TV and radio, and the usual social media saturation. I want you to liaise with Navin in marketing and produce a good promo video. Maybe one and a half minutes for TV and shorter versions for social media."

"Surely that would all come under the marketing team's remit?"

"Yes, and most of it will. But other than me editing the English version, I want you to manage it from start to finish. This is your baby, so let's see what you can do."

Anong blushed yet again.

"Thanks, boss, I won't let you down. I have a really good feeling about this book too. The first time I read it was in one sitting and I was up till 3am, determined to finish it. His English version is great but I don't think it quite captures the magic of the original Thai. I'd suggest we have one of our translators look at it and see if they can improve it before you start editing."

"For this book, you're the boss. If you think the translation could be improved, then assign one of the team to go over it with a fine-tooth comb."

"Tooth comb? What does this mean, boss?"

Tom laughed.

"I forget that sometimes there are words and sayings in English that even a fluent second language speaker won't get. It basically means to look at something in great detail."

"Ah, ok, I like that. I'll need to remember it, but I don't understand where it comes from."

Tom's laugh was louder this time.

"You know; I have no idea of its origins. I've just always known the phrase. Wait, let's both learn something new."

Tom turned to his laptop, opened Google, and typed the phrase in.

"Hmm, interesting. It seems to come from the idea of primates grooming each other for parasites and bugs and was then expanded to the use of a fine comb to search human hair for lice."

"But where does the tooth part come from? Were the combs made from animal teeth?"

Tom read further.

"No, I don't think so. Just seems to be an idiomatic referral to primates using their teeth as part of the grooming price. Oh, this is even more interesting. The first recorded use of the phrase was George Bernard Shaw. You've heard of him, yes?"

"Of course. Famous Irish writer if I remember correctly."

"Exactly right. Ok, the professor is due at 11am. We'll meet with him in here and then take him to lunch. Go and speak to the marketing team and put together some rough ideas so we can give him an idea of what we'd do with the book. Hopefully, everything will go smoothly and that lunch will include champagne if he's agreed to our terms. If he's said yes, and I see no reason why he won't, I'll have legal draw up the contract while we're at lunch. Then we can come back and get his name on the dotted line. I'll have your name added to the contrast as the supervising editor so this will be your first big signing. In fact, it will be your first signing full stop. So, there may be more champagne after the signing too."

Anong giggled.

"Oh, those bubbles go to my head. I may just have one glass with lunch and wait till the deal is done. I don't want the professor to see me too drunk."

"Whatever you want, Anong, this is your day as well as the professor's. Now go speak to marketing. I'd suggest a basic outline of a plan that includes a launch event, media coverage, interviews, and advertising. We can drill down into the details later, just as long as we have something to show him."

Anong left the office, enthusiasm clearly showing on her face. Tom had no doubt he was making the right decision. She was a hard worker, that much was true, but sometimes hard work wasn't enough. And he was pretty sure she had that something extra needed that would guarantee her a successful career.

He phoned for another coffee and decided to relax before the meeting so told his secretary to say he was out of the office unless it was Anong or the professor. Once his coffee arrived, he moved to one of the comfier seats by the window with that morning's copy of the Bangkok Post. The first few pages were the usual doom-laden headlines. Israel's war on Gaza continued unabated, with more children dying every day. The war in Ukraine seemed to be almost forgotten, relegated to a smaller article on page four. Tom often despaired for the world and found it ironic that his sexual tastes – and him – were judged and looked at in disgust. Yet the world was full of unnecessary suffering, people dying because their sky fairy was different from someone else's imaginary friend.

He'd managed to go through life with just that one regret, that one mistake, that one lapse of control that had led to him fleeing Thailand and not returning for two decades. Yet his crime was microscopic when you compared it to the misery that seemed to be prevalent in this world. And if it wasn't war, the news seemed full of extreme weather events, a climate change that many had denied and many more continued to do.

With a sigh, he moved on to the local news. At least it seemed to be less miserable than what was coming from round the world; *Politician arrested in corruption inquiry; New MRT line opens; $1 billion-dollar mall planned* (as if Bangkok needed another one); *Body found in canal, police suspect serial killer.*

That last headline caught his eye. Surely not. He focused on the details:

Police recovered a body from the Lam Phang Phuai Khlong canal close to the Chan Housing Village yesterday afternoon. The victim was a transgender sex worker who had been facing several charges of deliberately infecting clients with the HIV virus. Police Lieutenant General Apisitniran refused to give details. However, a police source did confirm that the victim's penis had been severed and was missing. The similarities to the murder of a policemen two weeks previously could point to a serial killer being at work in the city, especially given that both victims had been facing criminal charges.

This was ringing too many bells. He returned to his desk and went onto his laptop. He opened Chompoo's folder and went to the story he thought was ringing the bells. Opening the file, he quickly skimmed to a point near the end.

... the katoey spat in the direction of the figure in the shadows, straining against the ropes that bound her with little effect.

'You knew you were infected, yet you still fucked anything and everything, especially men who didn't want to use a condom,' the figure said.

'They asked for it,' hissed the ladyboy. 'How the fuck do you think I caught it in the first place? Some fucking farang offering 5,000 baht extra to fuck without a condom. It should be him you're hunting down.'

'As the old saying goes, two wrongs don't make a right,' whispered the voice. 'There's no doubt he's a bastard too but that doesn't change what you did. You could have sought treatment, seen a doctor. Instead you infected more than 15 men... and one of them was my friend.'

'So? I was angry and stupid. So what? What are you going to do, kill me?'

There was only silence from the shadows, answer enough for the bound prostitute.

Finally, the voice spoke again.

'In a way, you were unlucky. People can live for decades now without HIV developing into full-blown AIDS. But my friend already had a damaged immune system so the disease progressed quickly. Less than a year after you infected him, he was dead. You took his life as surely as I am going to take yours. I will show you some mercy though. He was full of morphine at the end, and I am going to do the same for you so you won't feel

any pain. You will drift in cloudlike dreams while my knife cuts into you.'

The ladyboy's screams were quickly stifled as the figure stepped forward and fastened a ball-gag round her mouth. Turning to the table behind them, the figure took an already-prepared syringe and injected the solution into the ladyboy's arm. As the drugs coursed through her system, her body slumped into what would be a welcoming unconsciousness.

Replacing the syringe on the table, the figure picked up a sharp-looking hunting knife. They turned back to the prone figure and cut away her panties, leaving her naked from the waist down. Pausing, they gazed at the flaccid penis as if in admiration but in reality, deciding where to make the first cut. They knew that the body could be discovered before they naturally bled out, so he had added some anticoagulants to the morphine to help things along. With a grim smile, they began to cut into the organ.

Jesus Fucking Christ!

This was just too much of a coincidence. Although the newscaster hadn't revealed any details of the killing – other than the severed penis – the stories were just too close to two killings now. Both with severed penises and both facing charges relating to sex, though he hated to describe rape as sex. It was a form of control; a dark side of the control urge that he had tasted only once and never would again. What was going on?

This was meant to be a transition from purgatory to redemption, a period of penance spent in a land he'd loved but had to flee from. But he'd seen opportunity too, a chance to shine and to make the Thai company a success, and to be welcomed back to London as a returning prodigal son. He'd thought the path was opening up too, but he seemed to have got lost in some very scary woods. He had a powerful politician – Lamonphet – who seemed afraid that Tom might reveal his sordid past, if it was only in the past. Then there was Hollings, free from prison and possibly looking for vengeance. His whereabouts were currently unknown though Tom hoped that situation would be rectified soon.

And then, Chompoo...

A mysterious girl with an amazing talent but whose writing seemed to have inspired a killer. Or was her involvement less innocent than it seemed? He knew that she had told him that several of her stories had appeared online including on her own blog, but he'd never seen any actual evidence of those claims. He looked back at some of his notes. No mention of a blog address. He turned to his old friend, Professor Google. But he realised he had little information to use for his search basis. He knew Chompoo wasn't her real name, but he wondered if it was the same pen name she used online. He searched and searched, using different Boolean combinations with the names of her stories. Nothing. But then he remembered that the online versions would be written in Thai so a search in English was unlikely to produce anything. For a moment, he considered asking Anong for help, but he was loath to reveal to anyone that there were possible links between the writer he had discovered and grisly murders.

Chompoo was not due to return for another 10 days or so. He'd get some real answers then, or so he hoped, but 10 days seemed like an eternity. It wasn't as if he had any choice though, not unless he brought someone into his confidence and that wasn't an option. For someone who loved control, who thrived on control, he felt utterly helpless. He was depending on the private detectives to find Hollings, the security firm to protect him, and on Chompoo being truthful with him when she returned. The only thing he felt in control of was the coming meeting with Anong and the professor, and even them he was sacrificing an element of control to the young Thai girl. It was strange, but knowing how helpless he was made him more determined to just get on with things and leave the other people to do what they did best. With a dark look on his face, he headed for his private bathroom to freshen up before the meeting.

1996

Tom couldn't remember ever being so busy in his life. There was a sweet irony in that just at the point he'd decided to write the book, a flood of paying work came in. While he could have afforded to turn the offers down, he knew that refusals could lead to the offers being less regular in the future. So, he'd plunged into both the paying work and a book that might never earn him a cent. The next day, he was due to take the train up to Lopburi to do a story on the macaques that seemed to rule the town. There was supposedly more than a thousand of them and tourists flocked to see them as much as they did to see the Khmer ruins in the old town.

He'd started the morning by planning what he'd cover in Lopburi. As was often the case, his point of reference was Lonely Planet, the excellent words of Joe Cummings the vanguard for so many visitors to the region. This piece would more be about the photographs, though he'd been warned that some of the monkeys would even try and steal your camera, or anything else they could get their paws on. He'd checked all his camera equipment and made sure he had everything he would need. And, after a tip from a friend, he planned on buying a couple of water pistols to deter any wannabe camera thieves.

He had a lunch date with Yevgeny – a supply run as well as a meeting with a good friend – but still had a couple of hours before he had to get ready. So, now was as good a time as any to start working on the book. Of course, there was not any actual writing, that would come much later, but he wanted an idea of the book's outline as well as some of the sources he might use for research. He knew that he wanted to grab the reader's attention from the start so decided that the first chapter, or maybe even the first two, would look at just how widespread the problem was. That meant collating data from as many countries as possible with a nice mix of developed and developing. He was determined that people realise that this was not an issue confined to low-income countries.

By the time he had to leave to meet the Russian, he had a rough outline. He was quickly realising this was going to be a lot of work. And it could be work that never saw a dollar in return, though he planned on raising that point with Yevgeny later. If his friend was going to use any publishing company for money laundering, the least he could do was make a sizeable donation to Maggie's NGO.

Walking down to the street, he hailed a motosai, the quickest – but also the most dangerous – way to get about Bangkok. He fiercely gripped the back of the bike as his driver weaved his way in and out of traffic, often missing other vehicles by what seemed like centimetres. Every time he took a trip on one of these death-defying rides, he swore it would be his last. But it was the only real way to get about the ever-growing city when traffic was heavy, which with Bangkok, was most of the day. There was a supposed mass transit system being built but Tom doubted it would be up and running by the end of the century. So, until that system opened, or some other solution presented itself, he had to take his life in his hands every time that he was due for a meeting, especially given Tom always left things till the last minute.

Despite what seemed like an endless procession of close shaves, Tom arrived safely in Chinatown and was dropped outside Daeng Racha Hoi Tod, one of Yevgeny's favourite spots. The Russian was already seated by the window nursing a cold Singha. He rose as Tom entered and embraced his friend, using the hug as cover to slip a bulky package into Tom's pocket.

"So, tovarich, love's young dream has come to life again?"

Tom laughed.

"Yes, Ireshi is home and everything is great. She even stood up to her father who was threatening to have me deported. She told him that if I was kicked out of the country, she would leave too and he would never see him again. You know, I almost feel sorry for the man. Ireshi's mother thinks the sun shines out of my arse and even the maid, Taeng-mo, thinks I'm wonderful. The poor man is outnumbered by three strong women, so he had no chance."

"Da, so many fools think we men are the strong ones when it is really the women who fill that role. If more of us accepted that and allowed women to be in charge, then the world would not be such a shitshow."

Tom sat at the table and Yevgeny called over the server, ordering a Singha for Tom and a fresh one for himself. He lowered his voice.

"So, as requested, 14 grams of charlie, and this is a particularly nice batch, and seven grams of freshly-cooked Ketamine. But I'll warn you again, this stuff is crazy. Do not do the same size of lines as you would with the coke. In fact, ease yourself into it and make the first few lines two parts coke to one-part K. That'll take some of the edge off it. Then, chop yourself very small lines of the K to try on its own, say a third of your usual coke line. No, wait, I've seen the lines you chop, so make it a quarter or less the size. Also, only do it at home, this is not a drug for the middle of a crowded bar or club, at least not till you're used to it."

"I'll be fine, Yevgeny. Jesus, you'd think I was some naïve idiot."

"It's nothing to do with naiveté. This is different from your coke or speed. It's closer to being a psychedelic than anything else. But fine, if you want to ignore my advice, go ahead. Just don't come crying to me later if something crazy happens."

"Ok, ok, I'll be careful. Happy? Now, is there any chance of ordering some food? I've not been here for ages."

Yevgeny called the server back over and ordered oyster omelette pancakes for them both as well as two portions of fried rice.

"You should always listen to your Uncle Yevgeny. I told you to give Ireshi some space and I was right. I tell you to tread carefully with this ketamine and I am again right. You may have done more in your life than most young men of your age, but I have been here a lot longer and have seen things you wouldn't believe. Christ, I sound like that replicant in Blade Runner, the one Rutger Hauer played. My point is that you should listen to the voice of experience and learn from it. If you do, you might avoid some of the mistakes I made when I was your age, mistakes that led to some rather uncomfortable scenarios."

"Yes, gramps," laughed Tom, "I do appreciate the advice, honestly. And if it's even vaguely psychedelic, then I'll be careful. I always am with acid or mushrooms and never do them outside my home environment. Well, apart from the crazy weekend in Wales camping on the side of a mountain, but that's a whole other story."

Their food arrived and they continued chatting casually while they ate. Once they'd finished, Yevgeny apologised, saying he had to rush to another meeting. Tom had already slipped him the payment for the powders but it was only after the Russian had left that Tom realised he'd forgotten to discuss the book and elicit a promise from Yevgeny for a donation to the NGO.

He paid the bill and emerged back into a busy Chinatown. Hailing another motosai, he took it the short distance to Siam Centre as he'd decided to spend a couple of hours shopping before heading home. Though now more than 20-years-old, it was still an impressive mall and Tom's favourite. He browsed the shops and then bought Ireshi some lingerie. She never tired of his taste in underwear, whether silk and lace or leather and straps. Of course, this was the gentler, more feminine variety. Tom didn't think a shop catering to the BDSM scene would go down well in such a family-orientated mall.

Looking at his watch, he realised he still had a few hours till Ireshi arrived home from work. He was keen to try this new substance and Yevgeny had said it didn't last too long. So, it was onto his third motosai of the day – with intrusive thoughts in his head telling him the odds of an accident were shortened with every trip – for the journey home. Despite the pessimistic voice inside his head, he arrived home safely, paid the driver, and headed upstairs to the apartment.

He jumped into the bedroom and changed his shirt, the humidity and heat having soaked the shirt he'd worn for lunch with sweat. Grabbing a bottle of water from the fridge, he made himself comfy on the sofa and unpacked Yevgeny's goodies. The Russian had packed the two bags of powder inside a larger plastic bag and sealed it with tape. He fetched his coke mirror, stashed on a shelf with a metal tube and a razor blade still on it. He lifted the blade and very carefully sliced the tape open. Removing the bags, he laid them on the table. At first, he couldn't notice the difference between the two and was grateful that he'd ordered a half ounce of coke and only a quarter of ketamine. But, as he looked closer, he could see differences between them. There appeared to be more crystals in the ketamine, and the granules were slightly larger. And once he shook the bag, he could see that the coke had some rocks in amongst the powder, as was usual with Yevgeny and a sign of good quality.

He thought back to his friend's advice and also remembered how bad he could be at taking advice. But the Russian had been unusually insistent so maybe this time, he'd break the habit. Opening the bags, he measured two small piles of powder onto the mirror, the coke one around double the size of the ketamine. He then chopped enough for two small lines from the ket and then mixed what remained together. Tom almost felt as if Yevgeny was behind him, making sure his instructions were followed. Chopping two small – at least for him – lines from the cocktail, he spent a few minutes making it as fine as possible. Some of those ketamine crystals looked as if they'd rip your nose open.

One or two? *'One!'* he could hear his friend shouting in his head. Oh well, it's not as if he couldn't increase dosage in the future. Taking the metal tube, he bent over the table, put the tube to his nose, and hoovered the line up in a split-second. Leaning back on the sofa, he waited to see what all the fuss was about.

He felt the coke first, or at least tasted it, that old familiar yet bitter friend making itself known at the back of his throat. The numbness came next, his nose and part of his mouth losing nearly all feeling. He could feel his heart rate start to climb and a wave of euphoric bliss swept through his head. Tom allowed a contented sigh to escape his lips. Fuck, he loved this drug. As he surfed the coke high, he began to become aware of something else, almost as if someone was hiding behind a person and you couldn't quite see them.

His vision was the first thing to go, objects all around him starting to blur and jitter, almost as if his drug reality was slightly out of sync with actual reality. Then sounds began to blur too, the voices from the television he'd switched on earlier seeming to slow down, to also appear out of sync with what he was seeing. He felt as if he was pushing to get out of his body and then, suddenly escaping his physical form, his spirit was floating near to the ceiling. This was something he'd not even experienced on psychedelics and his physical body sank further into the sofa as his spirit explored the room. A moment of clarity and a thought flashed through his brain; maybe this was the out of body experience many people experienced in surgery, after all, wasn't ketamine an anaesthetic at heart?

For around 30 minutes, he floated, nothing making sense while everything made sense at the same time. The floating sensation began to subside and he could see his body as he almost parachuted towards it. There felt like a moment, just a moment, when his two forms didn't want to come back together, but they finally rejoined with an almost tangible bump.

Although the journey was fading, he lay motionless on the sofa. That had been exhausting, well at least in terms of mental effects. And that was mixed with the coke to 'take the edge off' as Yevgeny had advised. Jesus, what would it be like with the edge on? One thing he knew for sure; sex on this new drug would be incredible though he knew it might take some persuasion for Ireshi to indulge too. But they hadn't had a proper session since before their holiday so Tom knew – or hoped – she would be up to some intense playing in the shadows that weekend. He had decided against another line, at least for now. He wanted to be fairly compos mentis when Ireshi got back and he couldn't be sure of that if he tried more.

Never mind, they had a long weekend ahead of them with a holiday on the Monday, so he fully planned on holding Ireshi's hand – or tying it to the headboard – and taking her exploring this new dissociative universe.

2023

Tom's phone rang and he quickly answered it.

"Hello?"

"Tom? It's Bill Hall here. I have some news for you."

At last, something good happening.

"So, we traced Hollings down to the Pattaya area. He extended his visa at Chonburi immigration to a one-year retirement visa and submitted a TM30 at the same time. The address he gave was a seedy little guest house on the outskirts of Pattaya. I had my guy in Pattaya visit and the owner said he left last week and said he was going to Bangkok."

Ok, maybe not as good as he'd hoped.

"Just in case, I've sent someone down to Pattaya to help our man there. They'll trawl all the main bars but also some of the less salubrious venues, ones that often operate illegally."

"Those places still exist?"

"This is Thailand, Tom. While the city authorities are definitely trying to turn the city into a family-friendly resort, there will always be black markets for everything under the sun, especially on the outskirts or even outside the city where the police might be more susceptible to bribes. Personally, I love the city now. Covid did for Pattaya what the 2004 tsunami did for some of the islands. A lot of damage at first but, ultimately, a cleaner sea."

"But I hear a lot of the young guys in the office planning weekends down there for fun."

"Hell, Tom, I said cleaner not clean. Sex sells and it always will. So yes, there are still a lot of sex workers in the city but they're not as much in the open as they there used to be, well, unless you dip your toes – and other parts – in the cesspool of Soi 6. Anyway, so I have two of my guys checking that area and I've sent out pics of Hollings with all my runners here. It will take two or three days to work their way round the city, but we'll have copies of his pic in every corner, every soi, and every khlong in Bangkok by the end of the week. If he's in town, we'll find him."

"Thanks, Bill, just keep me updated, will you?"

"Sure thing, buddy. As soon as I know, you'll know within minutes. Speak soon."

Tom placed his phone back on the desk and stared at the ceiling. Why couldn't his life be simpler?

There were still three days or so until Chompoo was due to return. Tom had found himself opening each day's Bangkok Post with a sense of dread. What would he do if there was another murder that matched one of the girl's stories? Would he go to the police? No, the girl's possible explanation had been fairly plausible. If someone was being inspired by the tales she had posted online, did she really have any culpability? Hell, there was enough violence in the world, whether the stark realities of the news or the glorification of killing in video games. If some sick fuck had read her stories and decided to copy them, could she really be blamed? The killer could just as easily have watched a film and decided to emulate the killings in that.

The only good news was that the professor had been more than happy with the deal on the table and had signed a contract for his current book and a further two, with an option to renew the contract if both parties were happy with how things went. Kevin had been gushing to say the least. Tom had sent him the manuscript the week before and his boss had been impressed, even more so when Tom tied him down to a three-book deal. The phone call from London had been enthusiastic.

"Tom, fantastic work. Your professor has a real way of words and the English version doesn't look like it'll take much editing."

"Thanks, Kevin. Before I even look at editing, I'm going to get the translation checked by one of the top services in the city. The last thing I want is some pedantic bilingual bastard of a reviewer pointing something out that we've missed. If nothing major comes from that, then we can dive into the editing. Anong has already started on the Thai version so I'm estimating we'll be ready to launch in about three or four months."

"Why are you in such a rush? We normally put a time frame of up to a year on a new book, especially one by a new author."

"I know, but hear me out. You've seen that his manuscript is pretty polished anyway and it's the first ever BIB in five month..."

"BIB?"

"Sorry, Bangkok International Book festival. I thought it would be perfect for the book's launch and for Green-Hayes to announce its arrival on the Thai literary scene, as well as launch our eBooks."

"Hmm, definitely. Good thinking, Tom. Another little coup like this and you may be heading home earlier than planned."

For a moment, Tom was tempted to tell him about Chompoo, about how he felt the girl could be Thailand's Murakami, albeit with a lot more darkness and violence. But there were still too many questions, too many things to be sure of. He'd tell Kevin when the time was right and he had the girl's signature on a contract. Plus, better to space his wins out or Kevin would be expecting more. Two big contracts in a few months would be two massive feathers in the board's eyes.

So he lapped up Kevin's praise and reined in his enthusiasm on other projects. He did report back that the process of converting their back catalogue to eBook format was well underway but that was fairly routine stuff. Once the business talk was over, they chatted generally about things, though Tom didn't mention that ghosts from his past were looking over his shoulder. He knew Kevin liked him, but there would only be so much his boss could do if the shit hit the air conditioning. He also knew that if it hadn't been for Kevin, he'd have been out the door faster than management heading for a complimentary lunch. If he had been sacked, there would have been little chance of getting a position at the same level as before, so he'd probably be working for some shitty little publishing house that released billionaire werewolf and alien erotica fiction.

Once Kevin has rung off, he ordered a coffee in and planned the rest of his day. He was going to go and see Anong later, now in her own – albeit small – office that had come with her promotion rather than in one of the faceless cubicles where the peasants slaved their days away. He also wanted to get some reading done. Two manuscripts had been passed to him in the last three days that supposedly had potential. But he had a feeling that he'd be seeing a lot of 'potential' being forwarded to him in the wake of Anong's success. He'd give it a month and, if the quality of the work being passed to him was more than 50% poor, he'd have a team meeting with an added side of bollocking.

The next morning, he was in the office early as he planned on leaving at lunchtime and catching a flight to Chiang Rai for a couple of days. He needed a break, not so much from the office but from all the other shit that seemed to be plaguing his life just now. As far as the office was concerned, Khun Aekarach could handle things. He was leaving strict instructions that work was only to call him in a real emergency. Knowing the Thai mindset, he was also leaving what defined an emergency in his eyes. There was no way he wanted a call just because someone had discovered an error in a file that had been sent to the printers.

He was so early that there were only a few other faces in the office. He noted that Anong was one of them, she hadn't let her promotion go to her head and seemed determined to make this project a big success. When he'd met with her yesterday, he'd been impressed by her plans beyond editing. She wanted teasers for the books on all the company's social media platforms – as well as any other relevant groups – to build anticipation for the book before it was even on the press. She had been the one who'd suggested that the official launch could be at the BIB festival itself. That would definitely grab the media by the balls and could catapult the book to the top of the bestsellers list in Thailand. He had a good feeling about Anong, she had the potential to rise to the top of the ladder. He'd see how this project panned out and would then consider what she could do next. If she coped well with two consecutive big projects, then he'd look at creating a team she could lead, he just wasn't sure what that team would cover.

Satisfied that he'd covered all bases for his absence, he gave Kanya a call. He hadn't seen her for several weeks and she'd been enthusiastic when he'd suggested three nights in the north. He'd booked a corner suite at The Inside House. It came complete with private pool and he doubted they'd leave the room that much. Kanya was bringing a fresh supply of coke and Tom was bringing – he cast an eye at his suitcase sitting by the door – everything that was needed to ensure Kanya would return home sore but happy.

He'd been unsure about security arrangements for his trip so had phoned Matt a couple of days before. At first, the Englishman had been none too happy at the idea of Tom taking a road trip, but when he'd found out where Tom would be staying, and that he didn't have plans to leave the suite too much, he'd calmed down a little.

"Ok, we can do it. We'll need to add the cost of flights and accommodation onto your bill. I know the manager at The Inside House so will call him and have a chat. We'll send a two-man team so that one is constantly on duty. If you want to travel outside the city, we'll add car hire on as I'd rather have one of our guys driving you. It's probably a quite low-risk trip as if there is anyone planning on getting to you, they won't know about this trip. Let me know all the arrangements and your driver can take you to the airport and make sure no-one follows you. You can meet the team at the airport too, they'll both be Brits as they'll stand out less at the hotel."

Tom glanced at his watch. He was due to be picked up in ten minutes, go and get Kanya from her condo building, then head to the airport. He shut down his laptop and packed it away, though he didn't plan on logging in until the last day, or even after he'd returned. Walking along the corridor, he popped in to see Aekarach before he left.

"Khun Aekarach, that's me leaving. I'm sure you can handle anything that comes up but if it's really urgent, you can reach me on my phone though it will be set to vibrate only. You can check on Anong in a couple of days but I have every confidence she won't have any problems. But it will probably help if she knows there are two management figures who believe in her. You hired her, didn't you?"

The older Thai man smiled.

"Yes, and even back then, three years ago, there was something... different... about her. All the other interviewees that day saw literature as a business and nothing more. Some even saw working for a publishing company as just a stepping stone to other areas of the media. But you could tell Anong had dreams in her eyes. When she spoke about books, there was a genuine passion in her words. For one so young to recognise the beauty of how a new book smells is unusual to say the least. Hiring her was the easiest, and maybe the best, business decisions I ever made. Have you read any of her work?"

Tom was startled.

"No, I didn't know she wrote anything."

"It's poetry, so sadly not very commercially viable. But she definitely has a way with words, a way of using imagery that almost transports you to the world her poems are set in."

"I'm not sure what you mean?"

"Ah, sorry, I should have been clearer. She writes poetry set in the past, but with no favoured period. Even her subject matter varies, from historical battles to court intrigue. Yet each of her poems can make you feel as if you're actually present. She writes some epic poems too rather than just a few stanzas. One of the pieces I read was around 14 pages long."

Tom whistled as the older man continued.

"I know one of your aims is to have us operating in the black, and I'm sure some of the board back in London only see figures on a balance sheet. But if the budget allows it next year, I'd suggest you put out a book of her poems, even if only a limited print run. She has the skills and commitment to be a great editor but I believe that somewhere deep inside, she craves some recognition as an artist."

"It's something to look into. I had thought about whether we should release some poetry, though I was more thinking an anthology of various Thai poets rather than a standalone volume. Maybe that would be a good first step for her?"

Aekarach smiled.

"Yes, I think that would be a very good idea. There is less chance of her being the target of the vicious barbs of reviewers, people who have no understanding of, or appreciation for, poetry in any form."

"Good. Let's have a meeting about it once the professor's book is launched. I don't want her facing any distractions during the next few months. There is one condition though."

"Yes?"

"This would be your project. I'd want you to choose the poems to be included and to edit the final work. Also, I have absolutely no idea if Thai poetry would translate well into English. I mean, I know the words would but translated poetry often loses much of its original meaning unless done well. Another idea would be to launch a competition for inclusion in the volume. Of course, as an employee, Anong would be excluded from that side of it but it would be a good way of getting poems from a diverse range of Thais, and it would also be ideal from a marketing perspective."

"Yes, Khun Tom, that would work well. Your heart may be soaked in literature, but your head remains dry and business-focused."

Tom looked at his watch again.

"I'm really sorry, Khun Aekarach, but I really have to run. Let's discuss this further when I return but don't say anything to Anong in the meantime."

Aekarach nodded.

"I understand. Have a safe trip and enjoy your holiday, Khun Tom."

‘

1996

Ireshi wasn’t overly enthusiastic at first when Tom told her of his plans for the weekend. Although she’d tried – and enjoyed – mushrooms a few times before, this new drug frightened her.

They myths that surrounded it, especially the only partially-accurate label of 'horse tranquiliser', did not sit well with her. It took all of Tom's persuasive abilities – and the odd white lie – to even get her to agree to a small sample. He knew it would be best that she tried it before the actual night and thought it best if her first line was 'watered down' with coke as she was a cocaine fiend once she got going.

The test went well, though Tom did feel slightly guilty that he hadn't had her try a line of K on its own. But he knew Ireshi loved altered realities, especially when her other senses were facing an onslaught from every side. He realised it had been a while since their last intense session. Not that their unusual – to some – predilections defined their relationship, far from it, but it was that mutual desire for control, her to be controlled and him to do the controlling, that had brought them together. They had evolved beyond that frantic fucking stage but it still remained the core, the berating heart, of the relationship that had formed.

For most people, BDSM was something they dipped their toes into once in a while. For many, it was just a kink to try, and sometimes to try again... and again. For some, it would become a weekly thing, or a monthly thing, or just an occasional thing. But very few would take it to the next level, a solid relationship founded on the trust needed to truly submit to, or be dominated by, their partner. Yet Tom knew that the control Ireshi gave to him was little more than an illusion, that she could set the boundaries or stop play. One word, well, in their case a phrase. One phrase and any session would stop immediately. Trust again. It could also be as non-sexual as it was sexual. Domination was not just a sex thing. Tom had known a few couples back in London who lived the life 24/7. As much as he loved being a dom, he didn't think he could go that far. The longest they had stayed in their roles so far was three days.

Only a few hours of that had involved anything sexual. It had been more about Ireshi serving him. In fact, that weekend had more been about Ireshi's fantasies than his own. She had taken on the role of a geisha, dressed in a beautiful white Yayoi Kusama kimono with red polka dots, her face an almost ghostly white after she had applied Oshiroi.

She had greeted him as he arrived home from work, bowing as he entered, her eyes cast downwards to the floor. She had led him to the bathroom, not quite a traditional suefuro but she had done what she could with the resources at hand. The bathroom was lit by multiple candles and flooded by what seemed like a hundred scents from the nerikō she had found somewhere in the city. He had agreed in advance that as this was her fantasy, he had to let her lead him until she told him she was ready. So, he had stood unmoving as she slowly undressed him, though his arousal betrayed that he was not fully impervious to what was going on. Tom had stepped into the steaming-hot bath, initially flinching at the temperature then sinking into it as he became accustomed to the heat,

She had then washed him with an almost maternal tenderness, ignoring his arousal and his growing desire. Once she has finished washing him, she nodded to the bathroom floor – she had not spoken a word since he came home. He'd stepped out the bath and stood motionless as she dried him before having him don a plain black silk kimono, her fingers teasingly brushing his penis as she tied it.

Ireshi had led him into their living area which she had also transformed with candles and scents to be her own version of a Japanese tea room. Still without speaking, she had performed every step of the ceremony without fault. While still conscious of the desire within him, Tom was immersed in the fantasy and had no idea what to expect next.

Once the tea ceremony was over, she cleared away the bowls and utensils. She returned to the room and switched on the stereo – Tom's pride and joy – filling the room with the percussive sound of Taiko. She then indicated he should move to the sofa. He sat back and watched her taking their small silver tray from a bookshelf. Tom saw that she had prepared a dozen lines of coke with their snorting tube laid beside them. She had knelt in front of her partner and offered him the tray. He'd hoovered two lines in quick succession before passing the tray back to Ireshi who did the same. Reclining, he put his head back on the sofa, staring at the ceiling as the first rush of the cocaine washed over him. Then he felt hands; delicate hands, inquiring hands, insistent hands. She untied his kimono and leant forward, taking him in her mouth as arousal returned.

Tom shivered. While that had not been their most intense weekend from a sexual perspective, it had been their most sensual. Most of their lovemaking had been at the same level of tenderness as Ireshi's initial bathing of him. They had only planned for the session to be the Friday night, but it had continued on into the Saturday and then the Sunday, the Japanese theme continuing throughout. His one regret was that his Kinbaku skills were not as good as he would have liked. There was a certain poetic irony that a dom who loved the idea of rope bondage was so inadequate at knots. It hadn't spoiled the weekend, nothing could have, but Tom still practiced his knots in secret, hopeful that one day he would be proficient and could surprise the woman who had given so much.

Thinking about that weekend made him decide something for this one. Perhaps Ireshi's fears of disassociation would be lessened if there was something familiar, something that she had loved. Walking through to their special room, he opened the wardrobe that contained, mostly, the many outfits Ireshi had accumulated in their time together. Pushing hangers aside, he found what he was looking for, the two kimonos Ireshi had bought for her Japanese weekend. Digging deeper into the wardrobe, he found a lacy little crotchless bodysuit she hadn't worn for a while and decided it would go perfectly with the kimono, the traditional merging with the downright slutty.

Let the games begin.

2023

As the flight touched down at Don Mueang, Tom smiled at Kanya in the seat beside him. That break had been just what he needed, the perfect mix of opulence and decadence with a side dish of debauchery. They'd eaten well, drank well, and fucked furiously. He'd felt the stress and worry ebb out of him with every thrust, the old Tom return with every gasp from Kanya.

His driver was waiting at the airport and Tom had almost forgotten that he had been shadowed on holiday until one of those shadows, an unsmiling former paratrooper called Mark, had jumped into the passenger seat. The downside of their return was that they'd taken a late afternoon flight, and the journey back into the city was rush hour, though the route into the city was nowhere near as congested as the roads out. But what was normally a one-hour journey was still closer to two and it was almost 6pm when he dropped Kanya at her condo in Sathon. He briefly kissed her, conscious of the two men in the front while not knowing why he cared what they saw. He promised her dinner at the weekend and then she was gone, leaving Tom back in the reality of his life.

The car took him back to his own condo, Mark going ahead to double-check the condo before giving Tom the green light by phone to come up. Realising he was exhausted, he ordered portions of Chili Rellenos and Berenjena Maria from Charley Brown's and settled down for a relaxing night on the sofa before returning to the office in the morning.

The next morning, Tom had a certain swagger as he walked into the office. Although it had been a short break, he felt he had a new clarity and that even a brief recharge would push him forward with all his plans. He was no longer worrying about Lam or Hollings. One could be ignored and there were plans in place to trace and neutralise the other. As for Chompoo, he wasn't thinking about the possible issues but rather her impending stardom. He was convinced that he could make her a star. Or at least, her writing would make her a star but he would help propel her to that level.

For once, he picked up that day's Bangkok Post without apprehension, with no thought to what it might contain. He strode through the office with confidence, bidding good morning to all the staff he passed. Stopping at his secretary's desk, he ordered a coffee before entering his office ready to face the day ahead. Checking his diary, he saw that he had no definite appointments booked for the day. That didn't mean he had nothing to do. He wanted to stop in for a coffee later with Aekarach and make sure everything had gone smoothly in the short time he'd been away. Then he wanted to have a progress meeting with Anong to see how her work was going. He really didn't want to be too hands-on with this project but at the same time, he did want her to know that he was there if she encountered any problems. Although he had complete faith in her abilities to see the project through to its – hopefully successful – conclusion, he was also aware that this was the first time she'd shouldered this level of responsibility. Tom hoped that she would see him as a mentor and that she would never be reluctant to come to him if anything was worrying her.

He'd just finished sending a couple of short emails to Aekarach and Anong to check they were available for informal meetings later, Aekarach just before lunch, though it might end up as a lunch meeting, and Anong mid-afternoon. A knock on his door was followed by his secretary bringing him his coffee. He thanked her and took the coffee and that day's paper to one of the armchairs by the window. His time was his now for the next hour or so.

The deflation of his good mood when it came was swift and vicious. He read in almost catatonic disbelief.

With the discovery of a third body yesterday, Police Lieutenant General Apisitniran confirmed that they are now hunting a serial killer. The body of businessman, Komsan Shoowong, 53, was found in a budget hotel in Bang Kae district around 4pm on Tuesday afternoon. Shoowong had been bound and beaten to death, but it was the removal of his penis that alerted authorities to the potential link with two previous murders. While Apisitniran refused to rule out a copycat killer, he did advise sex workers and anyone who uses sex workers to be aware of any suspicious behaviour. Shoowong had been charged with assaulting sex workers on four previous occasions but had only been convicted once after his victim spent three weeks in hospital with a broken arm and severe lacerations to the face.

No, this couldn't be happening. He didn't even have to refer to Chompoo's files as this, or a facsimile of this, had been one of the first stories she had sent him. While the emasculation seemed to be an M.O. particular to the real-life killer, the other similarities were too close. In her story, Chompoo had woven a dark tale of a man who got his kicks from hurting others. And while Tom knew that could almost have described him, the big difference, other than that one occasion, was consent. The other difference was that Tom never used sex workers, not because of any misplaced morality, but simply because it was transactional rather than genuine. Yes, Tom liked to inflict pain, but the recipients had to want to be hurt.

He sat and stared out the window for several minutes. A small part of him had always hoped the similarities were nothing more than coincidence, though his logic had increasingly seen that as unlikely. Any small shard of optimism had now evaporated in glaring reality. Someone had seen Chompoo's stories online and was either mimicking them or taking some form of twisted inspiration from their own lust for death. The big question was, what should he do? If he went to the police on his own, they'd likely dismiss his tale as the deranged ramblings of a drug-using farang. No, if he went to the police, it had to be with Chompoo at his side. The girl was due back tomorrow, so he would email her now to explain the situation and insist that she come to the office or meet him at the police station.

Chompoo,

Are you still returning tomorrow? There's been another murder, and all three of them bear more than a passing resemblance to events in your stories, too many resemblances to be put down to coincidence. I know we were going to take things slowly but this is now preying on my mind. I have to insist that you either meet me here or at the Royal Thai Police headquarters in Pathum Wan. If I don't hear from you, or if you refuse to come to the police with me, then I will have to go myself. If I don't, my conscience would be too heavy if another murder happened. There is one sick bastard out there, a bastard who has read your stories and is now bringing fictional deaths into the real world. I hope you will do the right thing.

Tom.

Do the right thing. What a fucking cliché. Maybe if he'd done the right thing two decades preciously, or if he hadn't done the wrong thing in the first place, then he might have lived a life untouched by the shadows of the past. Those ghosts seemed to be haunting him now, though he'd expected them to manifest as Hollings or Lam. For the next hour or so, Tom couldn't concentrate on anything, again staring out the window at the sprawling behemoth of a city while his thoughts plunged through maelstroms of doubt. Finally, a ping from his laptop told him he had mail, and he prayed it was from Chompoo rather than some invitation to a vacuous event.

Tom,

My God. I had thought you were being overly-dramatic when you said that murders were being committed that seemed to reflect events in some of my stories. Even after the second murder, I thought it was more likely your overactive imagination rather than someone using my ideas to actually kill people. My flight lands at 9am tomorrow morning. Let me go home and shower and change and I'll be at your office for 11am. I'll call when I'm outside and you can come down and meet me and we'll go to the police together. But I've thought about this, thought about nothing else since reading your mail. We can give the police all the information about the stories, and where they appeared, but there's no way of tracing anyone. The site didn't operate on a registration model so anyone could visit it. Still, maybe the police can do something, I don't know. I'll see you tomorrow.

Chompoo.

Tom felt palpable relief after reading Chompoo's mail. Knowing that the police would soon know everything took that Sisyphean burden from his shoulders. The fact that he would finally meet the mysterious girl, something he'd wanted for so long, was now secondary to passing what they knew to the investigating officers. He didn't miss the irony that she was now less of a priority though he knew that would change once this was settled. He realised he would also face a dilemma; would he have to remove the stories that were related to the murders from any book? Would he even have the choice or would the police insist. But the cynical marketer inside him also realised that this could be a major opportunity. If the police caught the actual murderer, and he truly hoped they did, then the connection to Chompoo's stories would come out and that could lead to huge sales figures. There would be massive media exposure and equally massive interest from the public. Many Thais had that 'rubberneck' obsession with the darker side of life. If you ever saw any sort of accident, then there would invariably be multiple mobile devices pointed at the action.

Although he felt slightly guilty of taking advantage of three murders, he remembered that the victims were hardly nice people. There was a definite sense of vigilantism to the killings, though he couldn't wholeheartedly approve. Still, their guilt would definitely assuage his own. The one hurdle he foresaw was the timeframe. Thai court cases had always been renowned for sometimes taking years, though a recently passed law was supposed to expedite cases in less than a year. He didn't think that her stories needed too much editing, but he would be toning down some of the more graphic details. While he hated the idea of sanitisation, he knew that she had gone a little too far when it came to her depictions of violence. The other thing he had to think about was the sexual content. He knew that Thailand could be quite conservative and had strict pornography laws but he was unsure what those laws covered. He'd have to talk to the company lawyer who looked over everything that had even the slightest stain of controversy. Still, that was something for the lawyer to worry about, not him.

He knew it was a cliché, but he really did feel that tomorrow was presenting him with a fork in the road, except he had no choice as to which road he would be cast upon. He did know that one direction would lead to smooth waters, satisfied police detectives, a happy lawyer, and Chompoo with her name in lights. Oh, and throw in a solid conclusion to the Hollings and Lam situations. In the other direction lay a threatening storm that could upset every point he had navigated until now. While the success of the professor's book might seem like something that would keep the rain at bay, the reality was that he had not been the one responsible for finding him, so only some of the rays of acclaim would reach him. The shadows of any scandal over the Chompoo project would likely be darker than the shadows hidden in his past.

1996

Tom believed that the relationship he had with Ireshi was based on more than the sexual tastes they shared. He thought they shared a love for an exploratory orgy of the senses, a desire to seek out new things in every area, from food to wine, from drugs to travel. He'd decided the night before that he was going to ask Ireshi to marry him. He knew their engagement would drive her father into an apoplectic fit, but that was not why he was doing it, though it would be fun to see his reaction. No, he had no worries about her father. With her mother and Taeng-mo on his side, he knew that Ireshi's happiness would be elevated far above any paternal rage. There was only one true reason he was going to ask her to be his wife; he loved her.

Tom had never thought there was a soulmate out there who could make him complete. After all, he was a deviant, a deviant who used drugs and who reveled in the feelings of power and control. Yet the discovery that she really was the yin to his yang when it came to that deviance had only been the first step on a journey of shared exploration. As well as a predilection for altered realities, though she was less into experimenting than he was, they had discovered that they shared a deep affinity for food. They'd eaten street food in Kuala Lumpur, lunched at a hawker's stall in Singapore, and been to every corner of Bangkok to sample the cheapest Moo Ping and the most expensive churrascaria. Food had led to wine and whisky, and he'd educated her in the different malts that he himself loved. Music had been another area where she'd proven a willing and compliant student, asking all the right questions when he played her Miles Davis, closing her eyes in quiet contemplation for the entirety of *Bitches Brew*.

While there were still some things that were solely Ireshi, they were still part of who she was. He'd often shaken his head when he found her in front of their aging television set watching some Thai soap opera, but he'd come to accept it, to realise it was a link to her childhood and many late afternoons spent with her mother. But nearly everything else was shared between them, and their often almost telepathic communication meant that they had a seemingly wordless symbiosis whether cooking for friends or finding new sensual delights.

All these things, from her smallest mannerisms to the things she did every single day, meant that he wanted this weekend to be perfect. He had booked them both into Shizukesa Spa and Onsen for three hours of sheer but separate pampering. Following that, he had booked a private room at Hanaya 1976, the city's oldest Japanese restaurant, for the finest sushi, sashimi, and sake. Once their culinary lust had been sated, it would be time to turn their attention to more carnal matters. Even the taxi journey home would be an entrée of anticipation as he would command her to remove her panties before leaving the restaurant and then to sit on his hand in the car.

Once home, she would shower and dress in the expensive geisha kimono – and the crotchless bodysuit – while he poured champagne, changed into his own kimono, and chopped the first lines of the evening. Once she was ready, he was going to propose, his thoroughly English upbringing dictating that he followed tradition and asked her to marry him while on one knee. Of course, he wouldn't be following the tradition of asking her father's permission; that would be the most pointless of exercises. But he'd discussed his plan with her mother whose only question had been as to how long before she had a grandchild. When Ireshi said yes, if she said yes... Jesus, he hadn't even considered rejection for one second. Once she said yes, they would finish the bottle of champagne and the prepared lines before the games began.

It would be the perfect day – and night – and the perfect proposal and, once her father had calmed down, it would be the perfect wedding and marriage. He hadn't thought about a destination for the honeymoon yet, though maybe they'd be able to answer her mother's question shortly after returning, but he knew that it would be the perfect honeymoon too. Hell, maybe her father would even pay for it, with a little persuasion from her mother of course.

He had everything meticulously planned, from the surprise visit to the Japanese spa right through to what toys he planned on using that night. He intended that this weekend would be indelibly stamped on both their memories as the culmination of one amazing journey and the beginning of another. He knew he would have little control over the wedding; Ireshi and nearly every female member of her family would be in complete control of that. He did plan on insisting on wearing a kilt, though. It was a family tradition and a nod to the McKays' Scottish roots. He'd have to remember to wear boxers though, at least for the Buddhist ceremony part of the day. It wouldn't be very respectful for a monk to be subjected to the sight of his waxed and unclothed balls. He could always slip the boxers off later and go commando.

Then there was the Sin Sod to consider. It was customary for the groom to pay a dowry to the family of the bride to thank them for raising their daughter. He'd asked a male Thai friend about this who had told him that it was often more symbolic than anything else. He'd be expected to attend a ceremony called Tong Mun where he would present Ireshi with 24-carat gold jewellery of some type. Once this was done they'd officially become a couple – ironic given that they'd been living together for so long – and have the title of Koo Mun, 'joined couple'.

When he'd first heard of Sin Sod, he'd laughed at the idea of such an outdated concept as dowry. But as he'd grown to know and love this country, he'd realised that he should instead be laughing at his own country where so many traditions had been cast aside. Since then, he'd learned just how much traditions were intertwined with modern Thai life. He'd more than learned though, he'd come to respect and admire the way the two worlds met without colliding. It went beyond his feelings though. He knew Ireshi, despite how much she embraced today's world, was a very traditional-leaning woman at heart. He also knew that if he followed all the traditional steps involved in a Thai wedding, she'd be extremely happy and that was enough for him, was all he really wanted.

Of course, there was still a ring involved in the process. He'd chosen a flawless 1.25 carat diamond on a simple white gold band. Ireshi had spoken of her love for white gold not long after they first got together so he knew she'd love this ring. Everything was in place for the greatest weekend of their lives.

2023

Tom woke drenched in sweat. Glancing at his phone, he saw it was just after 5am, too early to get up but probably too late to return to full sleep. His nightmares seemed to have worsened in recent weeks but last night's had been particularly horrific. A Krasue, a disembodied Thai spirit, had been chasing him down a deserted Sukhumvit road. As well as her organs floating below her, several bloody penises had also dangled from her neck, her malevolent gaze telling him that his would soon join them. He lay there for an hour, trying to put his night horrors aside as he planned the day out.

He hoped that their visit to the police would be a short one, but he knew that in the inevitable way of Thai bureaucracy, they would be slowly passed up the food chain until an officer senior enough to make decisions could deal with them. He also realised that, at first at least, no-one would believe their story. A vision of Chompoo trying to explain rose unbidden in his mind.

'Well, officer, I wrote some rather gruesome stories and somebody has used those stories as a template for killing people.'

It may sound ludicrous, but it seemed to be true. There was no other likely explanation for the series of bloody coincidences. But he wondered how many times they would have to tell the truth before it was accepted as such. He looked at his phone again. 6:25am. Maybe a shower would wash away the memories of the nightmare and ready him to face the day ahead, but he knew that no amount of scalding water would completely eradicate the Krasue from his mind.

Showered and with coffee brewing, Tom felt a lot better, though every time he closed his eyes, that damned Krasue returned unbidden. If he'd been Thai, he would likely have taken it as a portent of approaching doom, a harbinger of an uncertain fate. As he was Western, at least in most ways, he put it down to the events of the last few weeks and to Chompoo's imagination leading to a sojourn in a land of shadows where evisceration was an everyday occurrence. Could anyone escape the clutches of nightmares given the stories he had been reading? Both fiction and in the media? Tom didn't think so. He allowed himself a wry chuckle as he wondered if it was time they focused on children's stories. Nice fluffy bunnies and cute ducks rather than a bloody head with entrails and all sorts trailing beneath her. Funnily enough, he knew that a couple of the juniors were currently working on a children's' environmental series called Auntie Meng. As it wasn't really in his sphere of interest, he'd merely looked at the projected sales and, satisfied with what he saw, had given the project a green light. Maybe he should pay more attention and have pleasant dreams instead.

He called his driver and told him he'd be down in ten minutes; it was time to face the day ahead. He knew he wouldn't be able to focus on any work until this mess was behind him, though he knew it wouldn't be quite as easy as telling the police everything. There would likely be more interviews, not to mention a potentially lengthy police investigation into Chompoo and maybe even him. What would he say if they asked why he took so long to come forward? Would saying that he thought it was purely coincidence at first satisfy them?

As he took the elevator down to the lobby, he was still going over every possible permutation. He knew that he'd continue to do so all morning and that 11am seemed a long way off. The trip to the office was uneventful, Tom not even seeing the traffic as he navigated his thoughts on the day ahead.

By 10am, he was on his fourth coffee of the morning, the caffeine not helping with his anxiety levels. He wasn't too worried about it stopping him from sleeping that night; he had a nice bottle of 12-year-old Bunnahabhain sitting waiting to calm the day's mountain of nerves so it would also be the perfect antidote to being over-caffeinated. The sofa would probably be bed for the night, and he'd already accepted that dawn would bring a crushing hangover, unnaturally twisted limbs, and the inevitable river of drool that seemed to be a regular visitor when he overindulged. But all those bad things would be worth suffering if this mess was in life's rearview mirror.

He found he couldn't settle, constantly pacing his office or standing staring out the window at the city that offered so much yet demanded such a heavy price. Though he knew he'd had little choice in the matter, he still wondered why he had returned. He'd hoped that the ghosts of his past would have faded into nothingness by now, but Lam and Hollings were proof that they were very much still there. While he could understand Lam's fears, he was also sad as they had been good friends and he would never do anything to taint those memories. Hollings was a very different case. He felt no guilt in having been responsible for him being imprisoned. The man was a monster who had probably stolen the innocence of countless children. Yet he was walking freely because he had money and this was a country where money had a loud voice. He wondered if any of the victims' families knew that Hollings was not only free but maybe living in the same areas where he had preyed on helpless kids. Thailand was renowned for vigilante justice, especially in more rural areas where village headmen had more power than the local police. Nothing would make him happier than opening the Bangkok Post to read that Hollings' mutilated body had been found in some lonely canal. Though he knew that were vigilantes to target Hollings, his body would likely never be found.

10:30am. Thirty minutes till Chompoo was due at the office and they could begin to unravel the tangled threads between fact and fiction. Thirty minutes until this nightmare began to end. He just wanted this all to be over. Hell, he just wanted to be back home in London though he knew that was at least a few months off.

There was a knock on the door and his secretary entered, a worried look on her face.

"Khun Tom, there are two policemen on their way up. They want to see you."

Tom's heart sank. Was this the threatened move by Lam? Or was it something connected to Hollings? Why today, when he was getting ready to sort the Chompoo mess out?

"Ok, Mai, just show them right in when they arrive. Maybe bring us some coffee too."

The girl nodded, concern still etched on her features, and left to return to her desk.

Five minutes later, she knocked again and opened the door, two stern-looking policemen at her shoulder. Before she could say anything, they shouldered her aside and strode into the office. Tom nodded at Mai to reassure her and she shut the door behind her.

"Officers, how can I help you?"

The more senior of the two spoke.

"I'm Police Lieutenant General Apisitniran. Are you Thomas McKay?"

Wait, wasn't he the officer in charge of the serial killer hunt?

"Yes, I'm Tom McKay. What's this about?"

"Thomas McKay, I'm arresting you on suspicion of murder. You have the right to remain silent but any statements you do make may be used as evidence. I am also in possession of warrants to search your office and your condo. Do you have anything to say?"

The blood drained from Tom's face. *What the fuck? How could they possibly suspect him?*

"No, I have nothing to say other than that this is utter nonsense. But I don't want to say anything until I've spoken to a lawyer."

Apisitniran looked around the well-furnished office with a sneer.

"If you cannot afford legal counsel, which I very much doubt, then the court will appoint one for you. Now please, take a seat by the window while we conduct a search of your office. We already have officers at your condo to search it. I also need you to surrender your mobile phone. We will also be impounding your laptop."

Tom reluctantly handed over his phone and sat by the window as ordered. He was sort of glad they were taking the laptop though; all Chompoo's files and emails would surely tell the police the true story behind the murders. He watched dispassionately as the two policemen rifled through his desk drawers and moved every book on the shelves. The laptop, like the phone, went into a plastic evidence bag. He didn't have a clue what they hoped to find. Even if he was the murderer, would he keep a bloody knife or a trophy from the killings in such an obvious place?

The search of the main office only took ten minutes. Apisitniran pointed at the door in the rear wall.

"Is this a cupboard?"

"No, it's just a small bathroom so I can have a shower if it's a long day or I have to go on to a meeting."

The policeman frowned, maybe at the fact his own office didn't include such luxuries. He opened the door and began to search the small room. Tom knew it would only take a few minutes as it was a functional space more than anything. Maybe then they could get to the police station and sort this nonsense out.

He was gazing out the window again, thankful that at least the policeman spoke pretty fluent English. His Thai certainly wasn't strong enough to communicate well in this scenario. Telling someone you were innocent of a string of brutal murders was slightly more difficult than ordering some pad krapao. His thoughts were interrupted by a cough and he turned to see Apisitniran holding a clear plastic bag that seemed to contain a towel or something similar.

"Can you explain this, Mr. McKay?"

"Explain what? What is it? A towel from my bathroom?"

"Yes, it's a towel and it is from your bathroom. I was more wondering if you could explain why it's heavily stained with blood."

Tom stared at the policeman. Had he planted the towel? He'd only used the bathroom once that morning for a piss and he definitely hadn't seen that.

"I've never seen that before. Where did you find it?"

"It was hidden behind the cistern. You claim that you've never seen it before but it was clumsily hidden in your private bathroom, somewhere you'd not expect anyone else to use."

Apisitniran looked over at the other policeman and nodded. The man moved over to Tom and dragged him roughly to his feet before handcuffing him.

"Is there any need for this? I'm hardly going to run. I have no fucking idea how that towel got there but I haven't killed anyone. In fact, we were planning on going to the police today with information about these killings."

"We? Who else is involved, Mr. McKay? Cooperate now and things might go easy for you in court."

"For fuck's sake, I've told you, I'm innocent. The other person I'm referring to is a girl, a writer. Someone is copying what she wrote in some short stories. That's what we were coming to see you for."

"And who is this girl? Thai?"

"Yes of course. Her name is Chompoo. Well, that's not her real name but it's what I know her as. She was meant to be coming here at 11 so we could go to police HQ."

The officer raised an eyebrow.

"It's now ten past. Where is this girl whose name you don't actually know?"

"I have no idea. She was meant to be flying into Suvarnabhumi from Shanghai. Her flight was due at nine. Maybe the plane was delayed."

"Well, if what you say is true, I'm sure we can sort it all out but if it is sorted out, it will be down at the station. Let's go."

As the two officers marched Tom through the office, with almost every member of staff looking on open-mouthed, he was reminded for some strange reason of an incident at school when he'd been caught with porn mags and his housemaster had announced his crime to the entire school at assembly. While he knew there was no substance to the allegations, he knew that office gossip could take a long time to go away. The only thing he was grateful for was that, unusually for Thais, no one seemed to be recording the moment for posterity, though he was sure there would be some discussion on social media.

There seemed to be less reluctance in the building's lobby when it came to snapping pictures on phones. Tom was thankful when they left the building and approached the waiting car and driver, a Mercedes-Benz A Class that seemed appropriate for someone of Apisitniran's rank. He was bundled unceremoniously into the back seat and the scowling officer joined him while Apisitniran took the passenger seat.

Tom sat in contemplative silence while the car navigated the Bangkok traffic. *Where was Chompoo? Where had the towel come from? Why was this happening to him?* He thought only Lam could be behind this. Only he had the power to point the police at him and have a tame detective find something incriminating. That's if it was incriminating though he doubted someone would go to the trouble of planting the towel unless it put a big neon guilty sign above his head.

The car finally pulled off Rama 1 road and into the huge compound that was the Royal Thai Police's headquarters. It parked close to the door of one of the main buildings and the officer pulled Tom out the car with the same harshness as he'd used before. He was pushed through the door and upstairs to a sterile-looking reception area, its only colour and warmth provided by a large portrait of the former King.

They stood him in front of a desk, had him empty his pockets, then they searched him. A different officer then frog marched him to a row of cells, an odour of stale piss and human sweat hanging heavy in the air. There was a banging from one of the occupied cells, likely a drunk arrested the night before and wondering how he had got there. The policeman made him remove his shoes and belt and shoved him inside an empty cell. The air was even more pungent inside and the small room contained only a concrete bed and a toilet that hadn't seen any bleach in at least a decade. As the door slammed shut, Tom sat on the edge of the bed and put his head in his hands.

1996

The day had gone perfectly so far. Ireshi had been stunned when they'd arrived at Shizukesa Spa and Onsen. She'd thought they were going shopping for shoes for Tom and had planned to add a couple of pairs for herself. When the taxi pulled up outside the spa, she had looked puzzled at first and then delighted as she realised Tom had planned it as a treat. That delight had been amplified at the end of three hours of pampering when Tom announced he had reservations at Hanaya 1976.

She did wonder what was going on, though. While Tom always made an effort when they had a special session planned, this was more than she was used to. The food at Hanaya was, as always, superb. Ireshi began to realise that Tom had planned a meticulous indulgence of the senses. The spa experience had set a foundation for everything that followed, ensuring their bodies were completely relaxed and prepared for what lay ahead. The restaurant offered the chance to dive into their culinary loves, accompanied by a variety of the finest sakes. And she knew that once home, a rollercoaster ride through altered realities would culminate in imaginative and mind-blowing sex. She knew that there was a certain irony in that by the time the adventures had finished, she would probably need another trip to the spa as every part of her would have been used by Tom.

Too soon, the Japanese feast was over, though it was also perhaps not soon enough. As they sat and sipped their Kuusus, Tom leaned over and gave Ireshi a deep kiss before whispering in her ear. Ireshi smiled before standing and, with a bow to her dom, making her way to the toilets. She returned a few minutes later, one hand bunched in a fist. She approached Tom and knelt before him, passing him what was hidden in her hand. He gazed down at the scrap of cloth that had passed for Ireshi's panties, unconsciously licking his lips as he raised them to the face and drank in the aroma of fresh lust, a better aphrodisiac than even the most expensive perfume.

Tom decided to prolong the anticipation, knowing that this would annoy Ireshi but who could say nothing about it. He rang the bell for a waitress and ordered a Montecristo No. 2 for him and a Hibiki 17-Year-Old for them both. Once the waitress returned with their order then left again, he prepared and lit the cigar before taking a sip of the whisky. One final assault on the senses, at least for this part of the day. He closed his eyes as the tangy wood and sweet spices of the Montecristo combined with the different flavours of the Hibiki, though today he noticed the honey and smoke more than anything. Ireshi sat in silence with her whisky. When Tom was in his cigar and whisky zone, she knew it was like meditation to him, and she could him imagine him contemplating the later – and rougher – assault on the senses, her senses.

That meditative moment meant that Tom was also silent, the two of them comfortable in the lack of words the way only two close lovers can be. After about 15 minutes, he opened his eyes again, extinguished the cigar, and finished his whisky. He looked over at Ireshi and raised an eyebrow. She nodded compliantly. Tom rang for the server again and asked for the bill. She returned and he paid, also leaving a generous tip. He rose to his feet and offered a hand to Ireshi. As she stood, he pulled her towards him and again whispered in her ear.

"I love you."

She was a little surprised; usually by this point, Tom's asides would be lewder and sexually graphic. He certainly had his sweet moments but considering what was coming, they never happened at this point. He led her by the hand onto the street, the fourth taxi he waved frantically at pulling over and stopping for them. They climbed in the back, Tom putting his hand on the seat for Ireshi to sit on, before she gave the address to the driver. The drive to their apartment was only 15 minutes but she struggled to keep a straight face as she squirmed while Tom's fingers explored inside her. She was close to the point of orgasm when they arrived at their address, Ireshi mouthing a silent prayer to Buddha as she knew she would not have been able to control her screams had Tom made her climax. The driver paid, they climbed the stairs to the apartment, Ireshi walking in front so Tom could see up her mini-dress.

Once they were inside the flat and the door was locked, he turned to Ireshi and said, "Go and get ready."

She nodded again and headed to do her master's bidding. As she left, Tom smiled. Everything was going just as he'd planned. This would be a day neither of them would ever forget. Moving into the living room, he put Davis's *Milestones* on the stereo, the perfect soundtrack to the perfect day. He stripped down to his briefs then, after a minute's thought, removed them too. Now fully naked, he walked over to the drawer where he kept their drugs and took out the bag of coke. Emptying a sizeable pile onto the mirror kept solely for this purpose, he quickly cut and snorted a cheeky line for himself. He chopped the reminder into eight lines, then changed his mind and made a ninth which he swiftly hoovered up. As Miles went all melancholy on *Moon Dreams*, he slipped into his black silk kimono and made sure the engagement ring was in the pocket. Satisfied that everything was ready, he reclined on the sofa to wait for his partner.

When she entered the room, he remembered one of the reasons he'd fallen in love with her. While he'd only directed her to wear the kimono and the bodysuit, she had added her own sensual touches. She was wearing a Katsura geisha wig in the Geiko Shimada style, something he'd forgotten she had. The top front of the kimono was open just enough to display an enticing hint of cleavage and just open enough at the bottom that Tom could see the occasional flash of the bodysuit as she walked across the room. He noted with approval that she had also added retro seamed stockings, part of a haul that had delighted them both when they'd found it on a recent visit to Chatuchak market. She was wearing geisha makeup too, the Oshiroi turning her face ghostly-white while the striking red Beni made her eyes and lips stand out dramatically from the white.

Before he could even offer her a line, she knelt in front of him, opened his kimono, and began to fellate him. He knew that any release now would mean he would last longer later so sat back to enjoy her expertise. He laughed inwardly as he realised that any orgasm now might be the last as a mere boyfriend, well, if she said yes to his proposal. It wasn't long till he could feel his climax approaching, Ireshi was just too damn good at this. As he exploded in her mouth, she drank down his seed greedily and licked him clean. Moving back, she sat cross-legged on the floor and smiled mischievously at him.

"I think you like surrendering control too sometimes. I've noticed it before, especially when my mouth is involved."

Tom laughed.

"You really do have such a naughty mind. What have I ever done to deserve you?"

"You're you, that's enough. You make me feel complete. I know it's an old cliché, and one I never beloved in until I met you, but I know you are my soul mate."

"Yeah, it is a cliché, but I think the same. It's like we really were meant to be together. So, now that you've had your snack, would madam like a little line?"

"Little? You know I like my lines big and fat, just like your gorgeous cock."

He laughed again and wondered what her conservative parents would think to hear her. He passed her the mirror.

"Okay my lover, help yourself while I open the champagne."

"Hmm, just what's going on with you. It's not my birthday, nor is it our anniversary, but so far today, we've had a spa visit then some amazing food at Hanaya. Now you have champagne to wash down the coke, and the cock, with."

Tom smiled enigmatically. "Am I not allowed to spoil my partner now and again?" Still smiling, he headed into the kitchen to open the champagne, pour a couple of glasses, and put the bottle in an ice bucket. He returned through to the living room and passed a glass to Ireshi who was now leaning against the sofa. He placed the ice bucket on the coffee table and sat beside her. They clinked glasses.

"To my soulmate, now and forever."

They both laughed at Tom's words. It may have been an overused cliché but most of the time, it held little meaning. For both of them, it really meant everything. He felt in his pocket for the ring box. With it grasped in his hand but still hidden, he moved from his seated position to being on one knee in front of Ireshi. She looked at him in confusion.

"Ireshi, I never knew I could feel like this. Until I met you, all my relationships were fleeting and casual and I thought that was how it would always be. Given my tastes in the bedroom are somewhat unusual but important to me, connections with women have always centered on those tastes. But you tick every box when it comes to my ideal partner. The sex is great, better than great, but we've grown to be so much more than that. I never thought I would meet someone I'd want to spend my life with, to surrender the freedom I've always valued so much. But you are that someone. I want to be with you forever, to wake each morning to your smile. To share good times and bad, to share laughter and tears. Ireshi, I know this is not the normal Thai way but it's my way and am happy for the actual ceremonies to be Buddhist. Please, my love, say you will be my wife."

With those words, he took the box from his pocket, opened it, and offered it to his hopefully wife-to-be.

Tears were streaming down Ireshi's face. She hadn't expected this but the perfection of the day now made perfect sense to her. The fact that he'd planned the whole day with this as the climax, though she knew there would be other, very different climaxes to follow, made her feel like she'd never felt before. She wiped away some of the tears.

"Oh Tom, my dear beloved Tom. I thought you couldn't surprise me any more than you have done since we met. But today may be the most wonderful of my life and I doubt you can ever surpass this. My answer is yes, yes, a million times yes. I feel the same. I always thought my father would end up matching me with someone he saw as a good fit, someone from the same social class and who he viewed as enhancing his reputation rather than making me happy. I know mother loves you and that is enough for now. Father will come around, even if it takes time. He might not even fully accept you until we give him a grandchild. Even his cold and iron heart will be melted when he holds his luk khrueng."

She took the ring from the box and slipped it on her finger.

"It's beautiful. Tom, just what I would have chosen myself."

She moved towards him and kissed him with a deeper passion than he'd ever experienced. His mouth moved down from hers, taking first one nipple and then the other between his teeth, eliciting moans of ecstasy. He pushed her back onto the floor and slid inside her, the moans increasing in volume. Their lovemaking was slow and tender, no need for anything else after his proposal. When they came, it was together, their rising cries an expression of their bond. Tim collapsed beside her, both of them spent and satisfied and, as they began to doze off, he whispered in her ear, "I love you."

2023

Tom woke from a fitful sleep as the cell door clanged open. The officer standing there gestured at him to stand and follow him. Once in the corridor, the policeman motioned for him to place his hands behind his back and handcuffed him before leading him along the corridor and up the stairs. He was shoved into a small interview room, stark and bare other than a small table with a tape recorder on it and four chairs two on either side of the table. His escort undid the handcuffs then refastened them to a bar on the middle of the table, restricting all but the most basic movement, then left Tom alone with his thoughts.

He waited for what seemed like an eternity but was probably only ten minutes or so. Finally, Apisitniran entered the room with a younger officer Tom hadn't seen before. Both had stern and unforgiving looks on their faces and Apisitniran was carrying two evidence bags, one with Tom's laptop on it and the other with his mobile phone. Behind them was a man dressed in a well-tailored business suit who took the seat beside Tom. He whispered in his ear:

"My name is Adisak Chomklin. I'm your lawyer. Mr. Tortermvasana asked me to come down and represent you. Do not answer any questions unless I tell you to, ok?"

Tom nodded.

The two policemen sat opposite Tom and Apisitniran placed the bags on the table before switching on the recorder.

"It's Wednesday, December 6th, 2023..."

He glanced at his watch.

"... and it's now 9:24am. Present are Police Lieutenant General Apisitniran and Police Major Shoowong   Police Lieutenant

General Apisitniran to interview Mr. Tom McKay with his lawyer, Adisak Chomklin."

He stared at Tom intently.

"First of all, I want to establish some basic facts. Are you Thomas McKay, date of birth 14th of May, 1976?"

Tom nodded.

"Answer yes or no for the tape, Mr. McKay."

"Yes, that's correct."

"And you currently reside at Apartment 423, The Address, Sukhumvit 28, Bangkok?"

"Yes."

"And you are currently employed as general manager of Kram-roo publishing at M Thai Tower in Bangkok?"

"That's right."

"Thomas McKay, you've been arrested on suspicion of the murders of Sapsiree Pongprayoon, Sagat Kamsing, and Tawin Srichaphan. Do you know anything about any of these crimes?"

Tom looked sideways at Chomklin and raised a quizzical eyebrow.

"As I've not had a chance to consult with my client, I'd like to request some time to discuss the charges with him."

Apisitniran sighed but he knew they couldn't go further without complying.

"Interview suspended 9:34am to allow discussion with lawyer."

He pressed the button to stop the tape.

"I'll allow you until 10am to talk about the case."

With another audible sigh, Apisitniran and Shoowong left Tom and his lawyer alone, taking the evidence bags with them.

For close to 20 minutes, Tom told the lawyer everything he knew. He knew his story sounded unbelievable but insisted to the man that he was telling the truth. He looked at the clock on the wall and realised the policemen would soon return.

"Look, I'm being completely honest with you. It may sound like something out of a book but everything is centred on this girl. There are files on that laptop, both the short stories I've told you about and the messages between us. They will explain everything. Well, except the towel. I honestly don't have a clue where that came from."

Chomklin looked thoughtful for a minute.

"Incredible though your story is, I do believe you. Aekarach is an old and close friend. He said to believe everything you said, no matter what. If he has faith in you, then so do I. I just hope this policeman can be convinced too. I think we should be showing him what you have on your laptop first. But you have no idea what the real identify of this girl is?"

Tom shook his head grimly as the two policemen reentered the room, the evidence bags again deposited on the middle of the table.

Apisitniran sat opposite Tom and stared directly at him. He pressed the button on the tape machine.

"Interview resumed 10am. So, now that you've had a chance to talk to your lawyer, is there anything you want to say?"

Chomklin coughed. "After discussions with my client, we'd ask you to examine the laptop and mobile phone you confiscated. The laptop contains a file with all the stories Mr. McKay received from this girl going by the name of Chompoo. The Line app on his phone contains messages between the two which are also backed up on his laptop. While Mr. McKay doesn't know her real identity, perhaps your Cyber Crime Investigation Bureau would be able to follow her electronic trail."

"Very well. Let's look at the laptop first. And you say that the crimes in question somehow mimicked stories you'd received from this girl?"

Tom nodded.

"For the tape please, Mr. McKay."

"Yes. I'd noticed a similarity when the first crime was reported but put it down to coincidence. I confronted Chompoo after the second crime but she said that some of the stories had appeared on a website so anyone could have accessed them. When I saw the final murder in the newspaper, I insisted she drop her veil of secrecy and come to the police with me."

"Ok, let's have a look at these stories then."

Apisitniran took the laptop out the evidence bag and handed the power cable to Shoowong who plugged it into a socket on the wall. The senior officer then powered the device up.

"Your password, Mr. McKay?"

"Shibari23."

The policeman typed in the password and waited for the desktop to show. Tom was almost OCD-like in how he organised his files. He even kept submissions that had been rejected in case the writer came back later with a better manuscript. Given the promise he had seen in Chompoo's writing, she had a folder all to herself.

"So, what folder should I be opening?"

"It's labeled 'Chompoo' and is on the actual desktop itself."

Apisitniran peered at the screen for a few minutes and clicked on a couple of folders. With a bemused look on his face, he swung the laptop round so that the screen was facing Tom.

"There are numerous folders but none with that name. Could it be inside one of the others?"

Tom stared at the screen in confusion.

"No, I had it there, on the desktop. It must be there. May I?"

"Wait."

The policeman nodded to his colleague who got up, walked around the table, and stood behind Tom.

"If you attempt to delete anything, you could face further charges, not to mention being grabbed by Shoowong who is a former Muay Thai champion."

Tom moved the cursor around the screen, opening folder after folder in case he had moved her file accidentally. When he closed the last folder, he went to the search bar, entered *Chompoo*, and pressed *Enter*. The computer searched through the hard drives.

No items march your search.

"No, it has to be there." The expression on Tom's face was a mixture of bewilderment and despair.

"Wait, our emails. That's mainly how we communicated and how she sent her files."

He clicked an icon and Gmail opened.

"She first got in touch with me before my company email was set up," He explained.

His inbox appeared on the screen and he gazed in growing disbelief.

"This is impossible. Her folder, all her emails, they've all disappeared. Someone must have deleted them when I was away from the office."

The two policemen looked at him, almost matching sardonic smiles on their faces.

"We'll have our Cyber Crimes unit look at your laptop. If files have been recently deleted, they'll know."

Tom turned to Chomklin, a pleading look as his story began to evaporate. The lawyer maintained a stoic look though in his eyes, there was a hint of someone who felt let down.

"Well, since this seems to be a dead end, I propose we suspend the interview while we wait for the forensic results. Khun Adisak, do you have any objections?"

"No, none at all," replied the lawyer.

Apisitniran checked his watch.

"Interview suspended, 10:28am."

He stopped the tape machine.

"Shoowong, can you make sure Mr. McKay is returned to his cell."

"Cell? What about bail?"

The officer laughed.

"Bail? You're in custody on suspicion of three murders. The 'proof' that you're innocent has conveniently disappeared. You have adequate funds so that just holding your passport would be no guarantee that you wouldn't flee the country. No, Mr.

McKay, I'm afraid you will need to be our guest for a few days more."

1996

Tom woke with Ireshi's naked body still wrapped around him. He glanced at the clock on the wall to see it was just after nine pm. Still early. As he tried to extricate himself from his lover, she awoke too and looked at him with sleepy eyes.

"I think we had too much sake," she laughed quietly.

"That and mind-blowing sex, yes."

She looked down at her hand with the engagement ring on.

"I thought that I had dreamt that part of the day but it's real."

"Yes, it's real, very real. Do you want to continue our session or has today been too overwhelming?"

A wicked gleam appeared in Ireshi's eyes.

"Oh, sir, I want to play please. Let's make the night as memorable as the day."

Tom laughed.

"You're such a bad girl. That's just one of the reasons I love you. Do you want a shower before we continue or something to eat?"

"I'm definitely not hungry. In fact, after Hanaya, I'm not sure I'll need to eat for a day or two. No shower either, the smell of sex is turning me on again already. What I will have is a nice big fat line please, sir."

"That's an excellent idea."

Tom retrieved the mirror from the shelf and started chopping lines. Ireshi rose from the floor and walked over to the hi-fi.

"More jazz or something more soulful, sir?"

"Good question. How about some Otis? The Soul Album maybe?"

Ireshi nodded and flicked through Tom's vinyl until she found the Redding record. As the opening bars of *Just One More Day* emanated from the Mission 753 speakers, she came and sat next to Tom. He'd cut eight lines on the mirror and passed it to Ireshi who quickly snorted two of them.

"Well, that will certainly wake me up. Thank you, sir." She wiped the crumbs onto her gum and passed the mirror back to Tom who took two lines for himself.

"Shall we move into the playroom?" He suggested.

"Please, sir. I want you to use me however you want."

"Oh, I plan to, don't you worry. Now go and wait for me and I'll bring the coke and a bottle of whisky though. It may be a long night."

Ireshi obediently headed for their playroom while Tom collected everything they'd need. He put a bottle of Glenfarclas Single Malt on a tray along with two glasses and a jug of water. As an afterthought, he swallowed a couple of Epimedium tablets he'd obtained from a Chinese medicine shop. He'd initially bought it as he'd been amused by its nickname of horny goat weed but had then been very impressed by its actual effects which would counter the often impotence-inducing coke. He also retrieved the bag of ketamine and put it on the mirror with the coke. Satisfied that he had everything they'd need, he headed for the playroom.

Ireshi was sitting in the chair. Chair was perhaps too simplistic a name for something Tom had designed itself. While you could use it as just a chair, the various extra additions to the piece of furniture belied its true function. There were restraint cuffs on both arms and legs, and a number of hinges that allowed the chair to be adjusted from a sitting position to almost perfectly horizontal. And holes in the leather padding allowed access to any area of the body you wanted.

Tom smiled.

"Take off your kimono before I restrain you. I want to be able to reach every inch of that gorgeous little body."

Ireshi complied meekly, placing the kimono on the nearby chest of drawers and standing before him clad only in the crotchless bodysuit and the seamed stockings. She then sat down, her gaze on Tom the perfect mixture of submissiveness and lust. He moved forward and began fastening the in-built restraints, first binding her ankles to the legs of the chair and then her wrists to the manacles on the arms.

"Hmmm, almost but not quite perfect."

He went to the side of the room and wheeled the instrument trolley he'd bought from a medical supplies store. It was stainless steel and had four drawers and a top that could be used as a table. Tom opened one of the drawers and withdrew a ball gag and a blindfold. Fastening the gag behind her head with the straps, he stood back to admire what he viewed as a work of art.

"I think we'll leave the blindfold until later. Now I just need to choose some toys."

Turning back to the trolley, he began rummaging in the drawers, occasionally pausing and thinking before placing his chosen toy onto the trolley's top. This was why he'd delayed putting the blindfold on Ireshi; the anticipation in her eyes, and the wide eyes when he chose one of her favourites, was an aphrodisiac in itself. The nipple clamps awakened memories of sweet pain in her mind while the various vibrators and dildos made her wet without him touching her. Satisfied that he had enough for now, he turned back to his partner.

"I think we should start the evening with your first taste of ketamine. But we'll do it the same way as I did, a nice cocktail with some coke first."

There was some apprehension in her eyes but it was tempered by curiousity as to what awaited her. He walked over to where he'd left the mirror. Pausing, he filled a glass with whisky and added some water. There was little point in pouring one for Ireshi just now, not while she was still wearing the gag. He took a long drink then sparked a waiting spliff while he mixed the chemicals. Conscious of his captive audience, he gave commentary while he prepared the cocktail of drugs.

"It's hard to describe what this is like. These first lines will be fairly muted when it comes to effects as the coke offsets the more extreme feelings. Initially, you'll feel relaxed, though conversely there may be a little panic at something new. There will also be a feeling of detachment; that's the dissociative part of the k. You may even feel detached from your body. I felt like I was floating above the sofa looking down on myself. Depending on the dose you take, you might experience some hallucinations, both visual and auditory. The hallucinations aren't as strong as a good psychedelic, at least in my limited experience. Don't worry if you feel your heart rate increase, that's just part of the journey. Yevgeny did speak about k-holes, where you've taken too much and lose yourself. But we won't be going that far tonight."

As he talked to her, he was expertly mixing the two piles of the powder on the mirror, slightly favouring the coke when it came to ratios. He chopped four lines, leaving a small pile of the mixture as well as two piles of the original drugs. Standing, he walked over to Ireshi and leant over her.

“Now, it’s not going to be easy with you restrained so I’m going to have to help you. I’ll hold the mirror, put the note up one nostril, and pinch the other with the same hand. Just be ready to snort as normal.”

Ireshi nodded as he prepared her for her two lines. It was awkward, but Tom’s tenderness and expertise overcame any issues. She hesitantly snorted the first line, a look of almost pain coming over her face.

“Yes, sorry, I should have mentioned it’s not quite as smooth as coke on its own.”

He returned the mirror to below her nose and inserted the note again. There was less hesitation this time, less discomfort, and Tom grinned. He went to do his own lines then hesitated, his voyeuristic tendencies taking over. Instead, he placed the mirror on the trolley and sat on the room’s normal chair to observe the effects.

“Do you feel anything yet?”

Ireshi nodded. He could almost see her pupils dilate, though the dilation was less than with psychedelics. As he watched, she closed her eyes as the cocktail coursed through her system. Then she opened them again as the first wave of dissociation swept over her. He smiled again, job done. Satisfied that she wasn’t panicking, he quickly did his own two lines, grabbed his whisky and spliff, then sat back down to enjoy the euphoria.

Once he’d surfed the first waves, the play began. Over the next hour, he used the various toys he’d looked out, taking Ireshi on a sensual journey of the senses. As he began to feel the effects of the drug dissipate, he cut them both more lines of coke, followed shortly after by Ireshi's first lines of ketamine on its own.

As the night wore on, Tom felt that they were going further than ever before. Not just in terms of the actual sex but in terms of the altered realities they were both experiencing. He'd adjusted the chair several times and his lover was now prostate and face down so he could enjoy penetration as well as using toys on her. The gaps between lines of k were becoming shorter and Tom could feel himself imbued with an almost godlike power. Ireshi had refused the last lines he offered her but he didn't care. If this was the k-hole Yevgeny had mentioned, then he welcomed it with open arms.

He stopped for a minute to replenish his whisky and then drain it in one gulp. He looked at the mirror and thought *why not*, before hoovering another couple of chunky lines. Before returning to the chair, he plucked a long silk scarf that they'd occasionally used when experimenting with erotic asphyxiation. The combination of ketamine and sex had given him a maniacal expression, almost demonic, and one that would have scared Ireshi had she not been face down and blindfolded.

Approaching her, he wrapped the scarf around her neck and mounted her. As his thrusts increased in intensity, he pulled the scarf tighter and tighter, feeling like he was riding a dragon far above the earth. He was vaguely aware of a voice faintly screaming, *mai chai, mai chai*, but he ignored it as it meant little to him in the face of soaring in the sky. Pulling the scarf tighter still, he climaxed with a shout as it seemed every piece of energy left him. Spent but still mostly detached from reality, he withdrew from her and collapsed on the chair.

"Oh my fucking god. That was the most intense orgasm I've ever had. It felt like fireworks were going off in my balls. How are you, my love?"

There was silence.

Tom walked over to her, undid the gag, and removed the blindfold. She was breathing but unresponsive. From somewhere deep in his subconscious, a memory of her screaming their safe word through the gag rose to the surface. What had he done? He unfastened the restraints and lifted her onto the floor. She was definitely breathing but wasn't responding to anything he did. Had he taken the erotic asphyxiation too far? He knew the drugs weren't to blame though they did have culpability for him losing control. What should he do? His first thought was to call an ambulance but he remembered that her father was a senior police general and he knew he'd be lost in some dark cell, forgotten forever or even executed without trial or the opportunity to defend himself.

He checked Ireshi again. Her breathing wasn't laboured so he didn't think there was any immediate risk. *Think, Tom, think.* The more he thought about it, the more he thought about her father's likely reaction, the more he realised there was only one option. Panic. Run.

He rushed around the apartment, gathering a few clothes and any valuables he had such as his camera. He flushed all the drugs down the toilet, his weed, the coke, and every last crystal of that damnable ketamine. Everything he could think of taking went into his holdall. He didn't even want to stop for a shower, all that mattered for now was self-preservation. *Think, Tom, think. Ok, taxi to Don Mueang, first flight to the UK. In fact, first flight to fucking anywhere.* He had cash in the apartment and could take more from an ATM at the airport. He would also phone an ambulance from the airport, though he'd be sure to do so only when his flight was about to take off. He knew that her father had the power to alert the immigration department and to have him arrested.

Tom knew he was leaving so much behind. Hell, he was leaving Ireshi behind and he truly hoped she would be ok. But he also knew that her father's wrath would be unrelenting and that no amount of talking would turn him from his path. Arguing that there had been consent would not dilute the anger of a concerned father. Was it still consent when he'd ignored Ireshi screaming their safe word?

With everything packed he could manage, Tom grabbed his passport and money from the desk then returned to the playroom. Ireshi was laying where he left her and still breathing. He made her as comfortable as he could and fetched a quilt from the bedroom to cover her. He knelt beside her and kissed her tenderly on the forehead and then the lips.

"I'm sorry, my darling, sorry for everything. Sorry for hurting you but most of all, I'm sorry for being a coward and running away. I love you but your father would find a way for me to disappear. I promise I'll call for help before I leave. I just hope you are ok and that you can forgive me."

With tears streaming down his face, Tom got to his feet again. With one last, longing look at Ireshi, he left the playroom, grabbed his bag, and left the apartment.

2024

Tom tried to shut out the constant background noise but once again, failed. Whispered conversations, voices raise in anger, the cries of pain from violence or forced sex, the guttural shouts of sadistic prison guards; human instruments contributing to a twisted, never-ending symphony from hell.

It had been six months since the dark doors of Bang Kwang prison had shut behind him though there had been the trial which offered some respite, albeit a journey in a cramped prison van and the stinking holding cells that followed. The trial itself had been little more than a show trial. Tom knew that his guilt had been decided long before he faced the actual court. The forensic tests had shown that the blood on the towel found in Tom's office came from not one but two of the victims. And the Cyber Crime Unit had found no trace of Chompoo's files or messages, or so they claimed. Worse, their investigations had shown that Tom – or someone – had used the laptop to access violent pornography on the dark web.

The prosecution hadn't even bothered to present a motive. They didn't need to in the face of such conclusive evidence. His defence lawyer had tried his best, but his token protestations were drowned in the rising tide of assumed guilt. The judge had been impassionate when delivering both the verdict and sentence. Being found guilty was no surprise and neither was the announcement of the death penalty. There was a certain irony that the court case had taken only three weeks but that the appeals process could take two years, maybe even more.

He hadn't been abandoned completely. Aekarach visited every week and Anong had visited three times. They provided a vital lifeline to the outside world and, perhaps more importantly, they were a source of funds, something that was invaluable in Bang Kwang if you wanted to more than just survive. The fact that he spoke reasonable Thai helped a little too. Unlike the poor fools blinded by the promise of payment for carrying packages they well knew were heroin despite their protestations of innocence.

Tom even had a certain celebrity status among the prisoners, the mad farang who had killed three people. It didn't make his cell any comfier, far from it, but it did help ensure that he wasn't looking over his shoulder every five minutes, especially in the showers. During his second week, two unusually large Thais appeared outside his overcrowded cell and told him to come with them. He'd followed them apprehensively, wondering if this might be some sort of trap. Instead, he'd found himself outside a cell that looked more like a hotel room. The fact that it was single occupancy was one thing, but the real bed, the large television on the wall, and the various other bits and pieces made it clear that this cell belonged to someone not to be trifled with.

The cell's occupant was Nai Yai, who he later found out was a major figure in the Bangkok underworld and who still ruled his fiefdom from inside the prison. Nai Yai had no interest in small talk, he only had a take it or leave it proposal for Tom, though it was more a case of take it. He wanted 20,000 baht deposited in a bank account every month and Tom's safety was guaranteed. If he didn't take the deal, well... The choice was easy and Aekarach agreed to make the payments on Tom's behalf.

There was also a visit from a British Embassy representative, some underling whose responsibilities probably included ensuring the Chardonnay was properly chilled and visiting the prisons. Once he discovered that Tom had a support network, he lost interest and said he'd visit monthly to check if Tom needed consular assistance.

He'd had to wear leg irons for the first three months, a far cry from the designer socks that usually adorned his ankles. It was only three weeks after those leg irons had been removed that they moved him to death row. There were around 500 people, both men and women, on death row, though he was the only farang. 500 people wondering when their date with destiny would be set. The big advantage of the move was that the cells on death row were not quite as overcrowded as those in the main prison, 15 to a cell rather than 35 or 40.

Tom tried to look on the bright side and the fact that it had been six years since the last execution. Hardly a cause for celebration but it at least gave him some hope. If the appeals process failed, and he prayed to every deity that it didn't, then maybe he'd have some small chance of a royal pardon in the distant future.

To say that prison life was monotonous would probably be the understatement of the century. To say it was dangerous, at least for most inmates, would be entirely accurate. It was the boredom that destroyed Tom's soul more than anything. His visitors were not allowed to bring in books, though he'd bribed a couple of the guards to meet Aekarach outside and bring some in for him. Those same guards had accepted cash to smuggle him in notebooks and pens and Tom had finally started writing the novel that had been on his to-do list for two decades.

The appeal remained his primary focus. His lawyer had hired a private detective to see if they could uncover new evidence, though not the one that had been looking for Hollings. He still suspected that this was the man who was behind his demise, but he was still at a loss as to how evidence had been planted in his office. Lam was still in the frame too, though to a lesser extent than the man he'd helped put in this very prison. One of the things the PI was focusing on was who could have planted the towel in his bathroom and Aekarach had promised full cooperation.

He was sketching out some story ideas when a guard appeared outside his cell.

"Visitor," he said in Thai, gesturing for Tom to follow him.

Tom was confused. He wasn't expecting any visitors, at least for a few more days. Aekarach had been in yesterday, Anong last week, and he wasn't due to see his lawyer till Friday. Unless... maybe there had been developments in the case, maybe the private detective had found something, maybe there had been another murder that would show Tom was innocent, maybe...

He gave himself a mental shake. It was all too easy to cling to optimism when you were facing a death sentence. He knew that optimism offered faux sanctuary from reality and, while that was tempting, he preferred to remain grounded. Sighing loudly, he realised that the only real way to find out who the visitor was would be to go and see them. He pulled on the faded brown prison shirt that matched the faded brown trousers, put on the cheap trainers that were his best footwear, and followed the guard down the corridor.

He was handcuffed and shackled before leaving the block that housed death row. His walk changed to a shuffle as they moved through the prison. One thing he had noticed was that no matter where you went in the prison, the place had its own particular smell. Not the stench of too much humanity crowded into inhumane conditions. Not the smell of the overworked drains that meant you forever smelt piss and shit. No, this was the smell of despair, of people who had mostly given up on caring or hoping.

They finally reached the visiting area. Tom had once visited a friend in HMP Brixton serving a measly 12 months for driving offences. The prison authorities had recognised that visits were a time when families came together and had made the area bright and colourful with toys and activities for the children as well as various snacks on sale.

The prison authorities here had no such thoughts. They saw only the punitive nature of prison and that punishment extended to the families too. They even had a requirement that visitors change into the same sort of trousers as the prisoners wore. If the overall effect of the prison itself was oppressive and threatening, that was echoed in this sad area where families had the only real chance of connecting.

The guard escorted Tom to where his visitor was waiting and then stood at the back, ready to intervene if needed. Tom didn't recognise the girl waiting for him on the far side of the window that separated them. She looked to be in her mid to late 20s, dressed conservatively, and attractive in a studious sort of way.

He sat and lifted the grubby phone receiver that allowed them to talk.

"Hello, do I know you." His voice bordered on shouting, something that you needed to do in order to communicate in any way.

There was silence. He wondered if this was another journalist wanting some inside scoop, or merely a rubbernecker, fascinated by his supposed crimes.

Finally, she spoke but Tom couldn't make out any words as she had spoken too quietly.

"I'm sorry but you'll need to speak louder, these phones are shit."

The girl frowned, then spoke again, louder this time so Tom could hear.

“I said, hello Tom.”

“Do I know you? If you’re a journalist, you can fuck off. My lawyer is the only person who speaks to the press on my behalf.”

“I’m Chompoo.”

Such a simple statement but the effect on Tom was instantaneous. He stared at her in shock but also with some hope.

“You’ve finally come forward! Thank God. You have to go to the police and te...”

He stopped mid-sentence as he saw the girl holding a hand up.

“You already know that Chompoo is not my real name and I have no intention of telling you what that name is. I also do not intend going to the police to save or help you in any way. In fact, I am the reason why you are in here and why you will stay here.”

Ton was stunned. He’d always seen Chompoo as being key to this whole mess but he’d never suspected that her role was that of being the cause of his predicament. She continued.

“Do you remember Ireshi, Tom? She was my mother. You left her unconscious on the floor of your apartment and ran home like the snivelling coward you are. She never regained consciousness and remained in a coma. The medical staff reported ligature marks on her neck so I assume that you were both involved in erotic asphyxiation and the game went too far.

But that game deprived her brain of oxygen for far too long and she remained in the coma she arrived at hospital in. Then a few weeks later, the doctors were shocked to discover she was pregnant. Her father, the police general, paid for the best care available and nine months later, I was born. Yes, Tom, I'm your daughter but the only emotional attachment I feel to you is sheer hatred. My mother died a year later after contracting pneumonia and I was raised by my grandparents.

My grandfather made sure I knew exactly who was to blame for my mother's death. He tracked your life, your meteoric rise as an editor, every holiday, every relationship. Each day, he would attend the local temple and pray to Buddha that you would return to Thailand one day so he could avenge my mother. He even considered hiring someone to kill you in England, it would have been cheaper than the extortionate fees he paid to the private detectives who shadowed you. But he decided to be patient and that any vengeance had to happen in the country where his daughter died.

Five years ago, my grandmother died and then three years ago, grandfather was diagnosed with stage four pancreatic cancer. He knew he was dying and, on his deathbed, he made me promise to continue his mission, to await your arrogant return to our country and then exact the bloodiest of revenges. But I decided that just death, no matter how painful, was not enough. I wanted you to suffer for years on end just as I have done. The only way to ensure that was for you to be imprisoned here for the rest of your life. You won't be executed but you won't be pardoned either, my grandfather's connections will see to that.

Then my prayers were answered and the detective agency in London informed me that you were returning here to take up a new position. By that time, I had already come up with a plan and the whole Chompoo persona. And yes, that plan involved killing people but I made sure they were people who deserved to die. Everything worked as planned. You were so blinded by the potential benefits of discovering a great writer that you didn't see the ghosts approaching. But I also have to thank you.

I'm not sure if your genes are responsible for my literary talent but I had never thought of being a writer and had assumed my bank job was my future, albeit one with a good salary and promotions on the horizon. I fully plan on exploring my writing more, though I will move away from the dark bloody stories that ensnared you. I had considered just leaving you to rot, the uncertainty of what happened ever on your mind. But I decided that actually confronting you and admitting the truth held a far sweeter taste.

Oh, and don't think you're safe in here. I know about your deal with Nai Yai, I have eyes and ears everywhere. You can consider that deal as null and void. That gangster knows what side his bread is buttered on. You won't be killed, that would again be too merciful for you. But you face years of beatings and rapes, and every time some beast of a man holds you down, I want you to picture my mother's face as you left her."

Tom had sat in shocked silence as the girl had told him everything. There were tears in his eyes as he stared in disbelief at the daughter he never knew he had, the daughter who had engineered every step of this nightmare. He placed his hand on the glass in supplication but was met only by a look of disgust.

"I'm sorry, so sorry. I loved Ireshi, loved your mother. I panicked, scared of what her father would do to me. But at least I called her an ambulance."

"Yes, from the fucking airport, you coward. The doctors say they don't know if a quicker response could have meant the hypoxia could have been treated, but we'll never know, will we? You just ran, more concerned with your own well-being rather than the survival of my mother. And from the reports we had over the years, that selfish arrogance never went away. It's always been about number one with you. Drugs, alcohol, women, as long as you had what you wanted, fuck everyone else. There is a certain irony that you've always sought control over people, yet losing control, even if just for a moment, is what's responsible for you being in here. I'm going to leave now and I won't be returning.

But be assured, I will be getting reports on every incident in here that involves you, every fist, every boot, every sordid attack, and I will smile each time. It will never bring my mother back but at least I know her death has been avenged and that my grandfather will know his wishes have been fulfilled."

As the girl stood and walked away, Tom screamed after her, smashing the phone repeatedly against the toughened glass until the guard dragged him away back into the darkness of Bang Kwang.

Epilogue

The girl known as Chompoo unlocked the door to her condo. Once inside, she went straight to the bathroom and removed the wig and contact lenses that had subtly altered her appearance. While she was not overly worried about anyone listening to the rants and raves of her father, she knew it had been better to exercise a degree of caution when it came to the prison visit. Besides, if any report went higher than the prison, her grandfather's contacts would quickly quash any investigation and put the whole thing down to the desperation of a murderous farang.

Grabbing a bottle of water from the fridge, she moved to her work desk and booted up her laptop. She had no idea if her literary talent had indeed come from Tom or whether it had been borne out of a motherless childhood then the pain that had become part of her everyday life once her grandfather had told her the entire truth.

She was more concerned that she had inherited something else from her father's genes; a desire to be in control of every situation she found herself in. While she hadn't physically committed the murders, she'd found that there had been real enjoyment, almost sexual, from orchestrating each murder.

The murderers themselves had been surprisingly digitally adept. She'd found them on the dark web, a cutout process that protected both her and, to an extent, them. But although she had taken real vicarious thrills from seeing the murders reported in the press, she'd also felt it lacked the reality that she now craved.

Her plan had only been to take revenge on Tom. She didn't blame his sexual tastes, after all, her mother had enjoyed similar tastes and as the old cliché went, it takes two to tango.

No, what had been the source of her anger for so many years, what had fed the fuel of her single-minded path, was his abject cowardice. Nobody would ever know for sure if her mother could have survived had Tom called an ambulance immediately, but that uncertainty was enough. He had said he loved Ireshi, but given his fear of the repercussions had caused him to flee, that love must have been entirely superficial. There was no excuse for his actions.

Putting Tom out of her thoughts, at least for now, she began to surf the local social media and news pages looking for something that might give her path a new direction. It seemed to mostly be the same old gossip and stories that held little interest to her. Sighing, she moved onto the next page and saw...

Police Release Politician

Police today released Bangkok Metropolitan Council politician, Mongkol Wancharoen without charge. Wancharoen, 42, had been arrested on suspicion of domestic battery after his wife, Kanana, 37, had been admitted to hospital with several fractures and multiple bruises. Wancharoen had previously been arrested twice for assaulting sex workers but had never been convicted after paying compensation to his victims. A spokeswoman for domestic violence NGO, Yood Kwam Roonrang, said:

"Yet again, we see police turn a blind eye to violence against a spouse. Being a politician should not protect you from justice."

Mr. Wancharoen was unavailable for comment.

She smiled, but it was a smile devoid of any warmth whatsoever. She'd found her next story, one where she would be more than the writer.

SARASWATI PUBLISHING
Solutions For The Digital Age

Made in the USA
Columbia, SC
18 October 2024